SOME SECRETS MUST BE KEPT

MONTANAMO

CHRISTOPHER LEIBIG

TRAVELLER'S PLAYGROUND PRESS 2016

The very word "secrecy" is repugnant in a free and open society; and we are as a people inherently and historically opposed to secret societies, to secret oaths, and to secret proceedings.

— *John F. Kennedy, President of the United States*

The world is governed by very different personages from what is imagined by those who are not behind the scenes.

— *Benjamin Disraeli, Prime Minister of England*

The best place to hide a lie is in a pile of truths.

— *Phoenix Jamborsky, Mayor of Twin Rivers, Montana*

ONE

MAY 8, 2009 –
CAROLINE COUNTY, NORTHWEST MONTANA

"Sack o' shit!" barked Sheriff Pasquali. His rifle shot echoed through the morning valley mist. The eight-point buck stood about seventy yards away, in full view of Pasquali and his hunting companions. The buck turned its head as if vaguely annoyed and then arrogantly trotted into the underbrush. Gabriel Lantagne laughed softly, taking a deep breath of the morning mountain air. He lay between Phoenix and the Sheriff, the three of them hidden from the valley below by a huge fallen tree. He too gripped a rifle but had not even loaded it. The morning target practice was for the sheriff.

"Shit, Sheriff," Phoenix said, "you'd think by your age you'd a thought of a new epithet for when you blow a shot." Pasquali was sixty-six years old and always used the same gruff, three-word phrase whenever he missed. Phoenix had been hunting with the Sheriff regularly for three years and claimed she'd never seen him hit anything. She had, however, heard him grunt "sack o' shit" dozens of times. Gabe had no idea if Sheriff Pasquali directed the phrase towards the animal, towards himself, or towards whatever unknowable force had destined him to be such a piss-poor hunter.

Pasquali spit tobacco back across his body, strafing his protruding belly. "Epi-what?"

Phoenix stood up from behind the dead tree. "Your cuss of choice. Why don't you change it up once in a while? Maybe 'son of a whore' or something."

"You know I don't care for any of your fancy phray-zee-ology." Pasquali groaned as he hefted himself up with the help of the huge rotting log. He took out his flask, which Gabe could hardly see inside his meaty hand, took a small sip, and held it out to Phoenix.

"You know I don't drink during the day, Sheriff. I've got a job and whatnot."

"Didn't stop the last guy." Pasquali held the flask towards Gabe.

"I don't drink," Gabe said.

"Know what Frank Sinatra said? 'I feel sorry for people who don't drink. For them, when they wake up in the mornin', they know it's the best they're gonna feel all day.'" Pasquali's laugh bellowed through the woods and into the valley.

"Besides, I got a trial today." Gabe had not touched alcohol for four years but sometimes found his disciplined sobriety hard to explain. When people asked if he simply didn't like drinking, he sometimes said, "Problem is I love it."

"Grizzly Redford?" Pasquali said.

That Pasquali knew the name of his client who was going on trial that day surprised Gabe. But Pasquali, he was learning through Phoenix, knew lots of things. Phoenix viewed it as part of her job as mayor to hunt with Pasquali. The sheriff was, despite his anti-pretenses, an important man.

Phoenix lit a cigarette. "What would the town think if I showed up tonight half in the bag?" This jaunty, microphones-off Phoenix whom Gabe was only beginning to get to know contrasted with the earnest, almost shy city-manager type the town had elected a year ago. Correction, the almost shy but sublimely sexy librarian-type. Gabe studied her, the perfect posture and intelligent eyes, which betrayed a mystery beneath the down-home practicality she presented to the town.

"Same as they always think, darlin'," Pasquali said. "They'd think you're beautiful."

Phoenix turned towards the valley, where the mist had lifted as they spoke. "Looks got nothing to do with it, Sheriff. I got elected because I was on your ticket."

"That other fool had to go."

"This town meeting tonight is critical," Phoenix said. "You're coming, right?"

"I'm coming, but that don't mean I agree with you."

She exhaled. "You don't have a choice. The alternatives, I assure you, are gloomy."

"Maybe so, maybe so. But I urge you, madam, to keep your eyes focused on the traditions of this town even as you aim to end 'em."

"I don't aim to end anything. The future is coming with or without us."

The three stood quietly for a moment, looking into the valley together. Gabe knew he'd been invited on the early morning hunting venture because Phoenix wanted something from him. Just like she'd wanted him to run for the City Council and wanted him to be her assistant campaign manager when she had run for mayor.

In her first substantial act as mayor, Phoenix had jostled tradition by changing the town's name. Gabe's hometown had been called Weasel Junction since the early nineteenth century. Its new name, Twin Rivers, spearheaded Phoenix's efforts, as she put it, "to build a bridge to the twentieth century."

"Twenty-first," Gabe had said.

She'd smiled. "One step at a time, isn't that what they say?"

The town hall meeting to decide the name change had lasted past midnight, which qualified as an all-nighter in Weasel Junction, a far cry from Washington, DC, where Phoenix had worked as a staffer to Senator Beauregard Bryant before moving to Weasel Junction to be with her now ex-husband. "The funny part," Pasquali had said to Gabe in private, "is they ain't even fuckin' rivers." The town's new name referred to the convergence in northern Caroline County of the Fishtail, which had always been called a stream, and Wounded Man Creek.

The only remaining tribute to the old name was Pasquali's Weasel Junction Hunt Club, a large shack in the woods a hundred yards up the ridge from where the three of them now stood. The structure itself looked like something out of Deliverance, but inside, the shiny hardwood floors, oak bar, modern kitchen, pool table, karaoke machine, wide-screen TV, and rows of leather couches bespoke a hidden wealth.

"My idea can work," Phoenix said.

"It may work or it may not," Pasquali said. "This is a strange year, and apt to get stranger. But I'm talking about something you still don't understand, Madam Mayor. Politics."

"I don't understand politics?" She had a master's degree in public policy and had worked four years on Capitol Hill for the most powerful man in Montana.

"If you understood politics, you would have announced your plan Monday morning of this week, not in back in January. You gave this God-loving town all winter and early spring to talk it over. Plus all that national news crap? Half the town thinks Bin Laden saw that shit on CNN and plans to blow up the taco joint out on Route 3. The meeting will be packed tonight. If you'd waited until Monday, only the regulars, including those do-gooders you run with, woulda showed at the meeting. You coulda won the vote, and then maybe your plan could have worked in time to prevent you from getting thrown out of office at the next election. As it is now, you'll have a riot on your hands tonight. Don't forget the last time somebody had a revolutionary idea on how to save the town."

The last mayor had decided to float twenty million dollars in town bonds to help build a maximum-security prison in the hopes of securing contracts to house other states' prisoners. At a raucous town hall meeting, Mayor Pritchard had persuaded the town to vote for the idea. But now, three years later, the

Weasel Junction Detention Center, recently renamed Twin Rivers Maximum Security Penitentiary, remained empty.

"It's an important decision," Phoenix said. "Everyone has a right to be part of it."

"Yeah, you really understand politics." Pasquali spat a perfect stream of brown liquid onto the rotted log.

"Besides, the town elders see the need for change," Phoenix said.

Pasquali looked at her through squinted eyes until something turned his head.

"Sack o' shit!" Pasquali jerked around and grabbed his rifle from the fallen tree.

Down the slope, now more than a hundred yards away and partially shielded by tall overgrowth, stood the same huge mule deer, this time defiantly staring right their way.

Pasquali crouched, settling the rifle on top of the tree. Phoenix knelt, reached out, and touched his shoulder gently. When their eyes locked, she winked playfully.

Pasquali sighed. "Goddamn it." He moved aside as Phoenix settled in behind the rifle.

Gabe studied the dynamic between the old cop and the young mayor. He took a deep breath from the diaphragm, allowing osmosis to channel the still Montana air first through his lungs and then healingly along each and every vein and artery to his feet and hands. And eyes. Nothing he had ever felt in his life—not being drunk, not the excitement of winning big cases during the early part of his career, not even sex—pleased him like the utter stillness he felt whenever he walked the outskirts of his town.

Phoenix fired. The buck remained still for a second before keeling over in slow motion.

"I'll be goddamned!" Pasquali nimbly hopped over the log while drawing his knife. Phoenix stood, watching Pasquali amble down the slope hollering with pleasure. Before Gabe and Phoenix reached the buck, the calmness left Gabe, and he thought again about his normal life. That day's trial, the evening meeting, and why Phoenix Jamborsky had stopped him outside the courthouse the year before to recruit him into the inner workings of Weasel Junction.

"You got it from here, Sheriff?" she said. "I got work to do."

"You sure do." He ran his fingers along the edges of the antlers. "Not bad shooting for a Polack." No doubt the head of Pasquali's kill would soon join the rest of his impressive collection up at the Hunt Club.

"Doesn't take much to outdo a fat old wop." Phoenix turned away. "Don't forget I need you tonight."

Still squatting, Pasquali laughed as he cleaned his knife.

Gabe followed Phoenix back up the hill.

"See you tonight?" she said.

Weeks ago, he had said her, "Terrorists to Weasel Junction Penitentiary? You can't be serious."

"Twin Rivers, my friend," she'd said. "Twin Rivers.

Now he asked, "You really think you can do this?"

"Gabe, like I told you, I'm doing it." She winked at him.

TWO

Gabe took a deep breath and led his client out of the lockup and into the courtroom. Otis T. "Grizzly" Redford tried to straighten his crooked tie and smooth out his absurdly tight white button-down.

"Somebody's gotta tell 'em what's what," Otis whispered one last time as they approached the counsel table. Judge Floyd had given Gabe half an hour to talk Otis out of testifying. The state had rested its case, and everyone in the courtroom, meaning the judge, the prosecutor, Gabe, and the bailiffs, knew that Otis's only chance for acquittal, or even a hung jury, was to take advantage of his right not to testify. The state's case was purely circumstantial. Deputy Glower, having heard a series of rifle shots in the woods a few hundred yards up a ravine from his patrol route, investigated the matter. He stopped his cruiser at the end of the logging road and proceeded on foot. He discovered Otis, whom he knew well, standing over a dead grizzly bear and holding a rifle. Killing the bear was, of course, a serious violation of federal law. It was also common knowledge that Otis bore an unreasonable hatred for the species and had hunted them regularly for years.

"Dear God, Otis, ain't you ever gonna learn?" Glower removed the handcuffs from his belt and walked towards Otis.

Otis dropped his rifle and held out his hands for the cuffs. "I thought it was a blackie." Not an endangered grizzly.

Gabe had represented Otis before, always for some hunting violation or another. About a decade before, Sheriff Pasquali got sick enough of Otis's grizzly poaching to report him to federal authorities, and Otis had done thirty-three months in a federal low-security facility at Greenwood. Pasquali had felt bad about it when he heard the sentence. Otis was, after all, one of them. And so newly elected Mayor Jamborsky had persuaded the City Council to pass a local ordinance forbidding the killing of grizzlies, which allowed Pasquali to continue to arrest Otis for the crime but gave the town jurisdiction so that Otis did not have to travel to the less Otis-friendly federal court in Helena to face federal sentencing guidelines. "I don't condone the little prick's law-breakin'," Pasquali had said, "but we can handle it ourselves."

So Otis faced a maximum twelve-month sentence and seemed bent on making sure he'd serve all of it by testifying to the outrageous lie that he had believed the grizzly was a black bear. What Gabe had been unable to get through Otis's small skull—he really had a very small head, even for his wire-thin body— was that if he testified that he thought the grizzly was a black bear, the prosecutor would be able to cross-examine him about the half-dozen other times he had used exactly that same excuse. If he stayed off the stand, the jury would never hear that he had shot at a grizzly before or used the same lame ploy to get out of it. Of course, some of the jurors knew all about Otis, including his nickname (which had been excluded from evidence), but Gabe believed he could convince at least some of them not to convict if Otis would just keep his mouth shut. But Otis insisted on telling his side of it.

"I gotta see if I can beat this, Gabe! Sometimes you gotta do stupid things just to see how it'll all play out." Words to live by.

"Any luck, Mr. Lantagne?" Judge Floyd asked.

"None, your honor."

"All right, let's get on with it," Floyd said. "You're the one that demanded a speedy trial, so I guess I shouldn't feel bad for you if your client's not prepared." In fact, Redford had demanded a speedy trial, and Floyd had obliged him by setting the matter only three days after his arrest. Floyd was one of only two judges in town and had held the position since 1971. Gabe knew that Judge Floyd was not only familiar with Otis, but had also known Otis's great grandfather, who had shared Otis's deep running hatred for grizzlies. Back then, killing them had been legal. Floyd was a small bald man with a neatly trimmed white beard, very professorial looking, but no-nonsense in running the courtroom, where he rarely failed to know the family history of a litigant.

The jury filed in, smiling at both Gabe and the prosecutor, Maggie Smith. Maggie was shaking her head from side to side, not showing the slightest bit of anxiety about having to cross-examine Otis.

"I call Otis T. Redford," Gabe said. Otis proudly approached the witness stand. Gabe asked the basic but necessary questions. Otis had gone hunting, like he did every Thursday, and as he scoped for deer, a black bear rumbled out of the brush. "I swear, it was a black bear. I reacted and fired, dropping him. I had no idea it was a grizzly." At the end of direct examination, Otis looked right at the jury with a lopsided grin and broke out a gem of legal scholarship he must have picked up at the prison law library: "I ain't had no specific intent."

Maggie stood up and walked at an exaggeratedly slow pace towards Otis. Gabe waited for the expected litany of prior offenses. And prior lies. But Maggie took a slightly different approach.

"How long have you been hunting, Mr. Redford?"

"My whole life, ma'am. Since I was seven."

"And in that time you've shot many animals?"

"Damn straight."

"Rabbits?"

"Yes."

"Weasels?"

"Yes."

"Deer."

"Yes."

"Elk?"

"Not since it's been illegal, ma'am." Nice.

"And black bears, I assume?"

"Plenty."

"So you know what a black bear looks like?"

"Of course, everybody knows what a black bear looks like."

"And you know the difference between a black bear and a grizzly?"

"Yes, if I get a good enough look."

"And you would not shoot a grizzly bear?"

"Objection," Gabe said.

"Sustained." Judge Floyd did not make Gabe state the full objection. What Otis would or would not do on a different day was not relevant and triggered inadmissible character evidence.

"I'll go at it another way," Maggie said. "You shoot animals from a distance, do you not?"

"As far as anybody."

"A good shot?"

"The best." Otis gave the jury another spooky grin.

"Trained in the Army, correct?"

"That's right. Honorable discharge in eighty-eight."

"Trained as a sniper?"

"You bet."

"You're afraid to get too close, let's say, to a black bear. You take them from long range. Like a sniper."

"Afraid? Never. You shoot when you got the shot. Ain't no point in sneaking too close."

"But you'd prefer to shoot from far away, where the black bear has no chance to attack you?"

"Sheeeit. Everybody knows black bears don't attack."

"You're afraid to find out, aren't you?"

"No."

"You are a coward, Mr. Redford, hiding in bushes hundreds of yards away shooting black bears that can't even see you."

"That's crap."

Gabe could not understand Maggie's approach. Some jurors were noticeably reacting to the slam against hunting.

"You would never, Mr. Redford, have the guts to hunt a dangerous animal, would you?"

"Yes, I would." Otis was getting angry.

"You didn't know this bear was a grizzly, and if you had, you would have run the other way, am I right?"

"Hell, no!"

"You don't have the guts to hunt a grizzly, sir, do you?"

"You're full of shit! I've killed me a dozen grizzlies and you know it."

Judge Floyd did not even bother to reprimand Otis for the language. The jury laughed.

"Mr. Redford," Maggie asked politely, "would you like to change the story you told the jury on direct examination?"

Maggie was taking it a step further than she had to. Maybe she was giving Otis a chance to clear up the record, to come clean and help himself out at sentencing.

Otis looked at Gabe, who shrugged but objected.

"Overruled."

Otis took a deep breath. "All right, all right, I'll tell you what happened, but y'all ain't never gonna believe me."

More laughter.

"Try us," Maggie said.

"I was hunting Barney's Fall, looking for deer, but I won't lie, I hoped to see a grizzly. Just before quitting, downwind fifty yards, out comes that three-year-old. Took me but a second to get him in my sights, but, you know, you need more than one shot on a grizzly, and they's liable to charge after the first shot." Otis paused to look at the jury. "Y'ain't gonna believe me."

"Don't worry about what they'll believe," the judge said, "just tell the truth."

Otis shook his head from side to side. "I fired. As I chambered another round, the grizzly charged." Otis turned to the jury, animated. "They run a lot faster than you think. From, say, fifty yards, you only got a few seconds to react. I took aim, but before I fired, I heard a burst of shots to my left, maybe two bursts, a little bit up the ridge. Only, they wasn't rifle shots. It was like, it was more like…"

"More like what?" Maggie asked.

"Machinegun fire. The grizzly dropped like a stone, only twenty feet from me. I've never seen one go dead like that. I looked in the direction of the shots, and I saw him."

"Saw who?" Maggie asked.

"The Arab dude."

"Arab dude?"

"With a rifle like I never seen. And this is the hard part to believe. He raised his rifle at me, and I froze. Like one of them Al-Qaeda, come all the way from sand-land to wage war on us right here in Weasel Junction. I ain't never been scared of no grizzly, but I damn near shit my pants. I'm telling you ma'am, you may doubt it, but I got a knack for sizing up a man, and the second looked right into that fella's eyes told me he'd taken it upon himself to kill me. I know I'm as full of shit as the next man, but I've raised three kids and been kind to my wife, and unless God has an all encompassin' affinity for the Ursus horribilus, I deem my chances for paradise about even. So this is all flashin' through my head, especially when I noticed the thingamajig hanging off the side of the dude's barrel."

"Thingamajig?"

"Like a grenade launcher. My life flashed before my eyes until I heard Glower's car pull in way down by the end-way. I looked down at the car, and when I turned back, the fella was gone. Like he just disappeared without a sound."

"Why do you say he was a quote, Arab dude?" Maggie asked.

Otis thought about it for a second. "He had kinda dark skin. But I guess it was 'cause of the funny Arab hat."

Maggie paused. "And this…Arab dude, you never mentioned him to the police?"

"Nope."

"Or to anyone?"

"Nope. But I did ask my lawyer to check the ballistics on the grizzly. He said that wasn't no big issue."

Gabe cringed a little. When Otis's defense was that he had shot the bear thinking it was a black bear, it hadn't seemed ballistics would matter.

"Would you recognize this man again?"

"That face and eyes? I'll never forget him. Never."

"So instead of telling Glower the truth about the Arab dude, you told him that you shot the bear and thought it was a black bear?"

"It just came out."

"And when you said you thought the grizzly was a black bear, that was a lie?"

"Yes, ma'am.

"That's all the questions I have."

It was not the first time one of Gabe's criminal clients had self-destructed on the stand. Garbage in, garbage out, he told them. You have to tell me the truth. Gabe studied Redford, who watched him expectantly, apparently unaware he had just been humiliated by Maggie.

"Your honor, may I approach the bench?" Gabe asked. Floyd frowned, but motioned him and Maggie forward.

"Judge," Gabe whispered, "I move for a week-long continuance to investigate this new information. We could do an autopsy, and—"

"You gotta be kidding, Gabe," Floyd said, loud enough for the jury to hear. "Your client asked for a speedy trial and chose his poison. You actually expect me to order county funds to pay for an autopsy on an animal based on the fib this joker just told the jury?"

Gabe pleaded with his eyes. Maggie wisely stayed silent.

"Continue with the trial, Gabe," Floyd said.

As Gabe returned to counsel table, he knew that objectively, Floyd was right. So why did it feel wrong? When he turned back to face the court, he knew why. Sure, Redford was a liar. But after four years of acquaintance and several cases together, Gabe thought he knew when Redford lied. The Arab dude bit may have been crap, but Redford believed it.

It took the jury fifteen minutes to convict.

Judge Floyd shook his head. "Otis, you are a marvel. You can wait in jail for sentencing. In two weeks, if you can come convince me you'll give up hunting, I'll consider not imposing the maximum. That's not just for the bear, that's for lyin'."

Otis shrugged, not one to delve to deeply into the meanings of things.

In the lockup, Gabe had a moment with Otis outside the bailiff's earshot.

"What the hell was that all about, Otis? The Arab dude?"

"Gabe, I've known you for years and I know you know I'm full of shit. But on this one, I give you my word. That Taliban motherfucker aimed to blow my dick into the dirt."

"If you give up hunting for life, Floyd might cut you loose on probation."

"Not a chance, my friend."

When Gabe turned to walk away, Otis called out to him. "Hey, Gabe, you believe me?"

"No comment, Otis." Gabe's mind was already moving on from Otis to some of his bigger cases, including a rape case that would begin in a few weeks.

Redford called out again as Gabe left the lockup. "Hey Counselor, Glower never did no autopsy on that corpse. You really think a coupla bullets from a .358 Winchester killed that beast?"

THREE

The two young men flew along the ice, the sliver of a moon granting them just enough light to see their path. They were about the same age and yelled to each other over the loud whir of the snowmobile. The smaller man drove, with the bigger one gripping him around the waist, his mouth next to the smaller man's ear. The snowmobile dragged a large, swinging metal trailer. Anyone watching might have believed the pair slightly odd, speeding across the frozen lake in the middle of the night, too fast and too directed to be out for a casual ride. No, they were clearly not crossing the lake for fun. But no one would see them on the lake. The reservation police were not inclined to patrol the ten miles of frozen lake during the day, let alone at three a.m. And besides, two crazy Indians would hardly raise an eyebrow. After all, this was not the United States, not even Canada, but the sovereign Cree Nation.

The snowmobile reached the shore and bounced up over a small hill onto the American side of the reservation. Immediately, the driver whipped the snowmobile around and back to the edge of the ice, his movements, for the first time, suggesting uncertainty. Or, to a trained eye, panic. Both men dismounted and crawled to the top of the hill, peering down across the snowy plain onto the American side of the Cree Nation. After a few moments, the smaller man reached into a bag on the snowmobile and removed a small glass bottle. He looked back over the plain, then tipped the bottle back, taking a long drink. The larger man stood directly behind the smaller one, looking this way and that across the lake.

He too bent and fished through a backpack. The small man began to twist the cap back onto his bottle. Then his brains flew out of his head and onto the fresh snow.

Ahmed stood alone, staring all around, both north across the lake and south, over the small hill and across the empty plain. Nothing. Right before killing Adams, he had actually been impressed, for the first time, with the silly Indian's decisiveness. Not seeing his contacts on the American side of the lake, Adams had retreated a safe distance to assess the situation. This drug deal, and selling the American marijuana in Canada, would have earned Adams and his brother a lot of money. Yet Adams was willing to drive away at the first sign of trouble. The empty plain, for Adams, was a sign of trouble. Maybe he had not been such a monumental fool. Ahmed had paused before killing Adams. He had allowed Adams to get one last sip from his grubby little liquor bottle before he died. It was only fair. It was what Adams had loved most in life. But now, Ahmed needed to move quickly.

He crawled up the hill and looked across the snowy plain in the slender moonlight. Into America. Still nothing. He reached down and scooped up some snow. He was suddenly so thirsty. But as his heart rate slowed, he smiled to himself, the fresh powder tingling his teeth.

FOUR

MAY 8, 2009 – TWIN RIVERS, MONTANA

Gabe pulled into the overflowing Holy Redeemer parking lot. At least four hundred people had already arrived, and the meeting wouldn't start for half an hour yet. The beginnings of these things always made Gabe feel so awkward. The town leaders sat silently in folding chairs on the stage while the attendees filled the seats, socializing. Most of the meetings were held at City Hall, but the City Hall multi-purpose room wasn't big enough to hold that night's crowd. And so, for the second time in six months, Gabe watched Phoenix sitting patiently with her legs crossed, center stage, while the Holy Redeemer quietly filled with those Caroline County residents who cared enough about the pending issue to show up. Pasquali, the council members, Judge Floyd, and City Treasurer Marlin Stillwater were all late. Gabe nodded to people in the crowd while Phoenix waved. Her political wave. Gabe ducked back outside.

A year and a half earlier, he had stepped outside the courthouse during a recess in a jury trial.

"Hey, are you Gabe Lantagne?" Phoenix Jamborsky had been wearing jeans and a simple red blouse and carried a handful of campaign literature. Her own. She began to introduce herself.

"I know who you are," Gabe had said. "You're running for mayor."

"I met your father once, in Helena. During his last campaign." She smiled. "As if he ever had to campaign." In one sentence, this total stranger had touched not only on his father's career as Attorney General of Montana, but also on his death. His last campaign. Phoenix stood close, more familiar than most strangers.

Her blue eyes probed his, searching. His probed hers, curious. An older woman—a politician, for Christ's sakes. But a hot one.

"Can we have coffee sometime?" she'd said. "I admit I'm a shameless networker, but we have something in common. We both left big careers to come to Weasel Junction. Plus, I may need to recruit you to help save the town."

Martha Ann Tomkins, the wife of the owner of the town's only paper, *The Weasel Junction Wallflower*, pulled into the Holy Redeemer parking lot and threw him a kiss as she stepped out of her car. She was also the paper's only crime reporter and wrote stories about all of Gabe's trials, no matter how mundane. She had to be seventy years old, but with more than enough energy to treat the town's meager criminal docket as a real crime beat. She even monitored Pasquali's police-band radio and responded to drunk-driving arrests to get photographs.

"Any comment? Are you disappointed with Otis's verdict?"

Gabe put his arm around her and walked her towards the door. "I won't comment before sentencing, you know that, Martha Ann. I'll be in touch."

"Anytime, Gabe." She brandished her camera and walked inside.

"That woman is in love with you." Maggie leaned up against the door with an unlit cigarette in one hand and a lighter in the other. "No wonder they write up your losses as wins." Gabe shared a cigarette with Maggie and laughed as she parodied Otis's testimony. "What a freakin' piece of work," she said. "He's got Guantanamo fever, like some other people around here I could mention."

When they'd smoked the cigarette down to the butt, they walked back into the church, where Maggie went off to find a seat, and Gabe took his up on stage with the rest of the council.

"Miss Mayor," Will Jarvis called from the third row. "Go get 'em tonight!" Will owned all three of Twin Rivers' gas stations, each under a different corporate title. Martha Ann popped up from the second row, snapped a series of pictures of Phoenix, and gave Gabe a coy little finger-wave.

As the town leaders arrived, Phoenix spoke again to Evelyn Kerwinkle, the only solid supporter of her plan on the council besides Gabe. Jim Betterman, a wealthy retired rancher, would vote for her plan but say nothing. Egan Crowne, Twin Rivers' penultimate town elder, had openly opposed the plan all winter, and, as usual, had old Melvin Thompson with him. Egan was extremely wealthy and very active on the City Council. Thompson never attended a council meeting or campaigned for office but had more than a hundred relatives in Caroline County.

Treasurer Stillwater arrived and fed Phoenix his last-minute figures. Marlin typified the practical, small-town, honest frugality upon which Twin Rivers prided itself. His daily uniform consisted of high-water khaki pants, one of three colors of button-down shirt tucked in with a brown belt, and sneakers. He had been town treasurer for more than twenty years. His seven grown children, like many of their generation, had left town for college and never come back.

As seven o'clock approached, the pews filled, and attendees packed the sides and back of the church. Gabe saw an even mix of friendly faces, unfriendly ones, and unknown blank stares. The crowd buzzed loudly now. Out of the corner of his eye, Gabe recognized a surprise attendee and nudged Phoenix.

Phoenix rolled her eyes. "I don't need to see him, I can sense him." Her ex-husband, Michael Terwilliger. What used to be his father's ranch, and was now his, dominated the western part of Caroline County, one of the few remaining non-corporate ranches in Western Montana. Michael rarely left the ranch and, contrary to family tradition, was reputed to disdain town politics. He stood with his arms folded, but not in a way that suggested insecurity. "When Michael stands that way," Phoenix said, "he gives off this deceptive aura of cold substantiality."

"It's just about time, Phoenix," Marlin whispered from behind her, then scurried back to his own folding chair.

Phoenix rose. The buzz of the crowd faded quickly, and she stood at Pastor Jenkins's aged wooden podium, facing her town. "Welcome to the May 8, 2009, Twin Rivers town meeting."

"Weasel Junction," someone yelled out, followed by a smattering of claps, some boos, and a few laughs.

"We all know the purpose of this meeting and its importance to the future of our town, no matter which way it goes."

"Bullshit!" rang out under the guise of a cough. "Bullshit! Bullshit!" Coughs bounced around the room for a few seconds until Arnold Johanson stood up from the front row, turned to the crowd, and yelled, "Shut up, you ignoramuses!"

"Thank you, Arnold," Phoenix said. "Before I call upon Treasurer Stillwater to present the most recent Twin Rivers' financial figures, I want to discuss a bit of the history of this town. Weasel Junction was founded in 1869 by Emitt Johanson," Phoenix nodded to Arnold in the front row, "and George Carloff. They passed this way en route to Oregon, only to turn back. They remembered this spot, between the rivers, and the valley in which they had camped, where they saw…"

The room quietly laughed.

"Yes, we all know, two weasels mating. They believed that the place they named Weasel Junction would make not only a trading post, but a settlement. No soldier, no hunter, and no trader had noticed what these two men noticed about this place. They traded with the Flathead, the Cree, the Blackfeet, and the Cheyenne, remaining at peace with the tribes even at a tragic time of war about which America is still ashamed."

Heads nodded approvingly throughout the room. At least a third of Twin Rivers' residents carried some Native American blood, including town stalwarts such as Egan Crowne and Michael Terwilliger.

"And when the wars ended, Weasel Junction was not just a trading post, but a town—a town made up of almost as many Native Americans as whites from the East. Johanson and Carloff's town was different from many new towns in the West. For one, important decisions were made by town meetings. For another, Native Americans took part in those meetings. In the late nineteenth century, this idea was so radical that townsfolk lied about it to politicians from Helena, Bozeman, and Missoula, at one point literally holding sham, whites-only town meetings whenever somebody important came through." The phony town meetings were a famous story and a source of pride. Pride in the fact that Weasel Junction could keep a secret. "We all recognize the importance of tonight's decision."

"The whole freakin' country knows about tonight's decision," Angelo Martin called out. Angelo, like many, was angry about the national attention.

"I know, and I'm sorry about that. I had no choice there, if we wanted the opportunity to make this decision. Treasurer Stillwater, if you please, the financial report." Phoenix smiled and sat down.

Stillwater stepped to the podium to soft applause. "Ladies and Gentleman, Twin Rivers is in serious trouble."

The room roared with an acknowledging but disapproving groan of applause.

"Caroline County has nine hundred twenty-three residents, of which about seven hundred live in Twin Rivers. Three years ago today, three hundred and forty-seven people in this county worked, in some way or another, at either the Chrysler plant in Thomason, the National Park, some other tourist-based company up north, or the machine shop. As you all know, the Chrysler plant closed eight months ago, and the machine shop entered bankruptcy more than a year ago. The park is hiring, but people from all over the state are applying for those jobs and I haven't heard of a new hire in weeks."

"The jobs don't start until spring," Millicent Browner called out from the back of the church. Millie was one of those rare college students who had returned to Twin Rivers. She volunteered at Phoenix's office but wanted to be a park ranger at Glacier.

"The way I break it down," Stillwater continued, "twenty-six percent of Caroline County residents are over sixty-five, twenty-four percent are—"

"Drunks!" yelled Curly Bringham, standing and raising her hand to laughter. She owned Pandora's Box, the strip bar on the Caroline-Brody County line, as well as the motel behind it. The bar literally stood right on the county line, allowing Curly to pay the lower local taxes in Caroline but keep the east side of the bar open until 3 a.m. under Brody's more lenient liquor laws. Curly and her posse of strippers and waitress filled half a row. Solid Phoenix votes.

"The point is," Stillwater said, "to put it bluntly, without a new source of revenue, this town is finished, and we all know it. By the end of the year, we'll have no choice but to shut down funding for the after-school program at Ellman Elementary and Johanson Middle School, the drug and alcohol program on Dunbar, and Sheriff Pasquali's jail work-force program. We will also have to let go of two police officers, two courtroom bailiffs, and seven support staff at City Hall. That's more jobs gone. All snow removal outside Twin Rivers city limits ends today, and police patrol will likely only extend outside town on a call-by-call basis. By next spring, this town will no longer be a town, but just a strip bar, a motel, and a couple of gas stations. There won't be much of a reason to keep a name on it at all."

In the mammoth silence that followed these remarks, Stillwater unfolded an easel and placed on it a blow-up of a spreadsheet. "The County budget, showing what we pay for what: schools, the sheriff's department, transportation and infrastructure—all the expenses any town has. But our biggest cost is this one." He stabbed a finger onto the sheet. "The payments on the twenty million dollars we borrowed to build the Twin Rivers Maximum Security Penitentiary."

Stillwater stepped back and let the crowd heave in disapproval.

Mel Tarper stood, gesturing angrily. "I was always against that shit!"

"You should have come to the fuckin' meeting and voted then, peckerhead," Bill Stapleton said over his shoulder.

"Folks, quiet please," Stillwater called out. "As we all know, that prison has been built for nearly two years and has yet to house a single prisoner. I now will ask Warden Miller Haverford to say a few words."

The groans and boos exploded. Mayor Pritchard had hired Haverford to oversee the prison because he had an impressive career as a warden. He was an outsider from Eastern Montana, and the county was still paying him on his four-year contract. He reported to work every day at the empty prison, where he and his deputy nailed golf balls from the top of the prison yard.

"Fellow citizens of Twin Rivers," he said slowly, "I know my presence on your payroll has not been taken too kindly."

"Damn straight!" someone yelled.

"But I strongly believe that this town does not object to my citizenship itself, and I hope you believe me when I say I'm doing everything I can to secure a contract. The problem is, I'm failing. I've been to Washington, DC four times on my own dime, spoken to eleven state legislatures and many more corrections officials. Our prison has fallen between the cracks."

"We musta been smoking crack!" Curly yelled from her seat.

"I'm here tonight to assure you of one thing. I've worked in seven prisons in my career, all maximum security, and been warden of three. I've housed serial killers, death-row inmates, and even the Unabomber for a time. I give you my word as a fellow citizen and a man, the Twin Rivers facility is topnotch. I have never worked at a more secure prison. Harry Houdini couldn't escape from that joint. If any person here doubts me, I personally invite you to a free-of-charge stay at Twin Rivers, and you can try to escape. I'll use only one deputy, and I can guarantee not a one of you could get out, or even get from one unit to another without an escort."

"Why don't we lock you up and you try to escape," Myrna Flatcher mumbled loud enough to be heard.

"No thank you, ma'am. Nobody can escape from Twin Rivers. Nobody." Haverford returned to his seat.

Phoenix retook the podium. "This is the most critical vote that has ever come before a town meeting. None of you doubts Treasurer Stillwater's figures or his predictions. Caroline County will always exist, but in a year, Twin Rivers will be a ghost town unless something changes."

Silence.

Phoenix picked up a remote control, turned slightly, and triggered a projector which lit a large screen behind her. "This is the Guantanamo Bay prison facility. It opened in early 2002, and has housed between one hundred and four hundred alleged enemy combatants, almost all of whom were arrested in Afghanistan, Pakistan, or Iraq. The President has ordered this prison closed, and inmates will be shipped all over the world, including to prisons in Italy, Bermuda, Pago-Pago, Spain, France, and Turkey. No state, no city, no town, no prison in the United States has agreed to take any of the prisoners. Instead, our nation is paying extravagant amounts of tax money to other countries."

Phoenix clicked to the next slide, a document marked classified, privileged and confidential, and do not disseminate. Some murmuring and a few gasps rippled through the room.

"I have to be the only mayor in America who would share a document like this with all of you. Who could trust this information to an entire town? But we're no normal town." The document was a letter to Phoenix with financial figures, rules, regulations, and other stipulations concerning housing Guantanamo Bay detainees—essentially, a proposed contract.

"You can see a lot of fine print here, but I'm going to go through the important parts. First, contrary the reporting on CNN, our proposal to the Justice Department is not to house all of the Guantanamo Bay detainees, but only ten. None of us wants reporters flooding into town, we don't need that kind of tourist, nor to be on the news every night. We also don't need to be the focal point of any crazy terrorist who wants to make a point. I get all that. That's why I proposed we house only ten. We can keep our privacy and keep our town. Here's how. The United States government treats these prisoners differently than any other super-max prisoners. The rates are higher, the rules are stricter, and they are willing to shell out to make sure this gets done right. The Justice Department knows that whatever Twin Rivers charges for housing prisoners, it won't be as much as Pago-Pago."

She pointed to the key figure. "Three hundred ten thousand per prisoner per year to cover the actual costs of housing the prisoner, paid at the beginning of each year so that the municipality does not have to seek loans to cover costs."

Phoenix paused. Easy math for anyone. "Three point one million dollars a year. Some of this will go toward paying off the loan. Some of it will go toward paying the guards, at a starting salary of forty-one thousand a year plus benefits—and all of those guards will be currently unemployed Caroline County residents.

That doesn't include the clerical staff, kitchen staff, and the cleaning staff, who will be additional hires."

Phoenix clicked her remote. Another slide came up. "There are also upfront payments, as distinguished from the annual payment per prisoner, designed to make sure the prison is suitably staffed and secure to meet their guidelines. They cover any renovations necessary to comply with security requirements, and any extra staffing needs. For necessary renovations, the amount is one hundred forty thousand dollars per prisoner—even though Twin Rivers, as a new prison, already meets almost all the federal guidelines. For staffing, the amount is one hundred ten thousand dollars per new hire needed to meet the government's staffing requirement. The government's staffing requirements are slightly more stringent than for regular super-max prisoners—a five-to-one prisoner-to-guard ratio."

In the front row, Milton Dormington scribbled notes on a yellow pad he had laid out on his lap. Head down and hunched over, he wrote fast, his calculator balanced on one of his knees. Milton was an accountant, the only one in town, and his office on River Street serviced almost every business in Twin Rivers.

"The benefit to Twin Rivers mainly lies in the Justice Department's rigid regulations and definitions concerning prison capacities," Phoenix said. "Our situation is rather unique. The federal government insists that the task of housing Guantanamo detainees focus heavily on preventing them from having contact with any American prisoners. So while we will only be housing ten detainees, and thus receiving only three point one million dollars a year for housing costs, the upfront payments for renovations and employment are calculated strictly by overall capacity, and not just by the number of Guantanamo detainees." Phoenix paused. "This is true even if the prison is, like ours, presently under capacity. Our overall capacity is four hundred fifty prisoners."

The only notable sound in the room was Milton pounding the buttons on his calculator. Suddenly he stood up with his pad and stared at his calculator. Every eye was on him.

"Total upfront payment: thirty-one million dollars. Plus three point one a year." Gabe expected an uproar at this, but the crowd seemed dumbstruck.

"Thank you, Milton," Phoenix said. "The contract will create jobs and keep all of our county services open. But that's not enough. Right now, a lot of our citizens cannot shop at the stores on River Road, cannot buy new clothes for their children, go on vacations, get a new car, open a business, or just go to the movies once in a while. Therefore, upon securing our initial payment under the contract, I will give every adult in Caroline County a stimulus grant—not a loan, but a grant—of fifteen thousand dollars."

A wave of noise erupted from the assembly. Phoenix lifted her chin and waited. Just as quickly, the clamor died away.

"A week from Saturday, once the contract is formally certified, we will host the first annual Twin Rivers Day celebration in the town square. Within days, we will receive the first third of our initial payment, and the stimulus checks will issued forthwith— for the full amount. TR Day will mark the beginning of years of prosperity. But only if you trust me, and trust this plan."

Phoenix gravely scanned the completely silent audience, nodded, and returned to her seat. After another few seconds of stunned silence, the room exploded with loud applause. But for every smiling face, Gabe saw a skeptical grimace.

"All right then," Pasquali called out from the back. "Let's vote!" Gabe had not seen him arrive, but now he strode forward down the center aisle, commanding all attention. Perhaps he showed up late on purpose. Let Phoenix have her own show. As sheriff, he always supervised the town meeting vote. He carried the old wooden ballot box under his arm and placed it on the stage.

"All right, people, you all know the drill. Line forms up the middle. One vote each. Pens and ballots are being passed out by the deputies at the end of each aisle."

After voting, Gabe walked out the back door of the church, where he found Phoenix by Pasquali's Suburban. The other council members slowly joined them by the truck, forming a semicircle of eight. Gabe, the newcomer to the council, realized this was something of a ritual. Thompson and Egan made small talk, but for the most part, the group just stood, seeing their own breath and sharing the quiet anticipation. Gabe watched Phoenix smoke. She was a beautiful woman, but it was a beauty that grew from knowing her. Her stark blue eyes shifted with interest around the circle as her colleagues spoke. She finished a cigarette and flicked the butt towards an empty oil drum, where it smacked the rim, bounced into the air, and missed. She shrugged and looked at Gabe out of the corner of her eye, holding the look just long enough. She had caught him watching her. Her movements carried artistic flair even in failure, like those of a natural athlete gifted not only in sports but also in the normally mundane movements of regular life. Gabe may not have believed the crap about the town being so special, but the existence of Phoenix Eileen Jamborsky in Weasel Junction was an extraordinary event.

Pasquali finally sauntered out the back door of the church followed by Michael Terwilliger and Deputy Glower, who balanced the wooden ballot box on both arms like a Christmas gift. Pasquali scanned the group near his Suburban. "So this here's the town elders these days? They get younger every year."

"Speak for yourself, Grandpa," Thompson said, himself eighty-one. He smoked a cigar. "And let me get a hit of that flask, these meetings drive me to drinkin'."

"Since when do you lower yourself to attend a town function, your highness?" Thompson said to Michael, who just laughed and smacked him on the back. People used to refer to Michael and Phoenix as the King and Queen of Caroline County. That was before the divorce. And before Enos died.

"I'm just waiting for my daughter, big man. She's running around inside with the other banshees. Thought I'd watch what you important people do."

Pasquali tossed Thompson a half-full pint, which he caught with one hand. Thompson turned to Phoenix. "Thought I'd seen it all. Bribery! Right in front of everybody. Shit, boy, times have changed." He uncorked the bottle and took a swig.

Deputy Glower plopped the box down on the hood of Pasquali's Suburban and shined a flashlight as Pasquali dumped the vote box over, spilling the four hundred plus square sheets of white paper.

"Y'all can watch if you want," Pasquali said. He began sorting the ballots into two stacks, but stopped suddenly. "Almost forgot." He pulled a wad of white squares out of his back pocket. "Absentee ballots from the jail. Anybody contestin?" Gabe had seen this at the name-change meeting. The town rules allowed those serving jail time to vote, and Pasquali collected ballots from them.

Judge Floyd reached out his hand. "Somebody should check 'em." Floyd flipped through the ballots one at a time. "I recognize eleven of these names, and I take your word on the signatures, Sheriff, but I contest this one. Who the hell is Jonathon Scruggs?"

"Disorderly conduct. He's serving some time, sentenced by Judge Patrick."

"In any case, I don't know him. You're gonna need some proof he resides in Caroline County for that vote to count."

The Sheriff examined Scruggs's ballot, folded it, crammed it into his shirt pocket, then returned to the task of counting ballots.

The church door opened, and Michael and Phoenix's daughter Ayalette giddily skipped over to Michael, hugging him around the legs. "I'm out," Michael said. "See you captains of politics later." He scooped up Ayalette and disappeared around the side of the church. The church lights went off, and Glower's flashlight and a faraway streetlamp provided the only unnatural light. Gabe's eyes were drawn across the valley towards the mountains and above to the nearly full white moon.

FIVE

MAY 1, 2009 – CREE NATION RESERVATION, ST. REGIS LAKE, CANADA-MONTANA BORDER

It began to snow, not hard, but enough for Ahmed to be sure God was with him. Every second counted, as he had no way of knowing who might appear on the American side of the lake at any moment. Random eyes, even eyes far across the emptiness, could doom him. Be at Peace, Ahmed, Omar had said to him once, when Omar noticed the agitation in Ahmed's fingers during a weapons drill.

Ahmed had never been outside Pakistan in his twenty years, and here he was, standing over the body of a dead Indian—a North American Indian. He had volunteered to train at the camp north of his village two years before, leaving his mother and brother Abu on the side of the road in front of their home to watch him walk the entire way around the bend. He hadn't turned back, so his memory of them remained frozen in the moment he said goodbye, his mother sobbing and Abu stoically holding her hand, a book in his other hand.

You should never awaken a sleeping giant, Ahmed had heard the Great Leader say on the one of the two occasions he had been able to meet the man. Unless you know the giant will wake up and commit suicide. The Great Leader had smiled and laughed endearingly, standing and moving away from the circle of teenagers at the camp who hung on his every word.

Ahmed remembered the first time in his life he had laid eyes on men he knew to be mujahedeen. It was months after the attacks on the World Trade towers in America. Eleven years old, he was sitting in the café in a town far from his village, waiting for his father to finish some business. Watch those men, his father had said. Do not try to listen to them, just watch them, how they move, how they walk, how they watch. The three men sat a table drinking coffee and talking. When one got up, Ahmed saw what his father meant. The man did not walk like the workers he had seen in big towns like Islamabad, hurriedly, limbs cranking and creaking to get where they needed to be. Or like the arrogant businessmen, standing tall and walking slowly and erect in their suits. The mujahedeen walked like dangerous, wise lions with studying eyes and muscles relaxed yet ready to spring. They talked calmly, not gesturing and raising their voices like the other men in the cafés discussing politics. They spoke without fear even though the police here would arrest them here just as they would in Chechnya, France, Britain, or even America. The greatest infidels are the puppet governments of Muslim countries like our own, Ahmed's father said. Worse even than America, worse even than Israel. But the mujahedeen live without fear of them or anyone. Their souls are prepared for death. Can the same be said of the police and the army, who fight only for pay?

Ahmed knew that his father had once been to a camp, but many years before, and he had long since ceased walking like a mujahid. But he spoke with the deep wisdom of a man who understood the world. Soon after that day at the cafe, his father was arrested by police from Islamabad, right in their village in front of everyone. Ahmed never saw him again. When Ahmed turned eighteen, he left home for the mountains, with little more than rumors and old stories about how to find the camp that would teach him to wage jihad.

Ahmed stared at Adams's corpse. What a worthless man. He marveled at the entire decrepit Cree Nation. An oppressed people, like his own, but a people whose reaction to oppression was to live on the dark periphery, cringing with fear and drunkenness.

Ahmed knew that the North American Indians had once been a proud people, who fought the greedy Americans to the death in some of the most famous battles in the history of guerrilla warfare. Like Little Big Horn, where Sitting Bull's warriors had butchered General Custer's soldiers. Just like the mujahedeen, the Indians had fought for their homeland, and the soldiers had fought for money. The Indians could have prevailed, but plainly had lacked the will to continue the fight. Those Indians of old were people to admire though they had worshipped heathen gods. Adams and his Cree Nation would be better off today if their ancestors had kept fighting. Maybe Adams would have been a young soldier like Ahmed instead of a drunk who wore American rock band T-shirts and made his living smuggling drugs over a frozen lake.

Adams had even insulted Ahmed as they crossed the lake, referring to him as a homosexual merely because Ahmed held tight to his stomach to keep from being thrown off the snowmobile. "Does that feel good, you ass-pirate?" Adams had screamed, a phrase Ahmed only knew because Adams used it all the time.

At the camp, a man named Karim had discussed just such situations.

American and Canadian men make fun of each other with homosexual names, Karim said. If a man touches you, or sits too close, feel free to say, "What, are you some kind of faggot?" If you smile, he'll take it as a joke. Not like here, where you might be killed for calling a mujahid a homosexual.

Karim, half-Scot, half-Afghan, had, like Adams, been a drunk. Word among the brothers was that Karim traveled the world raising money for jihad. Karim himself bragged of buying weapons and collecting cash in western countries. He had attended college in England, had traveled in America, and even had an Anglo last name, McLanahan. In camp, he went only by Karim. His presence at the camp, Ahmed slowly learned, concerned his expertise in Western culture. Omar said Karim was a Muslim, but Ahmed never quite believed it. Karim lived in a separate cabin far from the brothers, and he owned luxuries like a television and a computer. He drank liquor, allowed himself to be fat, and made crude jokes. His skittish, suspicious eyes and silly comments made Ahmed suspect that Karim worked for pay.

But Karim McLanahan had been a valuable part of Ahmed's training.

The rules in America provide small, meaningless autonomy to the Indians to soothe American guilt for slaughtering most of them. So Indians can cross the border in the middle of the reservation without security checkpoints. Of course, the Americans have checkpoints entering the reservation, but not on the water. The Indians in Canada bring guns and whiskey into Montana across the lake. The Indians in the south sell them marijuana. Tons of it. Since September 11, the Americans have started watching the border more closely. But they don't really care about drugs, only terrorists. If they think you're a Canadian buying marijuana, they'll arrest you because prisons and courts are an important industry in America, but they won't suspect you're a mujahid. They don't expect a warrior like you in the middle of nowhere. But once the Americans decide to bring your brothers to the prison in Montana, they'll increase border protection. So remember, you're a Canadian pot smuggler. Act stupid. American police don't mind if you keep your mouth shut. They won't even torture you. They'll just give you a court date and then sentence you to prison for smuggling. They'll also force you to have a lawyer. Just tell your lawyer you're sorry, your father was a drunk who beat you, and that you only smuggle drugs because you're so poor you can't feed your children. For you, prison will be like a luxury hotel. Karim laughed and laughed at this. Sometimes, Ahmed could tell Karim knew nothing about the soul of a mujahid.

At the camp, most of the young trainees lacked any real education, spoke only their own languages, and trained to return home to fight in their own countries—Chechnya, Tajikistan, Afghanistan, Uzbekistan, Indonesia, Philippines, Yemen, Somalia, Sudan, Turkey, Egypt, even Iraq. Others though, had grown up in cities, even in Europe. Some had been to universities in Germany, France, or England. But Omar had noticed Ahmed right away. Also, while he could not follow all of the political discussions of the older brothers, he did know English. His father had been the wisest man in the village, and his mother, unlike most women, spoke English and taught at a school. Ahmed often wondered if Omar selected him because of his English or his physical strength and quickness with fighting and weapons, but Omar never gave either as the reason. He said Ahmed had the pure soul of a mujahid.

Omar asked Ahmed to accompany him and another soldier to Peshawar. Ahmed was honored to go on such a trip, but scared. Omar was famous and could be recognized by the police or the army. They attended meetings where dozens revered Omar, and they had more invitations to homes than they could accept. They also collected money. Ahmed was shocked that Omar carried so much cash in an old shoulder bag. Ahmed once mentioned robbery. Omar laughed hard at that. Death, yes, my friend. Robbery, I think not.

During the trip to Peshawar, Ahmed saw his own face in a mirror at a café. He had changed. The mirror reflected his long beard and hard eyes. He looked like a mujahid.

On the way back to the camp, Omar explained to Ahmed that he would be traveling on a foreign mission of the greatest importance. You are the best hand fighter at the camp, Omar *said. And good with weapons. But now your training will shift to explosives—and to American culture.*

Ahmed glanced across the barren landscape, the mountains jutting towards the sky many, many miles to the west. He had trained in the mountains, mountains as high as the ones in Canada and Montana. He could not deny the beauty of this land, all the more reason why Adams and his people should still be fighting for it. Allah could not look unkindly on a man like Adams, whose poor spirit and unholy habits were not all his fault. Unlike the leaders and capitalist classes of Muslim countries, who knew the Koran and God's way and yet sold themselves like whores, Adams was just a casualty of history.

Ahmed unzipped his backpack and removed a small wooden axe he had purchased at the Cree Nation general store. He fell to his knees on the edge of the lake and began to smash the axe against the ice, again, again, again, until the ice cracked. Then he stood on the cracked spot and jumped up and down until both feet broke through, one of them touching bottom six or more inches below. Again, with the axe, he pounded the edges of the cracked hole until he had a sufficiently large, raggedly hewn cleft in the ice.

He stood, breathing heavily. *Be at peace, Ahmed.*

He slid his arms under Adams's shoulders and dragged him towards the ice. Once he got the torso stuffed through the ice, he bent the lower body over and used all his strength to cram it in. On the horizon, the beginnings of sunrise slowly spread, but he still could not see the blood which he knew thickly stained the snow, the ice, and him. He would have to count on new snow to cover this problem, and also on the fact that the lazy citizens of the American Cree Nation did not often travel far from their stores and bars, especially not to the barely visible edge of the frozen lake. As for the Indians on the Canadian side, they would not venture this far across the lake unless they were making another drug run. It would take days for them to be even mildly suspicious about Adams's whereabouts. They ran their business like children, not even minding if couriers like Adams disappeared to get drunk for days or skimmed profits. He would have preferred to kill Adams with his hands, and could have just as fast, but had heeded Karim's advice.

They may find the first body before you finish your mission. A neatly snapped neck will create more suspicion than a gunshot. American drug dealers aren't trained soldiers, just idiots with pistols.

Adams breathed deeply again, and then stripped off his clothes down to the long thermal underwear, which was untouched by Adams's blood. He forced his clothes into hole in the ice, pushing them to the side so they wouldn't pop back up. He dressed again in clean clothes from his backpack, which he'd chosen to match Adams's manner of dress: black jeans, an Iron Maiden T-shirt, and a heavy red-and-black checkered flannel shirt. He then used a towel and some snow to clean the pistol and the axe. He picked up his thick down jacket and zipped it, and then returned the pistol and the axe to his backpack.

Standing straight, he looked around. No sounds, nothing in sight. Then he examined the trailer. It contained fifteen jugs of moonshine. A diversion, Adams had explained. *If the res police stop us, they'll just pinch a few bottles. They won't even search us.* Ahmed had no doubt the Cree Nation police were as stupid and corrupt as Adams said, but he did not have that belief about the American police. He decided to keep the trailer. It would be an eyesore alone on the empty plain and might draw attention to Adams's body. He would reconsider the matter if needed.

A mujahid must constantly assess, and reassess, Omar said. Some of your brothers are trained only for battle. They must shoot, run, and follow orders. But you are a lone soldier. Your brain is your greatest weapon, second only to your faith.

Ahmed saw the pint of whiskey sticking out of the snow. He scanned the ground until he found the cap, sealed the bottle, and slid it into the side pocket of Adams's backpack. Ahmed's religion forbade drinking, but on this jihad, no tools could be abandoned.

For the first time, Ahmed looked inside the main compartment of Adams's backpack. Neatly bundled stacks of ragged bills, probably from the casino. Two hundred twenty-five thousand dollars, Adams had boasted like a fool. Ahmed zipped the pack, secured both to the snowmobile, and climbed aboard. He started slowly, twisting the gas gradually, and pulled the machine up the little hill, giving him a full view of the American side of the Cree Nation.

In his village, he had ridden his father's motorbike from a very young age, and could not imagine that the heavy, low-centered snowmobile would present any difficulties. He turned sharply and headed down the hill, picking up speed as he proceeded further from the lake. The trailer leaned precariously to one side, but straightened out when he hit the level powdery snow at the bottom. Maybe later, further from Adams's body, he would cut the trailer loose. These poor Indians had so little to live for. No God. No country. No pride. Hopefully, one of them would find the moonshine.

Ahmed should have been hungry, thirsty, and exhausted. But he wasn't, not at all. He reached into the pocket of his jacket and touched his folded white topi, his prayer hat, and smiled. Omar's strict instructions included not possessing anything that could identify Ahmed as a Muslim. It was the one instruction Ahmed decided not to follow. The topi had been with him since childhood and reminded him of his father. And Abu.

He cranked on the gas, moving ever more quickly into America as the sun rose.

SIX

MAY 8, 2009 – TWIN RIVERS, MONTANA

Pasquali faced the shivering group. "You're not gonna fucking believe this." The moon was almost behind the mountains, and Gabe could now barely make out the faces around him. Deputy Glower held the two tallied piles of votes, one balanced on each hand, his fingers nervously gripping without crushing the flimsy ballots. Pasquali nodded to him, and he placed the ballots neatly back on the hood of the Suburban, weighting each pile with a rock. He handed Pasquali his flashlight. Glower then got into his patrol car and drove away without a word.

"Try us," Egan said.

"Two hundred seven to two hundred seven. With two ballots indecipherable."

Phoenix laughed quietly to herself, making eye contact with Egan.

"Let's see the indecipherables," Thompson said. "Maybe Floyd can decipher 'em."

Pasquali held up the first indecipherable ballot, and read aloud, "You're all a bunch of good for nothing faggots." He then unfolded a second ballot, reading, "God help us, and God bless America."

"Can you decipher those, Judge?" Thompson asked with true hope his voice.

Judge Floyd paused as if to consider the matter. "No, not enough to determine voter intent."

"Hold on now, Judge," Thompson said. "I agree you can't tell much from the first one, although I would call it a no vote, but the second one's different. God help us and God Bless America?

That's a vote against the plan. This voter is calling upon God to protect the country from terrorists."

Gabe could make out only Judge Floyd's silhouette. Floyd held his chin in his hand, like he did when he considered a ruling on the bench.

"This ballot contains two sections, Judge," Gabe said. "One says, 'God help us.' No reasonable finder of fact could determine, without knowing more, what this person wants help with. He or she may fear the terrorists, the economy, or even the apocalypse for all we know. The second part just says, 'God bless America.' A merely patriotic statement. That's it."

"It's a religious and a patriotic statement, Judge," Thompson said. "It calls upon our Christian God to bless our Christian country. What else is the point of writing it?"

"You can't say it calls upon a Christian God or any other specific God," Gabe said.

Thompson barked a laugh. "Oh please! This is Caroline County, son. There's only one God in Caroline County. Maybe a few atheists, but only one God, God damn it. Come on, Judge, what's the ruling?"

"There's no way to decide these voters' intentions by any reasonable standard," Floyd said.

"Fine," Egan said. "It's a tie. So the measure hasn't passed. End of story."

Glower's cruiser pulled into the church parking lot and parked behind Pasquali's Suburban. Another man sat in the back. Glower opened the back door and walked a handcuffed prisoner in an orange jumpsuit over to the group. The prisoner, in his mid-twenties, had shoulder-length blond hair and thick black-rimmed glasses.

"Thank you, Deputy," Pasquali said. "This here is Jonathon Scruggs, a man who cast his ballot from the jail."

Thompson yanked his hands from his pockets. "Oh, this is bullshit!"

"Settle down, Mel," Pasquali said. "Scruggs, the Judge here might have some questions for you about your residence."

Floyd stepped closer to Scruggs. Pasquali held the light on the ground between them. Scruggs face was not sullen or angry, but rather pleasant. He almost seemed amused.

"Where do you live, son?"

"Caroline County lockup, sir."

Everyone laughed, including Phoenix. Phoenix with that same little smile.

"Before that, you resided where?"

"Twenty-six forty Plainsville Road. That's Route 258."

"I know Plainsville Road," Floyd said. "What mile marker?"

"My mom's house is between 31 and 32."

"How long have you lived there?"

"Born there. Went to college at UM for two years. Dropped out. Moved back two years ago."

"Where do you work?"

"Don't. Take college courses from home."

"You're telling me you've lived on Plainsville Road in the county for a solid two years?"

"Yes, sir."

"You went to Weasel Junction High?"

"Graduated in three years, yes sir."

"Play any sports there?"

"No."

"Did you know Madeline Allman?"

"Who didn't? Head cheerleader."

"What kind of college can you do from home?"

"Computer engineering degree. I hope to go back to UM once I save some money."

"I thought you didn't work."

Scruggs hesitated. "Got fired from the car lot in January. Since then, odd jobs. Not much work in the county, but my mom can afford the online courses. Also applying for some loans."

"Why'd you finish high school in three years?"

"Wanted out, I guess. Weasel Junction had nothing left for me."

Floyd studied Scruggs. "Why haven't I seen or heard of you before?"

Scruggs looked down, but did not reply.

"When you gettin' out?" Floyd asked.

"Tomorrow."

"Any other criminal record?" Floyd asked.

"Got arrested in January. Embezzlement. Served one day, got bonded out, then all charges dismissed."

"If you hadn't been locked up today," Thompson said, "is there any chance in hell you would have voted at this meeting?"

"Wouldn't have missed it, sir."

Gabe watched Scruggs closely. If he was a random drifter, a conman set in motion by Pasquali, he was a damn good one. Besides, Egan and Thompson could check out his information easily. The legendary sheriff would never pull a silly con that stood no chance of working.

Floyd stepped away, turning from Scruggs and looking up at the clear sky. "I'd say he's a bona fide county resident. His vote counts."

"You cover your ass, I'll cover mine," Thompson said. "The Weasel Junction way. I'm against this proposal, and you all have heard me say it. One more question, Sheriff. Did the prisoners who voted know about the fifteen thousand?"

"The inmates got a right to know just like every other voter. I believe some of them might have heard something about the money."

Thompson threw his hands up in the air. "Jesus fucking Christ. I've really seen it all."

"We all know where we stand," Egan said with dignified resignation, as if to end the quarreling with an authoritative statement. "This is Phoenix's baby. Mel and I are against it. Evelyn's for it. And everybody else is neutral. Let's get on with it." He looked at his watch.

"I'm for it, too," Gabe said.

Egan barely looked at him. "I'm sorry, son, don't want you to miss the chance to be on record. Our town criminal defense attorney is also for it." Gabe's father had enjoyed a close professional if not personal relationship with Egan, but Egan had never granted Gabe a remnant of it. It had never bothered Gabe. Until lately.

Thompson turned on Phoenix. "One thing you haven't bothered to explain to us is why we're even going through all this shit when our friend Senator Bryant has already said no terrorists are coming to Montana on his watch."

"Obviously our friend Senator Bryant is wrong," Phoenix said.

Thompson's face darkened. "Just because you worked for him don't mean you know it all. I predict that none of your precious rag-heads get anywhere near Weasel Junction no matter what political gymnastics you cook up. Just remember, I warned you this could be a disaster."

"All right then." Pasquali tossed the flashlight to Gabe, wiggled his fingers into his shirt pocket, and pulled out the wrinkled ballot. He squinted to officially make out Scruggs's vote, moving it from side to side in front of his eyes as if to catch whatever small amount of residual light remained. "Looks like a yes."

Pasquali started his truck, revving it hard. Gabe and Phoenix stood by, the last two at the town elders' meeting. Pasquali's declaration of the winner had quietly and quickly scattered the others without argument.

Pasquali rolled down his window and leaned out. "It's not as if you're home free, Phoenix. Thompson's right about the Senator."

"So am I. I'll see the Senator tomorrow in Helena. He's home this month. I never said saving this town would be easy."

"You set up the appointment before even winning the vote?" Receiving no answer, Pasquali slowly pulled out of the parking lot. Gabe and Phoenix watched his taillights turn the corner, and walked together towards their cars. Phoenix stopped to light a cigarette, looking across the bare shadows between them and mountains.

"I married into this town," she said, as if she owed Gabe an explanation of a sort. An explanation, perhaps, of why she knew so much more about Gabe's town than he did. "But somehow it seems like I married the town."

"Is that why you're doing this?"

"I'm doing it 'cause I'm mayor."

She flicked her cigarette butt towards the same oil drum. This time it rang against the inner rim. "Want to ride with me to Helena tomorrow? We can talk on the way. About the future." Phoenix often mentioned the future.

"I got a case at ten," Gabe said.

"I'll call Floyd about that case."

"You're that powerful, huh?"

"The mission is," she said.

"You really got an appointment with the senator for tomorrow before knowing you'd win the vote?"

She opened her car door. "First of all, Grasshopper, I knew I was gonna win. Second, I don't need an appointment to see Senator Bryant."

They stood quietly for a moment. Then she said, "You're ready for something new, aren't you?"

"And you've got that thing?"

"Now that you mention it."

Gabe waited, still unsure if this were a serious conversation.

"I'm going to ask you to be my lawyer, Gabe. In a big case. A national case."

"You kill somebody?"

"One would think. But no. Tomorrow, when the Senator announces that ten detainees will be housed at Twin Rivers, a citizens group in Helena will file a lawsuit against the town and me personally, seeking an injunction to forbid me from allowing the Guantanamo Bay prisoners into Caroline County. We need to fast track the case and get rid of it. Delay will cause permanent damage to the town. We need the case gone within a week."

"I'm a criminal lawyer."

"So what? You used to be a fancy firm guy, right? And you're from Twin Rivers, and most of all, you're smart. Besides, the case is bullshit. They have no standing to even bring the suit."

"If they have no standing, what's the worry?"

"The people behind this suit know they can't win," she said. "They want to delay the contract and eventually kill it. Most of all, they want to scare me. They think I'll back down."

"Why would they think that?"

"Are you taking the case or not?"

"I'm asking questions to see if I'll take it."

"Attorney-client, Gabe. I need to trust you." She held two fingers aloft, intertwined. "Are you taking the case?"

"Do you want me, or do you want the son of Richard Lantagne?" He had asked clients that same question many times in his life as a big firm lawyer.

"That's below you, Gabe. Get over it. I could hire anyone I want. A national firm from DC or New York. I want you."

"You're telling me you just promised the whole town the prison contract by Twin Rivers Day, and that won't happen unless we win the case before then?"

"I'm telling you that if we can't get the suit dismissed by then, the entire contract will fall apart for good."

Gabe shook his head. "And none of that even matters unless you convince Senator Bryant to backtrack on months of public statements on this very issue?"

"Stick with me, Gabe. Now, are you my fuckin' lawyer or not?"

Gabe laughed.

She winked, got into her car, and began to drive away. "We cover each other's asses, my friend. The Weasel Junction Way."

After four years as a sober country lawyer, he had begun to wonder what was next. Maybe Phoenix Jamborsky knew.

SEVEN

MAY 9, 2009 – TWIN RIVERS, MONTANA

At 6 a.m. sharp, Will Jarvis flipped the closed sign to open on the glass window of the Shell station just as Gabe parked his jeep at the solitary gas pump. Gabe filled the tank, grabbed a coffee, paid Will, and was about to leave when Will reached out and grabbed his arm, his usual friendly smile replaced by a somber nod. "Good luck today, Counselor." Gabe nodded, surprised but not shocked that the whole town seemed to know he was driving Phoenix to Helena to see Senator Bryant about the prison plan.

Gabe spun back onto the road and past the Super 8 Motel, whose fluorescent vacancy sign remained lit as if to spite the bright morning sun. He accelerated his jeep into the foothills towards the Angel Sky Ranch, where Phoenix waited, having driven there early to have breakfast with Ayalette. Gabe had no idea how Phoenix planned to persuade Senator Bryant to endorse a plan he had lampooned on national news for months, but in the end, no one could say she hadn't tried. He lit a cigarette, turned on the radio, and extended his arm out the window to feel the morning air.

He pulled onto the long gravel driveway of the Angel Sky and, as usual, marveled at the beauty of the mountains, some still with snow at the very top. Cattle grazed on a sloping hill. The pasture wound far around the bend of the distant foothills, out of Gabe's vision. How could Michael afford to hold on to such a huge strip of territory? It had never seemed possible, but as for the Terwilliger finances, Gabe could only go on a comment Phoenix had once made. *These cattle boys are like the fucking Rockefellers. They can survive a generation or two* of incompetent management as long as they follow their golden rule. This rule is the first of the eleven commandments, and not one of them would dare break it. Keep it in the family. Period. Elijah, Amos, Augustus, Enos, they all knew the rule. I mean, who makes their son sign a prenuptial agreement?

Enos Terwilliger, Michael's father, had shot himself two years before, down by the Angel Sky stream on the lower west side of the ranch. It struck Gabe, who lived paycheck to paycheck on client fees, as strange that a man so rich and, despite his rumored drinking, so admired, could be brought so low. You can't understand these people, Gabe. Don't even try. The golden rule left Michael, who was so frugal he drove a 1996 Ford pickup, the richest man in Caroline County.

Gabe climbed the wide steps to the broad front porch of the main house, lifted the lasso-shaped knocker, and let it drop on the thick oak door.

Michael opened the door and slapped him on the back. "Gabe." Michael was always friendly to Gabe, who, though about the same age, felt worlds apart from this simple man. In town, Michael had the disposition of an unassuming ranch hand, saying "sir" and "ma'am" to his elders as he strolled around town for an occasional errand in his old jeans and boots. Gabe had been to the Angel Sky only a few times, but that was enough to see that Michael was a different man here, still humble, but secure in his castle, charging across his estate on his favorite horse, a man as mighty while he roamed his kingdom as he was quiet and gentle with his daughter. Unfortunately, Phoenix had once said, there is no deeper mystery. What you see is all you get.

Phoenix appeared from the kitchen. She looked thoroughly out of place in the towering, antique-ish western foyer with her tight city business suit. As usual, the youthful look of her thin body and firm breasts contrasted with the hardened wisdom glimmering from her big blue eyes.

Ayalette followed behind her. "Good luck, Mom. Hi, Gabe." She ate an apple and watched Gabe thoughtfully but without a care for what he was doing in her father's house so early in the morning. She wore her long brown hair like Phoenix often did, in one braid that swung back and forth behind her. She had Phoenix's intelligent face, but even at age seven, you could see an athletic build that came from Michael. She carried herself with the unapologetic posture of a ranch girl and not with the caution of one taught to be wary of appearances and to take up only a modest amount of space. Her limbs, like her father's, rambled with the unchecked confidence of one who cannot fathom an objection to where they might stray. A deeper look revealed a sliver of Native American ancestry from far back in the Terwilliger bloodline.

"Hey there, Ayalette," Gabe said, "you're looking relaxed this morning." Ayalette shrugged. *Why wouldn't I?* Gabe turned to Michael. "So what do you think of all this? How'd you vote?"

Michael did not respond, nor did he seem annoyed. As he often did, he just stood there, either too wise or too cowboy to say much.

Phoenix picked up her purse from the table by the door and said to Michael, "Some people in this town have to work for a living, my friend." Gabe had never understood these two, the stoic rancher and the worldly maverick. They were almost too clichéd to have ever been a real couple. Divorced without a visible flap. Could it be that their lack of commonality had, in their younger days, been trumped by nothing more than the fleeting bond of beauty?

Everyone knew that Enos Terwilliger, while an eccentric cowboy, had been connected to Montana politics, and that

Phoenix had met Michael when she was traveling through Weasel Junction as part of Senator Bryant's entourage in 1999, probably at some fancy event held at the ranch. Whatever passed between them had landed Phoenix at the ranch within a year. Gabe could not imagine what had led to Enos's going around the bend, but whatever it was, it had happened when Michael was away. Phoenix had been one of the first people to see Enos's body. Whenever Gabe got the chance to observe Phoenix and Michael together, he watched them for a clue of the emotional trauma that must have been associated with Enos's death and then the divorce. But beyond a casual sadness in Michael, and Phoenix's manic drive, he saw nothing but two successful people with a friendship and a pact to raise a child.

As they drove past the massive, carved wooden Angel Sky sign, Phoenix said, "I know, you don't get it. Neither do I. That man has never, in ten years, asked me a question about the life I led before I met him. Or after, for that matter. He's like, so there in the moment, but not all there, if you know what I mean. Weird choices. The story of my life." But she said it with pride. Pride in the come-what-may bizarreness of her trajectory. "Michael is a truly good man. He would kill for his daughter. It's almost like he's, well, more than me, or I guess I would say so focused on Ayalette. It's great." She shifted to a cross-legged position in her seat: the relaxed Phoenix. "So why haven't you considered a move back to the city? You could earn five times as much and still hang out in Twin Rivers when you felt like it. You're broke. And you don't give a rat's ass about the City Council."

"It's where I grew up," Gabe said. "Where my parents lived. Call it town spirit."

"Everybody your age who cared about being something left a long time ago."

Phoenix seemed to believe that *being something* was an urge unabashedly shared by all, with those falling below that bar doing so not out of choice but by failure. Or worse, weakness. He turned due south on route 620, one lane each way winding around the south end of Flathead Lake.

"Somebody's got to be the next generation around here," he said. Phoenix just nodded. Had he given her the impression that he figured he, rather than an out-of-towner like her, should carry the mantle for the younger generation of Weasel Junction?

"I got news for you, Gabe. You'll be the leader of this town yet—especially after we pull this off." We.

They passed a sign announcing ninety miles to Helena. "So, what's the plan?" Gabe asked.

"Let's just say the senator appreciates my discretion about certain matters and understands my plans for the future."

The town's future, or her own? "So you've got something on Bryant? It better be good. Did he sexually harass you or something?"

Phoenix lit another cigarette and looked out the window across the plains to the south. "Beau isn't like that."

They descended towards Helena. Around Phoenix—unlike with other people, especially women—Gabe found himself uncomfortable with long silences. This woman made it hard to think about anything else in her presence.

As they pulled into town, Gabe said, "So now he's running for President?"

"I'd vote for him. In Montana, who wouldn't?"

"Me," Gabe said. "He's a fuckin' Republican."

"That's not what it's all about. Beau could explain it to you."

"I doubt it."

"If someday you want to be mayor of Twin Rivers," she said, "or even more, you might want to reconsider that opinion."

"Mayor?" Gabe pulled up outside the Federal Building.

"You're a real leader in the legal community. And the number of people you've helped?" Phoenix smoothed her skirt and picked up her briefcase. "I'm on. Meet you at Arminger's?" A well-known Helena bar down the street from the City-County Building.

"How long's this gonna take?"

Phoenix handed Gabe a slim red file from her briefcase. "After today, the Citizens for a Safer Montana will file this complaint in federal court. We need to get it dismissed right away. Some of the shit in there, as you will see, is fucking scandalous."

"An advance look at their pleading? How did you get this?"

Phoenix got out of the car and leaned back in, hands firmly on the window jamb as if it were a podium. "Don't forget your number one asset, Gabe."

"What's that?" he asked.

"Me, Mr. Deputy Mayor."

"Twin Rivers has never had a deputy mayor."

"Twin Rivers has never had a lot of things. Attorney-client, don't forget." She again flashed him the entwined-fingers sign, then walked away with just a hint of a swagger, one clicking heel directly in front of the other, her long braid bouncing rhythmically against her back.

EIGHT
MAY 1, 2009 – OUTSIDE TEMPLE, MONTANA

Ahmed's arms throbbed from holding the steering bars straight. He realized that he needed to hold the bars softly, like a pistol or a rifle, and not with the rigidity that coursed through him. He was in no respect afraid for his physical safety, only apprehensive that his mission involved stealth rather than outright action. With his few weapons, he could likely defeat whatever police he encountered on the empty plain. On the other hand, Omar's words echoed. This was not a Chechen firefight. He was alone, on a complicated mission that required a series of perfectly executed steps. Of all his abilities, Ahmed most distrusted his skill in avoiding suspicion if faced with close inspection by intelligent, discerning Americans. The Cree Nation, full of drunk and trusting fools who accepted him without hesitation, had not been much preparation for what he would face in the days ahead.

He stopped the snowmobile and spun his binoculars across the snow in every direction. Nothing but white glare. There would be no actual demarcation between the Cree reservation and the United States unless he traveled a main road. Instead, he was likely to enter America before he knew it, a fact which bothered him because he did not know when to prepare himself for a possible encounter with American police.

He took a long pull from his water bottle and sat quietly in the broad emptiness, resting his arms. He had not prayed that day, but prayer at this moment was inconsistent with his mission.

Soon after he started moving again, the terrain changed. A road appeared ahead of him, running south to north, perpendicular to his path. Most likely this road formed a border between the Cree Nation and the United States. He stopped on the road, wanting to appear relaxed and unconcerned by anyone watching his progress from afar. Stepping from the snowmobile, he reached into his backpack, pulled out the small bottle of whiskey, and held it to his mouth. He swished the burning liquid around, but spit it off to the side before remounting. Any American watching him with binoculars would now know he was a member of the Cree Nation and lawfully entitled to cross out of the reservation into America. He then ripped hard on the gas, as he'd seen Adams do, and sped down the hill.

Temple, Montana is about thirteen miles due west of the reservation, but you will have no way to tell exactly where you are, Omar said. It was then that Omar had shown him the GPS device, a contraption from India that determined one's precise position from satellites in space. Ahmed's eyes had widened.

Ahmed pushed the GPS's ON button and preprogrammed it to map his current location with that of Temple, Montana. The device calibrated itself for a moment then depicted an arrow with his location and a three-dimensional pin in the center of the town. Ten point two miles, and Ahmed was barely south of the straight westerly path. The device also depicted roads, and Ahmed saw that in two miles he would reach an American highway, one that would certainly have cars on it now that the time approached eleven a.m. He accelerated and prayed. Despite the strong wind, he grew very hot from the sun reflected all about him from the brilliant, untouched snow. He was hungry and thirsty, and the adrenaline from his lake crossing had worn off. He cursed the nervousness in the pit of his empty stomach; while he feared no enemy, he did not fully trust his skills as a spy.

Language is your greatest obstacle, Omar said. You speak well, but too formally for a lower class American or Canadian. Your vocabulary is small, and not fitting with America. Your accent needs work. Perhaps most important is your demeanor.

You have never conversed with a real American. You lack in your very bones any real understanding of Westerners. For the next two weeks, Karim will focus on this part of your training.

Ahmed did not relish hour upon hour of language lessons with Karim, who, in any event, spoke almost incomprehensible Scottish English. But the training did not consist of merely conversing with Karim. Ahmed followed him into the back room of Karim's quarters. A huge wall-mounted television showed a news broadcast. From America. We'll meet here each morning, Karim said, after your breakfast and prayers. You'll watch CNN and American talk shows. Karim held a notebook aloft. Then you'll read these sentences and phrases into this tape recorder. After lunch, prayer, and further training with Omar, you'll watch an American film with me then read more phrases into the tape recorder. Each morning, before the news, you'll listen yourself from the day before. Tomorrow, you'll sound like a Muslim from a poor village in Pakistan. In two weeks, you'll sound like an infidel from East Armpit, Wyoming.

CNN was not altogether new to him, he had seen similar news shows in the café with his father. But he began to pay closer attention. The discussion centered mostly on American politics, but one of the segments depicted the President's trip to Israel and Palestine. He saw the President sitting comfortably talking to King Abdullah of Jordan, who would be willing to wipe his backside with the Koran for another such moment on TV with the American President. The President praised Abdullah and discussed Islam as if Abdullah had anything whatever to do with Islam. His father had said that nothing is worse for the struggle of true Islam than the secular frauds who control the Muslim nations. Their own people hate them but are bombarded daily with the message that alliances with the West will bring material rewards like those enjoyed in America. For the women, the perils are even greater.

Karim turned to a show where a man sat on a couch talking to various American fools about sex and other unseemly topics. Ahmed was astonished when he saw one woman discuss with her husband how she had been having sex with his brother. Then, the brother appeared and proceeded to explain to the cuckolded man what he liked about his wife's private areas. The show got even more obscene as a teenage boy explained how he wished to undergo surgery to become a woman. As Ahmed watched, Karim studied him from across the room. He had no fear of Karim, as they both understood he could break the man in half in less than a second, and yet Karim's sidelong glances and perusals for Ahmed's inner reactions bothered him

Ahmed stopped the snowmobile and ate some snow to conserve water. He checked the horizon. His back stiffened when he saw two snowmobiles approaching from the southwest. They moved slowly, but unmistakably towards him. Be at Peace, Ahmed. Ahmed sat backwards on the snowmobile, took off his wraparound sunglasses, wiped them clean, and put them back on. Shit, junior, those glasses are right on you, man, Adams had told him. Ahmed only knew they hid his eyes and made him look more like the young men who strutted around the reservation impressing the girls. He could feel the chill of his sweaty body under the thick clothes. He took off his knit hat, reached slowly into his backpack, and pulled out a baseball hat, turning it around backwards on his head like some of the relaxed Americans from a comedy film Karim had showed him, Old School. He then removed his gloves, knowing they would present a major hindrance in his handling of his pistol. He pulled the whiskey bottle out of the side compartment of Adams's small pack, held it loosely in one hand, and kicked both legs onto the covered trailer in a pose of complete relaxation. He took a deep breath, sipped the whiskey, and then took a longer drink from his water bottle. As the snowmobiles got within twenty meters, he saw that their riders were indeed uniformed policeman.

Karim had routinely lectured Ahmed on police encounters in the West. *The Reservation police won't be a problem, they'll think you're an Indian from the north side. Just tell them you're looking for work. But in America, you'll be at risk until you get to a town and take your cover to the next level. The Americans who patrol the reservation's borders might be federal immigration agents, who will take seriously the mission of discovering your identity. You must pass for a Canadian Indian traveling to visit friends or relatives. You're not allowed to work in America, so don't use this excuse with an American policeman. They'll never suspect you're a mujahid, but they'll arrest you if they think you entered the country illegally. As innocent as you seem, their procedures and computers will see through your story. So no matter what, don't let the immigration police arrest you. If an encounter with a routine patrol escalates to checking identification, assume you are about to be searched, and kill them. Then hide them well, because killing federal agents will bring a raft of trouble, all the way from Washington. If local police try to arrest you, shoot them with their own weapons and set up the bodies to look like they got into a fight with each other. Stuff one of their pockets with a few thousand dollars, which will baffle the local police and make the media believe the killing is linked to corruption. If you encounter police near the reservation, act friendly, like an Indian, and like you have been drinking a little, but not too much. Americans love it when you smile. And never, ever offer a bribe to a policeman in America. High-ranking officials in America make their living from bribes, but many low-ranking officials actually believe in the integrity of the system.*

As the policemen pulled up, Ahmed lit a cigarette, careful not inhale and provoke a coughing fit. Both snowmobiles stopped, and the policeman dismounted, removing protective helmets. Both wore pistols but foolishly did not unfasten the protective leather clips on the holsters as they approached him. They also failed to remove their bulky black gloves.

"How are you doing this morning?" Ahmed said.

"We're fine this afternoon," the bigger, fatter policeman said. "It's near one."

"Really?" Ahmed said. "Time flies."

"It sure does," the thin cop said.

Ahmed's pistol, tucked safely into his belt below layers of clothes and barely noticeable while riding, suddenly felt bulkier than an Uzi.

"I hate to be this way on this fine day, son, but my partner here saw you drinking from that bottle. You know it's illegal to drink and drive out here?"

Months of training, and his first question was beyond comprehension. Illegal to drink? What of all of Karim's talk about drunk Indians?

"Oh, yeah, just a sip, Officer. Hard day of riding, you know. I drink water too." Ahmed held up the water bottle.

"Tell you what. Since we didn't see you driving, we can't arrest you for DUI, but if you blow too high on the AlcoSensor, we're gonna have to order you not to drive for a few hours. And don't think we won't be back this way, so you better not be gone for at least two hours."

What was the policeman talking about? Ahmed's elbow touched his pistol. He glanced around, feeling, for the first time, like he might look nervous.

"You're lucky Boswell's not out here," the fat policeman said. "He'd run you in just for fun." Both policemen laughed, but not in the way policemen in Pakistan laughed. Not nastily, not at his misfortune. The fat policeman handed him a metal contraption, and Ahmed cautiously held out his hand to receive it. He could still kill both men without his pistol way before they could react.

"Just blow, don't be shy, and after five seconds, hand it back to me."

Ahmed had no idea of the purpose of blowing into the small machine, but he did as he was told, holding his other hand on his hip in case he had to reach for the pistol, and keeping both eyes on the policemen's hands, knowing they could not see them through the dark glasses. After five seconds, he handed the small machine to the policeman, who examined it closely.

"I'll be damned, you're fine. Point zero, zero two. Hell, you really did have only a sip."

Ahmed smiled. His shoulders relaxed, and his elbow came away from the pistol.

"Yeah, man, like I told you. Water." He again held up the bottle.

"So what you got under the tarp?" the thin policeman asked. Ahmed did not sense a threat in the man's voice, only curiosity, but his shoulders clenched again.

"Oh, man, this is my friend's ride. He left it with me and just wants it back. I don't mess with his stuff."

Ahmed cringed at his horrible answer, but he had tried to follow his training. *Americans, especially rural Americans, do not expect crisp answers, Karim said. Make small talk. Answer without answering. Most of them consider it rude to ask too many personal questions if put off in this way.*

Of course, that wouldn't apply to policemen, who wanted their questions answered and were trained to notice evasive responses. Think. Think. Be at peace. Be at peace.

We'll now watch some American films, Karim announced one morning after prayers. Americans model their speech after the actors in the films. Watch their movements, their lazy speech, everything. Of all the television Ahmed studied with Karim, he remotely enjoyed some of the films. They were fictional and this provided more freedom to study, to listen to the nuances of the words. Unlike the political discourse and live shows, the films relaxed him. He watched some of them more than once, trying to copy the words and even the movements of certain characters. One was entitled Die Hard, where the main character, a policeman, used his toughness and skill with weapons to prevent a robbery. Ahmed liked imitating John McClane's words, gestures, even his jokes. McClane thwarted the less intelligent enemies by using his wits and courage and yet seemed to enjoy himself while doing so. It's just a movie, my friend, Karim said when he caught Ahmed watching it for the third time. Ahmed shot him a dark look, but continued to watch.

Ahmed liked another movie, also about a tough policeman, Dirty Harry. You've got to ask yourself one question: do I feel lucky? Of course, the criminal would not have been able to move as fast as the policeman and lacked the courage to try. Ahmed imagined having a similar encounter with the men who arrested his father. Karim annoyed Ahmed while watching Dirty Harry, pointing out that the policeman should have just killed the criminal instead of playing a silly game with him.

Once Karim actually turned off a film Ahmed liked, Scarface, about a Cuban refugee who became wealthy selling drugs and outdoing the Americans at their own decadent culture. The man was an animal, a godless monster who wore a crucifix. And yet Ahmed was mesmerized by the film, by the man's personality. Karim called it waste. It's about an Italian pretending to have a Cuban accent, he scoffed. What'll you learn from it? But Ahmed, seeing its application to his mission, had finished the film later. Another film that stuck in Ahmed's mind, There's Something about

Mary, was about a group of homosexual men who competed to marry a pretty but vulgar woman. Ahmed laughed out loud several times, along with Karim. In fact, the viewing of that film had been one of the few times he enjoyed spending time with Karim.

Ahh! Omar said, smiling and smacking Karim on the back, after hearing Ahmed recite a paragraph of banal American speech at the end of the two weeks. We have an infidel among us. Omar's friendly, deep laughter filled the courtyard at the center of camp.

"Mind if we have a look?" The thin policeman now paced around the trailer. Even worse, with one policeman close and one out of reach, he could not kill them both quickly. If the thin one were extremely skilled, he actually might be able to draw his pistol by the time Ahmed killed his partner. Or he could run, forcing Ahmed to shoot him down before he used his radio.

Ahmed stood and bent down as if to loosen the string ties on the tarp. What would the policemen do if they saw the moonshine? "Why not, man, your guess is as good as mine." He fumbled awkwardly with the tarp, rubbing his hands together. "Cold, man, give me a second." He pretended to work the knot.

Suddenly, the fat policeman moved his hands—to look at his watch. "Give him a break, Jess. I'm gettin' hungry." Was that slang for something? But the policeman was walking away.

"You sure?" Ahmed said. "No big deal." Pride welled inside at his boldness.

"Enjoy your day, son. No more whiskey while driving."

"Lesson learned, man, lesson learned," Ahmed said.

Then, in another gesture of nonchalance, he turned his back on the policemen, ready to mount the snowmobile.

"Hey, one more thing," the thin one called.

Ahmed's hand moved for the pistol.

"You know there's a helmet law out here?"

Ahmed slowly wiped the ball cap from his head and stared down at it as if he'd never seen it before. "Aw, yeah, man, forgot my damn helmet." Now, he was in violation of an actual law. They would ask for his identification, and whether a Canadian driver's license would suffice was far from clear. The fat policeman reached behind his own snowmobile, probably for an automatic weapon. Ahmed cursed himself for letting them gain the advantage of distance. The policeman tossed something into the air towards him—but it was too big and light for a grenade. Ahmed raised his hand and caught it.

"Nice catch," the policeman said. "My son's helmet, pal. Return it to the Temple Police Department when you get to town or he won't have nothin' to ride with. Leave it off for me, Officer Bard."

"Thanks, man."

The policemen sped away.

Ahmed put on the blue helmet and motored quietly towards Temple. He'd been lucky, but was not pleased to now have made the acquaintance of two policemen from town. Temple would be nothing but a part of his history by morning.

Soon, Ahmed drove alongside a small highway. Ahead, a culvert run under the road—just the sort of thing he was looking for. He glanced east and west, then swerved off the road to the mouth of the culvert, where he tore away the tarp, and, three at a time, transferred the fifteen gallons of moonshine from the trailer to just inside the pipe. He then re-covered the trailer, pulled away, and traveled along the side of the highway at full throttle until he saw the beginnings of the town.

He could have driven the snowmobile on at least some of the town's streets, as matted snow covered even the busy highway, but the encounter with the policemen had educated him as to his lack of knowledge about the petty laws in Montana, so he chose instead to park the machine next to a dozen others in a lot near the main road. As casually as possible, he unloaded all his gear, stuffing everything, including Adams's backpack full of cash, into his own larger pack. Under the guise of cleaning the snowmobile, he wiped every spot which could conceivably been touched by his bare hands. Minutes later, striding the main street in Temple, he tossed the whiskey bottle into a trashcan.

People in Montana do all kinds of outdoor sports, Karim said. Not for training, not for any purpose, just to do it. Even old women and fat men hike in the mountains and ski. When you're on foot, with your Western clothes and fancy backpack, you'll look like a typical young idiot. Walk slowly and keep a simple look on your face.

Ahmed stopped at a small gas station with a store. In Canada, he had become familiar with these stores, expensive little shops that sold trinkets and horrible food for twice the price of a regular store. The members of the Cree Nation loved to eat at these little stores, spending their small amounts of money on awful little sandwiches. Ahmed approached the food counter. An old woman waddled over to him.

Ahmed read the signs near the food. "How about…four, ah, all beef hotdogs and a large water."

As the woman filled his order, he felt in his pocket for the small amount of cash he had kept on him. Small, considering his mission, but enough to feed a family in Pakistan for a year. He paid the woman, carried his bag of food and backpack outside, sat on the curb, and devoured the sticks of meat and bread. In the camp, the food was often bad, sometimes even containing living bugs, but there, with the brothers, Ahmed felt a sense of wholeness, of wholesomeness. Here he felt like a decrepit beggar eating stumps of meat near smelly gas pumps. There had to be millions of such gas facilities in America, all running on the lifeblood of Muslims, the birthright of Muslims.

He hoisted his pack and walked along the sidewalk until he found what he was looking for. Ahmed entered the lobby of the motel, paid cash for a room, and allowed the manager to make a copy of his Canadian driver's license. The picture resembled Ahmed, but was actually of the man named in the license, Arthur Macow. Macow would not be calling the police about his missing license.

Once in his room, Ahmed stripped naked and showered quickly. He preferred cold water. It felt like swimming in the frigid ponds near the camp, the full exhilaration of cleanliness, body and soul. He dried himself, put on some thin pants from his pack, knelt on the ratty motel carpet, and prayed. At the end of the prayer, as he always did, he thought of his mother, his father, and his brother. He stripped away the thick colorful top blanket, lay down on the bed, and slept.

NINE

MAY 9, 2009 – HELENA, MONTANA

Gabe, sitting at Arminger's, took a long drink from his club soda, lit a cigarette, and opened Phoenix's file.

> Citizens for a Safer Montana versus Twin Rivers
> Municipality and Phoenix Eileen Jamborsky
> Complaint for Permanent Injunction, Temporary
> Injunction, and other Appropriate Relief
> The plaintiff, Citizens for a Safer Montana, alleged
> against the defendants as follows:

Gabe read the entire complaint, making careful note of the specific allegations about Twin Rivers and Phoenix. About an hour later, Phoenix appeared through the crowd, climbed onto the barstool next to Gabe, and sighed deeply.

"That was short," he said. "What happened?"

She ordered a Knob Creek sour.

Suddenly the volume on the TV went up and people quieted. Senator Bryant appeared on the steps of the Federal Building with Montana Congressman Tad Walpole. The CNN caption below read TERRORISTS TO MONTANA?

"Today, Congressman Walpole and myself met with officials from Twin Rivers to discuss the town's proposal to house enemy combatants at Twin Rivers Maximum Security Penitentiary outside that town. The meeting was productive, and I have become convinced that the prison facility and the town are more than capable of safely housing any detainees within the facility's maximum capacity. The prison is safe. I have also consulted with Senator Marion and Governor Hyde.

After consideration of the entire situation, including Twin Rivers' need for the revenue that could come from such a contract, I have decided that I still cannot support the idea of bringing these terrorists into our very backyard."

Gabe looked at Phoenix, who calmly sipped her drink.

"My concern," Bryant continued, "is that contrary to the views of this administration, housing these detainees on US soil risks direct terrorist action against the places that hold them. Some say the chance is remote, but let me just say that I have been on the Intelligence Committee for four years, visited the Middle East extensively, and studied the history and evolution of our enemies in the War on Terror. I believe housing the detainees creates a risk that the people of Montana have hired me to prevent."

Gabe turned to Phoenix again. "How—" She stopped him with a finger to his lips and a shake of her head.

"However," Bryant said, "while as Minority Leader I am uniquely situated to advise, persuade, and perhaps influence this decision, I lack the constitutional authority to prevent Twin Rivers from seeking, or even securing, a contract from the Department of Justice. I have implored the President not to risk American lives by creating terrorist targets in Montana or anywhere else in America, but the President has made it clear he intends to proceed, absent a legal obstacle. As of this afternoon, Twin Rivers has decided not to heed my warning, but to formally seek the contract."

The buzz around the bar picked up, and then Phoenix appeared on CNN walking along the sidewalk. She stopped, smiled and spoke briefly to a group of reporters, but CNN only showed a snippet of her comments, something plucked from the middle of her statement: "Twin Rivers has decided not to shrink from any risk that could be involved, but we also believe that the Twin Rivers facility, indeed the entire county, can be made perfectly safe and secure with the additional law-enforcement resources the contract will bring to the town. We are not afraid. We are proud to step forward and help make our country and the world a safer place."

Phoenix turned on her stool and lifted her highball glass— round ice, crystal bubbles, lime. Gabe lifted his club soda. They clinked glasses.

"How'd you do it?"

"Attorney-client?" she asked.

"Of course."

"Really, it's not a big secret. It's right for the town, right for the country. We're not the only municipality in the country that will do this. Beau just needed to cover his ass. That's politics, Gabe. It'll be the President's ass, not his, if terrorists blow up the rib joint out on Route 606." She took a sip and glanced down at the file he'd been reading.

"Under the rules," Gabe said, "we're entitled to an almost immediate hearing. Given that they seek a permanent and a temporary injunction, the court has the ability to consolidate the entire issue almost at once. Literally, this could happen in days. The Citizens' claim of irreparable harm to the state is ridiculously speculative."

Phoenix lit a cigarette. "That's simple to prove. But if the suit doesn't end almost immediately, the feds won't honor the prison contract, and Twin Rivers is screwed."

"But the plaintiffs have exactly the opposite side of that coin going for them," Gabe said. "If the prisoner contract becomes official, the alleged danger begins. They will suggest to the court that the contract be *temporarily* enjoined because if the prisoners actually arrive, their legal position is destroyed—no judge will allow the prisoners to arrive and then order them removed."

"So how do we block the temporary injunction?" she asked.

"It's more than that. We're screwed unless the court not only denies the temporary injunction but also agrees to expedite its ruling on the permanent injunction, and dismisses the entire case. That's legally possible, but only if we make a very difficult showing."

"Showing of what?"

"That the mere pendency of the suit will cause irreparable harm to Twin Rivers."

"That's easy, I just told you, we'll lose the contract."

"Agreed, but it's a rare remedy. I'm not saying we can't win it, I'm just saying it would be a big victory."

"Great, that's why I hired you." Was she pretending not to understand his point, or did she always expect the nearly impossible?

Gabe continued cautiously. "About the discovery. They request various town records. How are they relevant?"

"Exactly. They're not. They're just screwing with us. Hoping to intimidate me."

"Can't we just provide the records?"

She impatiently blew smoke at the ceiling.

"They also want to depose you and Michael," Gabe said. "What's that about?"

"Harassment. This is high politics, Gabe. The people behind this group have an agenda, and it does not include me or Twin Rivers succeeding. Period."

"But why Michael? You've been divorced for two years."

"Who knows? The suit is bullshit. But they're threatening to plow forward in a losing cause to force the discovery. To scare me. They don't really care about the prisoner issue at all, what they care about is me."

Gabe marveled at Phoenix's lack of self-consciousness in making the bold declaration that a huge federal class action suit was just a ploy aimed at her, personally.

"This Citizens for a Safer Montana appears to be a real group," he said. "They sued six years ago to prevent out-of-state sex offenders from being housed in Miles City."

"And lost."

"My point is they're a legitimate group of Montanans. And they don't like prisons on their turf. They probably have support on both sides of the political fence. Even liberals hate the idea of bringing the rest of America here, especially the dregs."

"Legitimate or not, in this case, they're a pawn." Phoenix eased off her stool and said, under her breath without moving her mouth, "You're about to see I'm right." She squared herself towards a man who approached her, a tall, older gentleman in a cowboy boots, a cowboy hat, and neat black suit.

"Mayor Jamborsky."

"Ron." Phoenix tilted her head most imperceptibly to the left and up—a very slight look of defensive judgment. Of wariness. This wasn't the laidback, Twin Rivers Phoenix, but a harder, more determined woman.

"Shall we talk privately?" the man said.

"This is my lawyer, Gabriel Lantagne," Phoenix said. Gabe shook the tall man's hand.

"Pleased to meet you, Gabe. Ron Westerman. Who are you with?"

"I have my own firm. In Twin Rivers."

"Great. Good for you." Ron gestured towards an empty booth alongside the bar.

Phoenix led the way to the booth. Ron gestured for Gabe to go ahead. This was the first time in his career that Gabe had been imprudent enough to enter into a meeting without knowing what it was about.

At the table, Phoenix's pursed lips signified a waiting—*Get on with it, motherfucker.*

"I don't know how else to put it," Ron said. "But this is your last chance. I spoke to Egan this morning and implored him to reason with you. But apparently you've got him wrapped up in this nutty scheme."

Gabe crossed his arms.

"If you move forward with this we are going to fucking ruin you. And not just you. The town. And Michael. You must see that. This is crazy. Think of your daughter."

"Is that it?" Phoenix asked.

Ron removed his hat, set it next to him on the table, then leaned across the booth, his face only inches from Phoenix's, and spoke in a slow, confident drawl, like a real Montana cowboy. His thick, neatly trimmed, and probably dyed moustache suited him well in the manner of Magnum P.I.

"You got a nice town up there, Ms. Mayor. Let it die quietly. Or don't. But if you proceed with this, you will not only fail, ma'am, but one year from now your lawyer will be visiting you in a fucking federal prison, not in the governor's mansion."

No response.

"Don't say I didn't warn you. I respected Enos, and out of that respect I'm giving you one more chance. For Michael. But I suppose you'll ruin him along with yourself. But then you wouldn't care about that, would you?"

Phoenix's narrowed eyes flickered away from Ron Westerman's. "Done yet?"

Ron stood and picked up his hat. "Mr. Lantagne." He nodded to Gabe, then turned back. "Lantagne, is it?"

"Yes," Gabe said.

"Are you…?"

Gabe nodded coldly.

"Your father was a heck of a guy." Ron placed his hat on his head and walked away without looking at Phoenix again.

"Let me guess," Gabe said. "Citizens for a Safer Montana?"

Phoenix sighed. "Citizens for a Safer Montana is a bunch of fairies. They're the type of people who would vote to criminalize farting in public. But Westerman is a political goon. He's using them. Pathetic. Lucky I got a great lawyer." She winked.

Phoenix stood, leaving her second drink half-full on the table. Even after four years, Gabe marveled, as he often did, at how anyone could walk away from a half-full glass of liquor. Or abandon the last sip of dark red wine. Or even leave an inch in the bottom of a beer can.

The TV cameras' lights imparted a garish glare to the sidewalk outside the bar. A uniformed deputy stepped towards Phoenix. "Phoenix Eileen Jamborsky?"

Phoenix smiled. "That's me."

"Service of process, ma'am." He extended a packet of papers.

"I'll take that." Gabe gruffly snatched the papers from the deputy and escorted Phoenix away from the crowd, where he scanned the pleading while they walked.

"You'll do great, Gabe. I wouldn't have asked you if I didn't know it."

Gabe started the car, and moments later, they cruised north on the mostly empty highway out of Helena.

"One thing, though," Phoenix said.

Gabe raised his eyebrows. "You're gonna school me now?"

"Just a little."

"Well, go ahead then."

"Never, ever, act on your anger. Meanness can be by an ally, but anger is always an enemy."

"I'll remember that." Why did he find it relatively easy to hear such a lesson from this woman barely older than him when he often bristled at orders from much older men? That trait, he had always known, was a large part of the reason he worked for himself.

Gabe did not ask Phoenix any more questions on the drive home. Not about Ron, not about the lawsuit, and not even about the requests for discovery he had seen in the newly served pleading. They wanted to depose Phoenix and Michael about Enos Terwilliger's suicide. They rode in silence. Only the headlight beams pierced the darkness on the way back to Twin Rivers.

TEN

MAY 2, 2009 – TEMPLE, MONTANA

Ahmed removed his topi gently and folded it on the shabby motel table. Morning prayer finished, he surveyed his equipment. His arsenal of supplies looked dull. Old. Not up to the challenge.

Technology improves, Omar said. But the weapons of a true mujahid like you lie inside.

He picked up his pistol, cleaned it, and polished it with a white towel from the bathroom. He repeated the cleaning with the rifle, a semi-auto with a grenade launcher. He would have preferred a Kalashnikov—the Russian weapon used by the brothers at the camp—but the gunrunners using the Cree border sold American weapons. Ahmed took stock of his other possessions. Of paramount importance was the American cash, the neatly bundled stacks of grubby bills. Ahmed could feel the dirt, the moral filth, emanating from the money, each bill of which had once been in the sad little pocket of a degenerate gambler. Now, sidetracked from their purpose, they would be the grease for the mission of a mujahid.

When Ahmed dressed and left his room, he carried twenty-five thousand American dollars in Adams's small backpack and one thousand dollars in his pocket. Spending money. He knew he needed to get further from Adams and closer to his mission, but not before shopping for some critical items. Strolling down the main street, he quickly found what he needed. A cheap clothing store, Walton's.

Americans don't picture you when they think of a mujahid, Karim said. They imagine a sophisticated spy, a well-dressed intellectual like Atta with his glasses and leather briefcase. You're a street soldier, not a blowhard Saudi professor. You won't look like a Mujahid to the average American. By merely being yourself, you'll appear to be a standard, uneducated, Native American drifter, albeit a strong one. As such, you should wear cheap clothes and live only in dirty places with the lowest in their society. You'll be invisible in those settings.

Ahmed entered the store and quickly located the men's section, where he selected four pairs of jeans, six collarless long sleeved shirts of various colors, and two colorful flannel collared shirts of the type favored by Adams. He picked out a long, black coat with black lining, warm but not memorable, which if buttoned, covered his body down to the knees. Finally, a dark blue knit hat that fit snuggly on his head, covering his ears. He approached the counter.

"Big shopping spree, huh?" The teenage girl smiled at him. "You headed on a camping trip or something?"

Ahmed tried to grin, but it felt fake.

You may be the perfect fighting machine, but you're not much of an actor, Karim warned him. So don't try too hard. Faking a smile can make you look creepy, especially to women. You don't have a light heart, but a serious one. Be yourself. You're shy, the strong, silent type.

He looked down at the clothes. "Just picking up a few things."

"Have you seen our sales? We have some pretty cool jackets back there, better than the one you have here. Sure you don't want to check 'em out?"

"I'm sure. Thank you, though."

"Suit yourself." She read the price tags with an electronic gadget.

"That's exactly what I'm doing," Ahmed said.

The girl looked at him blankly for a second then laughed. "Cute. Not from around here, are you?"

Ahmed cringed. He could not even withstand the scrutiny of an uneducated teenager. A girl no less.

"Up north," he said. "The res."

"You don't sound like you're from the res. You grow up there?"

Ahmed began to feel a burning annoyance at the talkative girl. How could she speak so incessantly about nothing? He looked at her plastic nametag. Winnie. He also examined her face more closely. What a fool he was—her friendly features plainly said she had Native American blood. He cursed himself again. Attention, attention. *Be at peace, Ahmed.*

He peeled off a hundred dollar bill and handed it to her.

"Nice roll." She punched a few buttons on the register.

It took Ahmed a moment to figure out what she meant—another mistake, showing too much money. He began to sweat, and left the store quickly after paying. Now, he needed a phone.

All Americans have a cell phone, Karim said. Most cell phones you buy through a phone company, which requires a contract, identification, and even a credit check. But other phones, called prepaids, are sold at small convenience stores for cash. You'll need an American phone, not a Canadian one. You'll need a phone number to get any sort of work or place to live.

Ahmed walked back to the gas station where he had bought the all-beef hotdogs, and sure enough, the store did sell prepaid telephones. He approached the counter. "A phone, please."

"No problem." The clerk—an older man this time, perhaps the store's owner—handed him a written contract and a pen. "Just fill this out, son. How many minutes you need?"

"Just a few." Ahmed calmly scanned the form. Karim had said nothing about filling out a form. They had discussed rudimentary forms, such as that needed to get a cheap motel room or a simple job. He pulled out his Canadian driving license and carefully copied its information into the blanks on the cell phone form.

"Minimum's a hundred minutes."

Ahmed clenched his teeth—another mistake. The question about minutes did not concern how much time he needed to fill out the form, but the calling minutes he wanted to buy for the phone. "Sorry, two hundred dollars of minutes, sir."

"Canadian, huh? What brings you to Temple?"

Again, Ahmed marveled at the constant talk without meaning. "Thought maybe I'd do some hiking. Lost my damn phone."

"I hear you. In the good old days, a telephone was attached to the wall and couldn't walk away. Guy your age probably doesn't remember though."

Ahmed gave the man the thin smile he was perfecting.

Once the man did whatever he needed to do to charge his phone, and showed Ahmed the phone number on the top of the form. "Don't forget it now." He laughed. "You should write it down. You'd be surprised how many people come in here and ask me for their phone number. I don't have it."

"I'll do that, thank you."

Americans, Karim said, have terrible memories. Television and the Internet bombard their senses and rot their brains. You have a quiet mind. Memorize everything.

Ahmed left the store. Even simple interactions in America will be tiring. He took a deep breath. One more purchase, and he could get away from this town. Further from the reservation. Away from Adams.

Buying a car will be the hardest thing, Karim said. Worse than renting a room or getting a job. By law, car dealers have to know your identity. You can't use your Canadian driving license because there's a real chance they'll notice it's not yours. You have to find a way to buy a car without identifying yourself— without using a dealer. For this you will pay a healthy price. If at all possible, buy your car from a Native American or an old country white man. Not from a woman or a younger man. I'll leave that to you. You also need valid license plates. Pay the seller extra to keep the license plates for a month and promise to mail them back later.

Ahmed stood on the corner and looked up and down the street. It was late morning, and the urge to leave the town was almost overpowering. He turned around and walked back into the gas station. Cars and gas? Made as much sense to him as any other plan.

"Hey, pal," Ahmed said to the old man. "Know where I can buy a used car around here?"

"Can't help you there. There's a used lot out on Greenway. You lose your car too?"

"Naah, man, it died. I thought it had a few more kilometers remaining."

"Kilometers?" The old man furrowed his brow. "If you just need something to get you around for a few days, and then back home, I might have a deal for you."

"Oh, yeah?"

The old man waved Ahmed through the back room and out a metal door that led outside behind the store. What he saw there made him smile. Not the serious smile of quiet prayer, but a real smile, one that reminded him of being a boy.

After prayer in his room, Ahmed stood naked in front of the bathroom mirror. He breathed deeply, relaxed his muscles, and studied his new look. The changing of his appearance was one of the last parts of his training. Both Karim and Omar had extensive advice on the matter.

As for changing your appearance, enter America with long hair and a clean face, which allows for more changes in your hair and beard along the way. Make a substantial change in your hair soon after you enter America. After that, use your best judgment. But remember that American Indians grow little or no facial hair.

Ahmed's thick black hair covered the sink and counter. He rubbed his hands over his newly shaved head. The shaved head, the first in his life, felt good.

Ahmed dressed in his new clothes, new coat, and new hat, and shouldered the two backpacks. Driving in America worried him a great deal. As a boy, he had driven his father's car as well as his family's motorbike. But he was intimidated by the aggressive driving he had seen in American films. And by the possibility of police.

The easiest way to be harassed by police in America is to drive too fast on the highway, Karim said. For you this is an even greater problem because police are much more likely to stop a Native American, or anyone with dark skin, than a white person. Once they stop you, they'll check your license and try to search you for drugs, and you'll have your weapons with you. Be very, very careful.

As he was about to walk outside, the policeman's son's helmet caught his eye. He shook his head—so many petty obstacles to deal with, and since he was leaving Temple forever, this one was unnecessary. He picked up the helmet and carried it outside with his gear, where he loaded the sidecar, careful to pull the tarp over everything and seal it tight around the edges. He clipped the policeman's helmet to the handlebars, put on his own helmet, and turned out of the parking lot onto the street.

It felt good, riding a motorcycle instead of driving a car. It reminded him of his father. And his mother. He recalled a long-ago memory of her laughter as she and his father pulled away on the motorbike while Ahmed held his brother's hand. She had been so happy about the motorcycle ride.

Ahmed turned on his GPS device and found the listing he needed. He parked and strode confidently into the Temple police station, feeling strangely detached from the weapons in the backpack. Unworried. Unafraid.

"Officer Bard asked me to drop this off for him, ma'am," he said to the uniformed woman behind the counter. He smiled more broadly than he had for the store clerk or the gas station owner. The smile did not feel forced nor, as Karim warned, creepy.

"Thanks, I'll make sure he gets it," she said without paying him any real attention.

Minutes later, Ahmed was on the quiet road out of town, driving only sixty-three miles an hour but hurtling towards his destiny all the same. He wasn't due at his next rendezvous until the next morning, but it wasn't wise to stay in Temple. Besides, he wanted to ride.

He prayed as he rode, but kept his eyes open, scanning the road ahead, the mountains in the distance, and the endless flat land in between. This land of the infidels was truly as beautiful as his country.

America is a massive land with beautiful nature, Omar said. The people benefit greatly from their isolation from the rest of the world. Until now, North America, with its resources and protecting oceans, has always been able to hide from the conflicts that mark the complicated histories of our brotherlands.

Ahmed prayed again, and then looked at the GPS device. Twin Rivers, two hundred sixty miles. Not far on such a marvelous vehicle, and he had several days for the journey. Ahmed enjoyed the loud and constant rip of the engine and the cold wind on his face. He checked the speed again. Sixty-two. In an hour or so, he'd find a roadside motel. Be at Peace, Ahmed, Be at Peace.

ELEVEN
MAY 11, 2009 – TWIN RIVERS, MONTANA

The Monday after the trip to Helena, Gabe surveyed his office from behind a desk which had once graced the corner office of the Attorney General of Montana. His father's office. Now the desk occupied the second floor of an old townhouse across the street from the Twin Rivers Courthouse. Despite his recent boredom with his practice, Gabe still loved the office. The huge windowed room with hardwood floors and an old maple fireplace were wholesome symbols of the two biggest decisions of his adulthood. First, to quit drinking. Second, to quit Seattle and move home. To become an important fish in a small pond.

Gabe's assistant Myrlene filled him in on missed phone messages. But Gabe's mind wandered to the difference between his trial lawyer life in Seattle and his small-town lawyer life of the last four years. As he often did, he thought of his last day at his firm, the day he made his decision to quit instead of attending a firm-sponsored inpatient alcohol-rehab program. *You're one of the best lawyers we've got, the very best in your age group. But it's been stressful. Get healthy. You have a long future with us.*

Gabe rejected the generous offer, instead quitting the firm, and booze, on his own. In four years in Weasel Junction he had made a fine, if unexciting, life. Early nights, respect in town, and the feeling of dull, predictable healthiness each morning. But yesterday's jaunt to Helena, the press, and Phoenix had his mind cranking again.

Myrlene went through the assorted messages. Nothing big: a few new clients on small cases, a call from the prosecutor's office, and business solicitations.

"Grizzly Redford called twice yesterday from the jail phone. Said you'd know what it was about but he didn't want to talk about it. Said the call might be recorded. Dude's crazy, right?" Myrlene ran her fingers through the temples of her frizzy red hair.

"Yes, but I don't trust that phone either. Never have."

Myrlene frowned. At twenty-eight, she, like Gabe, didn't quite fit in Twin Rivers. Though she had tried. Until the year before, she had been dating Levi McManus, a second cousin to Melvin Thompson. Myrlene claimed to be considering law school but had been saying that for three years now. Instead, she continued to work for Gabe with the title of legal assistant and the salary of a secretary. "You're sayin' Pasquali violates the fucking law by monitoring the attorney-client phone calls?"

"I'm saying Pasquali does what he wants. As for Redford, he's fine. I'll go see him when I can. We got a new case. A big one."

"Cool."

"It's a civil matter in Helena Federal Court. We're gonna represent the mayor and the town against a group that wants to block the Gitmo prisoner contract." They spent half an hour discussing the legal research Gabe needed on the injunction issue.

"Basically, we gotta stop this thing before it starts," he said. "Find all the precedents on getting a full hearing without discovery under this section. We're entitled to a hearing ASAP, and I want to request one for next week. This is gonna be a mess, and I assume the national press will be onto it by today."

"You gonna get famous? Has Phoenix admitted it yet?"

"You're reading that all wrong." Gabe liked that Myrlene believed Phoenix's interest in him and his career meant she had the hots for him. He suspected otherwise, beginning to realize that Phoenix operated on a far more complicated level.

"Watch out for her, Gabe. I don't trust her."

"I know you don't."

"Not that it matters to me. If you want her, go for it. She's going places, but she's not your type."

"I hear you." Gabe smiled as Myrlene walked away. Her thin frame, long red hair, and habit of wearing jeans and T-shirts to work could easily make a stranger peg her as a college student. She was, however, capable of doing better legal research than most first-year law students. Gabe had hired Myrlene out of college, and in four years had watched her grow up. She was not striking, like the typical Western beauty at UM, or sexy and mysterious like Phoenix. She was, rather, an earnest girl with a thin, freckled face and a cynical sense of humor. The fabulous underachiever type. Somehow too cool for the world but, just under the surface, seething for its acceptance. She probably thought the same of him.

Gabe picked up the phone and made an appointment for five o'clock. Then he bore down on the complaint in Citizens v. Jamborsky, scratching annotations in the margins of his copy, a to-do list of sorts. As he went, he used the Internet for basic searches.

As he often did, Gabe zoned in on the task at hand, unaware of his surroundings. He had the opposite of ADHD, his last girlfriend had declared, and not as a compliment. She referred to his ability to completely ignore everything else while focusing on a task, usually a criminal case.

Myrlene buzzed him from downstairs, and he was surprised to see it was past three o'clock. He had forgotten lunch. "It's her highness," Myrlene deadpanned through the intercom.

"Hey, Phoenix," Gabe said.

"Any word?"

"Doing some background stuff. I entered my appearance on the court's electronic filing system this morning and plan to call opposing counsel before the end of the day. I say we should file for next week for a hearing on the merits without discovery."

"Next week is perfect. We can get rid of this mess before TR day. I thought I should tell you I spoke to the Justice Department today. Once we certify the contract, we can get the first payment, one-third on the upfront fee, within days."

"Days?"

"Days. They want to do a final inspection by December and have prisoners here by mid-January, but I can't certify the contract until this case is gone. What day can we set the hearing for?"

"The clerk is calling me back about the calendar, but the code suggests this needs priority on any court's docket. I'll write the thing tomorrow and aim for next Thursday as a hearing date. Which reminds me, I need a list of things from you."

"Shoot."

"I need a notarized affidavit outlining the reasons why delaying the resolution of this matter would cause irreparable harm to Twin Rivers. We'd lose the contract, etcetera. And, briefly, how the payments will help the town. I'll file that under seal, but you have to figure the press will eventually get hold of it, so be careful."

"I'm always careful."

"We also need to go through the topics they want to depose you about and develop short explanations of why the information is irrelevant."

"That's easy. The town's finances, the finances of the leading businesses in town, and Enos Terwilliger have nothing to do with whether the prison would create a danger for the citizens of Montana."

"So you know they added Terwilliger's death as a topic for discovery."

Phoenix hesitated. "It's come up. There's always been a silly conspiracy theory about Michael's father. That he was murdered or that he killed himself over family finances. It's a non-starter. Michael won't even hear it."

"I know it's personal," Gabe said, "but I need to sit down with you and Michael and talk about this before we file. How it happened, when it happened, where everyone was, the details. Just so I know. We can't be sure the judge won't ask a question about it."

Phoenix sighed. "Agreed. But you're not going to be talking to Michael."

"No?"

"Michael can't talk about it. Not even to me. Never has."

Gabe paused."Then I need the details from you."

"I said fine. Do you know which judge we'll have?"

"No. I have calls in to a couple friends to get some intel on the judges in that court—Bernstein, Morgan, and a recent appointee, a woman named Reynolds."

"I've met Reynolds," Phoenix said. "Tough lady."

"How well do you know her?"

"Not well. Beau got her appointed at the end of the last administration. I shook her hand at a fancy function last year. Former US Attorney."

"You know what, it doesn't matter in the long run. The case is bullshit. Any judge will eventually toss it. The question is whether we can avoid the lengthy process and get it done right away."

"The town expects a certified contract on Twin Rivers Day, and we need the revenue right away. Do you have any idea what will happen if Justice finds out that due to passage of time, we can't even fulfill the contract? That the prison is being foreclosed on?" Phoenix laughed. "No pressure or anything. I know you can do it."

"Thanks for your vote of confidence."

"Am I a high-maintenance client yet?"

"Breaking all records."

"We haven't discussed your fee."

"Good point. I charge four hundred an hour."

"Has anyone ever paid that?"

"No, but that doesn't mean it's not my rate."

"I got a better idea. I'll pay your hourly rate, but if you get the case dismissed by the end of next week, I'll change it to a flat fee of a hundred."

"Dollars?"

"You're funny."

Gabe was silent. He had earned twice that at his Seattle firm. But per year, not per week.

"I need this case gone by next week, Gabe," Phoenix said.

"I'll do my best. We'll win. But as for next week—"

"Next week." Phoenix hung up.

Gabe went downstairs where Myrlene was reading legal opinions while leaning back in her chair, feet on the reception desk.

"This suit's really a joke," she said. "We're entitled to an expedited hearing as a matter of law, and provided we can show irreparable harm from the delay, the court has to hear the permanent injunction issue forthwith."

"That's how I read it."

"They could defeat the motion, though, if the requested discovery is material to the issue, in which case we can still get the trial calendared fast, but not fast enough—maybe three months instead of the usual year to dispose of a civil case in that court."

Gabe was impressed. "How do you know that?"

"I called a friend in Helena. He's a lawyer. Goes to that court."

"Who?"

Myrlene looked at Gabe sideways, running her fingers through her hair again. "I have to tell you about all of my friends?"

"What else?" he asked.

"Your job is to make it clear the discovery is irrelevant. The suit alleges a likelihood of physical harm to Montanans. It does not even allege financial harm, and even if it did, the town's finances are irrelevant. I think you should file Rule Eleven on them."

Gabe smiled. "Great fucking idea." Rule 11 under the Federal Rules of Civil Procedure allowed for sanctions against a party that files a frivolous lawsuit or pleading. "Draft that. I'll work on the motion to dismiss and expedite. Oh, and we got Gillespie coming in at five."

"What the hell for?"

Roland Gillespie dressed like a cowboy, complete with hat, boots, and stitch-patterned button-down shirts. He was actually a retired cop from the Crow Indian reservation near Hardin and the only private investigator in Caroline County. He sat before Gabe's desk next to Myrlene and listened. Gillespie was an aggressive listener. He rarely took notes, but nodded slowly after each important chunk of information. Gabe had never known him to forget a name, a date, or a critical fact. His crinkled brown eyes watched Gabe. Gillespie had the wise, tanned, alert, and wrinkled look of an old Indian—like the old pictures of Red Cloud, calmly holding a rifle across his lap. Gabe had always thought it was strange that a career Indian cop would move away from his connections within the tribe, where he would certainly be viewed as a leader. It was a forced move, Gillespie had said. It's so beautiful here.

"So I'm thinking you trust me because I'm an outsider," Gillespie said, summing up Gabe's precise thought on the matter.

"I trust you, period, Roland. You've always done right by me. If this job isn't for you, tell me, and I trust you'll never mention this meeting to anyone."

Gillespie looked at the ceiling and held his hands together in front of him, fingers touching, as if to contemplate.

"I'll do it. Hell, I've wondered about some of this shit myself."

"Just be careful."

"One question, Gabe. Who am I working for? You, or your client?"

"I'm acting to protect my client, but no one except the people in this room need to know a damn thing about this investigation."

Gillespie nodded as he shook Gabe's hand. "We'll be in touch." He picked up his hat from the desk and left Gabe's office unescorted.

Myrlene pretended to try to hide a curious smile.

"What?" he said.

"Our argument is that the discovery requests are irrelevant to the lawsuit, so the actual answers to the discovery questions don't matter. Why are you, Phoenix's lawyer, paying somebody to dig into this shit?"

"I want to know why my client is scared of the answers."

"Why?" she said.

Gabe stood and grabbed his jacket from the antique coat rack.

As they had on occasional evenings in the last few months, Gabe and Myrlene sat in the far right corner of Ramhead's, a bar on the corner of River and Centennial.

"One Stoli martini up with olives," Gabe said to Nelson, the owner. The place was filling up, but not like it used to, not like before the town started to die. The drink was for Myrlene. Her favorite. "And a club soda."

"Check it out." Myrlene was watching the television above the bar.

"Hey, turn this up," somebody said, quieting the bar.

"That's Pandora's," someone else said. Sure enough, Caroline County's strip bar was on CNN. An incident. An attempted murder? A strip bar bouncer saved a stripper from her jealous husband.

Gabe pointed to the mug shot on the TV. "Hey, I've represented that guy." John Gallager, a local degenerate who went by the nickname Gracie.

"Apparently he ain't rehabilitated," someone said, raising a twitter of laughter along the bar.

"I had him two years for domestic violence against his wife," Gabe whispered to Myrlene. "I hope I don't get appointed to this case tomorrow. We got enough going on."

Myrlene squinted at the TV. "Don't sweat it, look at the date, a week ago, guy must already have a lawyer. Man, this town used to be boring."

CNN showed a local clip of Pasquali speaking to reporters. "We got the suspect in custody. A young man employed at the establishment disarmed and disabled him until police arrived. The suspect's charged with brandishing a firearm and attempted murder, as of now. Nobody except him was injured." Pasquali looked old and tired on the news, much more so than in real life.

"Go get 'em, Sheriff,' the barroom loudmouth said.

"Since when does Twin Rivers get on CNN?" Myrlene said. "News from the strip bar? Week-old!?"

"Get used to it," Gabe said. "Background. We're famous now." The screen changed to a clip of Gabe and Phoenix walking along the street after they had been served the lawsuit papers. Then they showed a still shot of Twin Rivers prison next to a an overview photograph of the prison facility at Guantanamo Bay. A reporter, standing on the street in front of the Federal Courthouse in Helena, discussed the lawsuit.

Gabe and Myrlene talked until late—about the suit, Enos Terwilliger, and the mysteries of the town into which neither of them had ever been invited.

Gabe brushed his teeth while standing naked in front of the mirror. He felt perfectly comfortable with his decision to investigate the facts of Phoenix's case. He, not his client, was in charge of case strategy. In fact, he felt invigorated. The next day, he would draft the motion to dismiss. The opponents might even waive a hearing and concede.

He opened the door to his dimly lit bedroom. Myrlene sat at the foot of the bed; even in the dark he could tell her thin frame was naked. She sat Indian style, her feet hooked into the crooks of her legs as if to meditate. Instantly aroused, he slid onto the bed next to her, gently pushing her up towards its center. Her hands manically gripped his buttocks as he took her breasts into his hands and mouth and softly touched her back and the insides of her legs. She pushed against him roughly, and he rolled. She took all of him into her mouth, quickly moving up and down. She gave the best head he had ever known, somehow more exciting for her seemingly quick desperation which contrasted starkly with her normal stoic demeanor. It was, as usual, too good, and he gently pulled her head away. He rolled her over again, communicating his desire with their shared, practiced movements. Her thin legs squirmed, churning to get them where she wanted. Gabe then placed his face into the fresh warmth between her legs, and she engulfed him with her mouth again. They moved quickly together, and Gabe lost himself, now lying on his back beneath her. Her sudden series of rapid shivers alerted him, and he turned her again, entering her easily and thrusting hard, their mouths finding each other. Myrlene cried out, her whole body shaking. She squeezed him harder. Gabe finished and rolled over, leaving his leg on top of her. He knew he would sleep quickly. The next morning Myrlene would probably be gone, casually reading the morning paper when he arrived at the office, her feet up on her desk, sipping her tall mug of coffee. This had not always been Gabe's kind of thing, fucking his secretary. A strange year, and apt to get stranger. Gabe shut his eyes.

TWELVE

MAY 3, 2009 – OUTSIDE CUT BANK, MONTANA

You will meet three counterparts in America, Omar said. Karim sat behind Omar in a chair, his arms folded over his belly. Your main contact will meet you near Caroline County—near the location of your jihad. That contact will provide you with supplies and possibly with the opportunity to speak with Karim on the phone about last-minute details. Before that, within days of arriving in America, you will meet your first contact. This person will provide you with lawful identification. He is a Muslim whose family is sympathetic to our cause. He works for the agency that issues driving licenses. He will have received your photograph and created a driving license for you. He will also give you some false pay receipts and other documents that will make it appear you have lived and worked in eastern Montana for some time. The brother's name is Yusef Hadid. After your mission, your driving license information may lead the FBI to Yusef, who has knowledge of some of our brothers in America. In any event, Yusef will meet you at a roadside stop on Route 2 between the border crossing and your destination on your third day in America. If either of you fails to meet, you will repeat the same meeting time and place the next day. Yusef, however, will not fail to meet.

Ahmed enjoyed riding immensely, but he felt the need to clean himself, as even just an hour on the motorcycle had caked a thin layer of highway dirt on his face. The GPS told him that Cut Bank rest area approached. He'd left the dingy motel when it was still pitch dark outside, and he was now more than an hour early. He hoped the rest area would include a bathroom.

He had not encountered many cars on Route 2, especially before dawn. It was a frigid, bland morning. A certain emptiness left Ahmed with a yearning inside, one he had felt before, but not recently. He never felt it while training, praying, or studying, but the long dark drive had brought it out of him. He had felt the same way when he walked alone from his village to the training camp.

The rest area was completely empty at 6 a.m. It resembled a park, with benches, drinking water dispensers, and a wooden cabin. Light barely appeared over the mountains, but the wooden cabin had lights in front of it and inside the wide passageway which cut it in half. Restrooms on either side, and machines that dispensed drinks, candy, and some food. Ahmed saw no cars and no people, only an occasional car speeding along Route 2, fifty meters away. He washed his face in the bathroom and then walked out behind the wooden cabin. A steep slope led to heavy green underbrush. Garbage—aluminum cans, food wrappers, cigarette butts, condoms—littered the area. Ahmed trudged down the hill and into the underbrush. *I was just going to the bathroom because the one in the cabin is so disgusting,* he would say if a policeman pulled into the rest area and questioned him. He soon found what he was looking for and returned quickly to the cabin. He decided, without apprehension, to pray, but without his topi, which lay folded in the pack with his weapons.

When he stood, the empty feeling was gone. The sun had risen. He walked to the machines, pulled out some coins, and bought a bottle of water and a wafer wrapped in shiny red paper. To his surprise, the wafer contained some frosty sugar. He sat on one of the benches in front of the cabin, paying close attention to each car that flew by on Route 2.

He checked his watch—two minutes after seven. A blue sedan turned into the rest area. It moved quickly—too quickly, for Ahmed's taste. Ahmed stood casually, stretched his arms as if bored, and walked towards his motorcycle. He stood where he could retrieve his pistol quickly while keeping the motorcycle between himself and the approaching car.

The blue car parked astride two slots, and a thin, balding man with a small moustache got out. Immediately, Ahmed relaxed. The man posed no danger. He was about fifty years old and wore tan pants, white sports shoes, and a tight blue coat. The man moved toward Ahmed in short, hasty steps, eyes darting around. He was neither a mujahid, a policeman, nor a man trained for fighting. Quite the opposite.

"Jimmy? Is that you?" The man spoke in a whisper, hesitantly, as if he'd forgotten his script. "Why are you here? I mean, what are you doing so far up here?" The man carried himself like a nervous American.

"Waiting for you, brother," Ahmed said quietly in English. He gestured towards the bench. "Let's talk."

The man had already pulled a folder out of his jacket and attempted to hand it to Ahmed before even shaking hands. Ahmed stepped back.

"My friend, relax. Sit." Ahmed then turned his back on the man. The man followed. He sat on the bench next to Ahmed, shivering, and not just from the cold. He could not control his shaking jaw or hands.

"What is your name?" Ahmed asked.

"Is that—well, no offense, but, sir, is that really necessary?"

"It's okay, I already know your name, Yusef."

Yusef grimaced. He turned his small, timid brown eyes to Ahmed's. "Please, please, brother. My family. I just need to go." He again thrust the folder towards Ahmed.

"Relax, my friend." Ahmed took the folder and opened it. He carefully reviewed each document, especially the Montana driving license clipped to the corner of the folder. He raised his eyes again to the road. One speeding car and nothing more.

"Jeremy Blain," Ahmed read slowly.

"That's what I was told. Blain's a common last name in Billings." Yusef now held both hands on his shaking knees. "For Indians."

"Thank you, Yusef." Ahmed placed the folder into his own jacket, then zipped the jacket to the top. This moment, he knew, was one of the most dangerous of his mission.

"May I go now?" Yusef asked, clearly wanting to stand while not wanting to be disobedient.

"Almost, Yusef, but first, your pay."

"Pay? I am not doing this for pay. It's my family. We respect you, but I—"

"You deserve to be paid. For your risk. Follow me." Ahmed stood, patting Yusef on the back softly. He glanced again at the empty highway. He feigned nonchalance, but silently cursed Karim for authorizing the choosing of such a bad meeting spot for him and Yusef.

"But why...I, I don't need pay."

"I'm not here to harm a true believer, a brother. If I planned to harm you, you would already be dead. They told me to pay you, so I must. Your cash is by the restroom, in a bag in the trashcan. You know, in case of the police." As Ahmed walked, he led Yusef towards the cabin with a light hand still resting on Yusef's back. They passed Yusef's awkwardly parked car.

"Please, please, my children." As if to demonstrate the truth of his claim, Yusef gestured to two colorful stickers attached to the rear fender of his car. *Amhurst Junior High Lions.* Junior high, a school. *Denver Broncos.* Perhaps another school. They named their schools and colleges for animals, something Ahmed vaguely remembered learning before.

"My brother, do not be afraid. Let's get your money and be on our way." Ahmed glanced at Route 2 one more time before turning Yusef towards the cabin. Yusef followed obediently, but Ahmed heard him praying softly. Ahmed's chest tightened with anger. Karim claimed to know America, and yet he allowed this meeting to be set in broad daylight under such absurd circumstances.

Yusef followed Ahmed through the tunnel and behind the cabin. Ahmed gently urged him ahead as they reached the incline above the underbrush. He then reached his right arm over Yusef's shoulder, placed his left hand on the side of Yusef's head, and snapped his neck. Yusef fell gently into Ahmed's arms; he had bony arms and legs and a soft, round stomach, the result of an American life. He hoisted Yusef and carried him on his shoulder down the hill and through the underbrush for about thirty meters until he found the grated drainage ditch he had scouted an hour before. He dropped Yusef gently in the dirt and shut the man's eyes with the palm of one hand while patting his pockets with the other. He then shoved a wadded up newspaper page in the man's pocket, direct advice from Karim.

Americans often meet each other randomly for sex. You may find this distasteful, but pick up a copy of the Helena Times and look for the advertisements placed by homosexual men—"men seeking men" and such things. Circle some of the advertisements and leave the paper with Yusef. The police will spend days investigating homosexuals while you continue your mission.

Ahmed grabbed the slats of the rusty grate. It took him three tries to budge and then slide the thick metal. He pushed Yusef's body into the dark well and heard it hit shallow water a few meters below. Ahmed then replaced the grate and returned the same way, back through the cabin tunnel, and out into the now bright sun.

Several cars passed moving at least seventy-five miles an hour. Ahmed walked quickly to the sidecar and removed a small knife and a pen from his pack. He also found his guidebook and tore out the last page, which was blank. *Be at Peace, Ahmed, Be at Peace.* He jogged to Yusef's car and used the knife to remove both number plates. He then bent over the car's hood, thanking God for his good memory for words and numbers.

Ahmed, eight years old, turned to the classroom, smiling into the applause.

"Excellent, Ahmed. Excellent," his teacher said for all to hear. They studied writing letters, but his teacher sometimes made it fun, like with the memory game to see who could write the letters in order after only a quick glance. "You must have a photographic memory, Ahmed. I cannot wait to tell your mother." The tiny classroom had open windows which allowed for an occasional breeze, and at the moment Ahmed felt such a breeze, sweetly running across his face as the class clapped. "Maybe you shall be a scientist." Many days, hardly anyone came to class, but Ahmed's mother made him and Abu go. Every day.

Ahmed drew thick lines on the blank page, which took several moments because the pen drew only thin marks. He had fallen into his frantic movements, those Omar viewed as a sign of an unsteady heart. Not a soldier's heart. He placed the sign he had made under the windshield wiper, opened the car door, wiped the guidebook against his jacket on both sides, and tossed the book inside.

Route 2 was still clear. In seconds, Ahmed spun the motorcycle and, moments later, pulled onto Route 2. Only one car was ahead of him in the far, flat distance, and none visible behind. Thankfully, he soon approached a cement bridge over a medium-sized stream. As he sped over the bridge, Yusef's license plates sailed into the water below.

Ahmed hoped his own ingenuity made up for Karim's idiocy in selection of the meeting place with Yusef. It bothered him that Karim would create such a weak plan, one that had such a high chance for exposure or failure. *As to the specifics, I leave that to your wit and skill.* Fine, but why place him in a situation that made the mission so hard?

When the police found Yusef's car and the sign—For Sale By Owner, 406-265-3120—they might actually believe someone was selling the car, and so see no need to search the area. The phone number would lead them to a random motel in Billings. In any case, Ahmed needed only hours to distance himself from Yusef.

Ahmed tried to manage his nerves while he drove. He checked the GPS and his speed. His stomach clenched and unclenched, and warm bile tried to force its way into his mouth. He forced it down again and again, until it stopped. About fifty miles later, he stopped to buy gas. After filling the motorcycle, he entered the dirty bathroom at the back of the gas station. He washed his face then stared into his own eyes. Even the washing felt frantic. Not like a soldier. Suddenly, he vomited, barely able to spin in time to get half of the vomit into the toilet.

A soldier must get proper rest and food, Ahmed. In times of need, a mujahid can fight with no rest and no food, but during jihad you must care for your body as well as your mind.

Ahmed knew he was hungry, maybe enough so to vomit and have shaking hands. He cleaned the sink and toilet with paper from the metal receptacle.

In several hours, he would get a motel and eat—Jeremy Blain would get a motel and eat. His tight stomach and rushing chest made his arms feel tingly and weak. He gripped the handlebars tighter.

A freedom fighter does not falter, Omar said. Of all of his weapons, his heart is the one which separates him from an infidel. His heart is the reason he cannot fail. Tell me boys, do each of you have the heart of a mujahid? The four new trainees, eyes pointed obediently ahead, responded loudly in the affirmative. Omar then called out to Mahmoud, who trotted over obediently. Only a few years older than Ahmed, Mahmoud had led the first week of training, which included daily excursions up into and around the mountains.

Mahmoud and his men have a captured an Indian soldier, Omar told the new trainees. They are holding him at the northwest satellite camp. Which of you wants to execute him? Omar looked coolly at the Kashmiri boy to Ahmed's right. The boy had related to Ahmed the murder of his three brothers by Indian soldiers. Ahmed had been able to feel the boy's hatred. The boy planned to return to India, to carry on the fight for his homeland against the Indian army. But now, the boy would not meet Omar's gaze. Eyes downcast, his enthusiasm buried deep under his fear, he did not speak. Omar kept his stare fixed on the Kashmiri boy. Finally, Ahmed broke the uncomfortable silence. I will kill the infidel, take me to him, God willing. Omar nodded, but his cold eyes stayed on the Kashmiri. He then put his arm around Ahmed and led him to a jeep.

Ahmed, Omar, and Mahmoud drove west toward the low-lying hills. But once outside camp, Omar told Ahmed the truth. There was no Indian. It was a test, good friend. You have passed. The Kashmiri has failed. Pray, do not tell the others.

Yusef had not been a brother. Yusef had been an American, an infidel with his fancy schools and cars and nervous ways. Ahmed reached into his back pocket and flung away his Canadian driving license. He enjoyed seeing the way it spun through the cold wind and off the road.

THIRTEEN

MAY 12, 2009 – TWIN RIVERS, MONTANA

As always, Gabe awoke at five-thirty, and Myrlene was indeed already gone. *The only thing you have to change is everything.* A famous slogan for addicts.

An hour later he was finishing the first part of his workout. He swung as hard as he could, delivering an uppercut into the heavy bag, lifting it slightly into the air. He followed with rapid jabs and ended the flurry with a hard left hook. He then backed up, breathing heavily. Soaked with sweat, he bounded up the basement steps, put on a light sweatshirt, stepped out into cold early morning, and started running. Boxing followed by running—his normal routine since he had moved back to Weasel Junction—was one of the dividing lines of his life. Before drinking, after drinking. Again he thought of his old life in Seattle. His last name, as well as his own talent, had him trying big cases by age thirty. The late hours, the busy social life, the women, and inextricably intertwined with it all, the drinking. "The machine," a co-worker had called him for his ability to work twelve hours, close down a bar, and then do the whole thing over again the next day. Every time Gabe congratulated himself on his conversion—from manic workaholic and urban partier to responsible small-town councilman—a momentary sadness followed.

Gabe sprinted the last quarter mile, bursting back in his front door. He checked his watch, though his timing was usually perfect. He had an hour to make the council meeting. He grabbed a bottle of water and stood shivering in his kitchen. No hangover. This was his life now.

May you live in interesting times, an ancient Chinese curse. Gabe never enjoyed the Twin Rivers City Council meetings. Held one Saturday a month, they were, during uninteresting times, nothing more than hours of pointless discussion about property lines and zoning. But this meeting was different, and Gabe's fleeting thought of the Chinese proverb concerned Phoenix's grandiose minimization of the pending lawsuit.

Phoenix stood at the head of the U-shaped table, concluding her remarks. "My hope is to distribute the first third of the payments to county residents the following week, and to make that announcement during my speech. Warden Haverford is taking applications immediately for the staff positions, as well as arranging for a two-week, in-county training program for the actual prison staff. All of this will appear on posters around town and on the Caroline County website today. Because Twin Rivers Penitentiary is technically a private prison, owned by the town, we are allowed to discriminate in favor of hiring Caroline County residents. Nonresidents will only be considered if there's a shortfall in applications, which I seriously doubt, given the salaries and benefits."

Egan sat upright, yet relaxed in that stately way of his, at the far right end of the U, opposite Gabe. "Ms. Mayor, can we be assured the contract will even be certified by Twin Rivers Day? It would be a disaster to promote the event only to cancel it. My feeling is that your whole point was to make Twin Rivers Day a celebration of the funding. You need a lock on it first, right? Plus we promote other festivals for months. Four days?"

"I know your position and took your advice in postponing it until after the lawsuit. Our case should be dismissed Thursday in Helena. People are excited about this, Egan."

"You still setting up on River and Rhodes? Like MountainFest?"

"Actually no, we thought we'd set up at the end of River, with the stage facing up the street and the mountains in the background. It will—"

"I want to head up the security detail then. Along with Pasquali, of course."

"I thought of that job as rather below you, Egan." She winked.

"Not at all, Ms. Mayor. Especially not under these… circumstances. You won't have your roving band of overpaid border patrols trained by then. I'll bring in my team. We'll need the press away from the stage. And I meant it when I said I'm worried about safety. We need screeners around the stage. And a firearm ban inside the town for that day."

"I'm borrowing fifteen thousand from the emergency fund for the event. You're in charge, Egan, along with Pasquali, of course."

"So what's the setup?" Gabe said.

"We're building the stage as we speak," Phoenix said. "Egan and Michael have been kind enough to donate some labor for that. They're also installing a temporary chain-link around the festival spot, with only two entry points to the grounds. We'll kick off the day with speeches at noon. Stillwater, briefly on finances, no real details, just the improvements. We have a couple of awards. Jon Bradley from Twin Rivers High will get a scholarship. I'll give an award to that bouncer who saved the stripper the other night. And then I'll speak. We got all the networks from Missoula, Helena, FOX, CNN, MSNBC, everybody."

Gabe watched Phoenix's excitement build just talking about it.

"Gabe, you should give a speech before mine. Get your face shown around. Son of Attorney General Lantagne, born in town, now back as a town leader—Deputy Mayor, yes?"

"Maybe next time. Kind of busy this week." Gabe was still amazed at Phoenix's brazen confidence, planning Twin Rivers Day before disposing of the court case.

Outside City Hall, Gabe waited for Phoenix. As Egan walked towards his truck, Gabe called out to him.

"Let me know if you need any help, Egan."

Egan turned and smiled. "Thanks, but we need your attention on the case, right? I got it covered. Nobody I don't know is getting near this event. That's an advantage of small town life. I'll even get some cowboys and farmhands on a few rooftops for you."

"This town is never gonna be the same, is it?" A worthless question, but Gabe wanted to see Egan's reaction.

"Hey, man, you guys won the vote. You pull this off in the court case, and we're on. We can disagree, but once we decide, we move forward together."

Egan strolled towards his truck. "Egan!" Gabe called out. The old man was now further away, crossing River Street. He craned his head back at Gabe as if, what? Annoyed? But his face showed only the same sage composure.

"The case will be over by Twin Rivers Day," Gabe said. "I'm in for the security committee."

"Whatever you like," Egan said, barely loud enough for Gabe to hear.

"I asked you for a briefing on the discovery requests," Gabe said. He and Phoenix sat across the conference table at the back of the large first-floor room. Myrlene, far across the hardwood floor at the reception desk, answered the phone with her back to them.

"And I just gave you one," Phoenix said. "Only two points merit attention. First, Twin Rivers has an A-plus credit rating that dates back twenty-six years. Our books are done by Dormington on River Street and protected by the attorney-client privilege."

"I need more than that. I don't know what they're gonna toss at us during the hearing. We'll only get their written response pleading a day or so before. Break it down for me. Revenues? I mean, you said yourself the town collects no taxes from businesses on River Street."

Phoenix took a long pull of her coffee and leaned back. "Attorney-client, right? This doesn't leave this room. Not in court, not under seal, nothing."

Gabe gave her a small nod.

"Caroline County uses a very unique revenue generating plan," she said. "A special tax, you could call it."

"How special?"

"I call it an extremely graduated flat tax. We tax the very wealthiest residents of the County at one rate, and everyone else at another rate."

"I paid less than two hundred dollars in local taxes last year, and I've gotta be in the wealthiest one percent. Shit, most of the people in the county are dirt poor by national standards."

"More graduated than that. Very, very graduated."

Phoenix was having too much fun with this. "Cough it up," Gabe said.

"The Angel Sky, Egan Crowne's farm, and Thompson's farm pay the town a combined flat tax each year. The modest gentry of the county, like you, pay half a percent income tax."

"That's about one percent of the county," Gabe said. "The rest?"

"Pay nothing. No business tax, no property tax, no payroll tax, no income tax. Nothing. They pay state and federal taxes of course. I mean, if they work, I assume they do."

"So how much is the combined flat tax?"

"About five million dollars." Phoenix stared calmly at Gabe, who searched her deep blue eyes. They danced like lively little mirrors.

"How long has this been going on?"

"Since the seventies."

"River Street, the town square, the schools, the police department, everything? Funded by the graduated tax?"

"Plus payments on the prison."

"They pay voluntarily? Why?"

"You can't believe they love the county? Love the town?"

Gabe did not answer.

"Think about it," she said. "We have the cutest little town center in Montana, great schools, a decent police force. And yet we have no outside retailers. No chain stores. No developers colonizing us with condos or McMansions. And we live in some of the most beautiful country in America."

"It's still not sustainable, three citizens funding a whole town? In exchange for what? And if they stop?"

"Control, Gabe. The council. And until lately, the mayor's office."

Gabe looked at her quizzically.

"I thought you might have seen this coming, Gabe, but Mayor Pritchard wanted to end the graduated tax, to try to make Weasel Junction into a regular town."

"And you disagreed?"

"He was right, as you are. It's not sustainable. What I propose is to end the graduated tax and save the town. But Pritchard had no vision. Or influence over those who mattered."

"Egan, Thompson, and your ex-husband? They're good with this? With ending it?"

"They know it can't go on. Don't forget what I told you about these old cowboys. They're conservative, in the real sense of it. Meaning they hate change. But they're also conservative, meaning they're cheap. They're reluctant, but relieved, to let it go."

"And so the prison plan."

"Save the town, end the tax. My idea. And not one they saw coming."

"And so you…"

"Ended it. In one move. I am, after all, the mayor." She smiled. She so clearly loved the feeling of a swinging set of nuts. "In days, the town will be free, but has only months left to live without the Guantanamo contract."

"It's not even about the economy, Chrysler, or the plant closing?"

"It never has been. Not for the town. Maybe for the workers. But hell, layoffs have happened all over the country. The point here is, Twin Rivers is special. We will get jobs for our people, and without selling the town to outsiders."

"Who in town knows about the graduated tax?"

"Almost nobody. They think it's just a well-run town."

"Stillwater?"

"Of course. That's why he's Town Treasurer for life."

"So what's the big deal if the graduated tax got exposed? Why do they think you're scared of this issue?"

Phoenix again just stared at Gabe. He thought of the vast acres of the Angel Sky, Thompson's properties in North Caroline, and Egan's huge farm in between.

She stood."I gotta go. When are you filing?"

"We're not done, Phoenix. What about the Terwilliger matter?"

"He was depressed. He shot himself. It was really sad."

"Sorry, Phoenix, but I need more than that."

Phoenix gave Gabe a deliberately phony smile. "Michael was away. I heard the shot. I got a call from the top hand—you know, Manuel. I rode down to the stream. Manuel had found him by the stream bank. Happy?"

"Was it investigated? Do they believe Manuel killed him?"

"Shit, Gabe, Manuel Foreva's family has been with the Terwilligers since Elijah. He's as loyal as they come. Ask Pasquali, he investigated the shooting. Enos killed himself. What my friends in Helena need to realize is, I got nothing to hide. But neither do I scare. And I got ammunition they blatantly fail to appreciate."

"I don't get it, Phoenix. Why do these anti-prison people, who are not really scared of a terrorist attack according to you, care if Twin Rivers brings in the Guantanamo prisoners? There'll be prisoners in Illinois, Kansas, and likely Virginia. What, in the end, is the big deal?"

"The future, Gabe. The future of Montana. You're right that they don't fear a terrorist attack. They're politicians for Christ's sakes. But they do have a fear. And I'll tell you why—because they're smart. It's very important to them we don't succeed, and they're willing to ruin me and even the son of an old friend to make sure we don't."

When Phoenix left, Myrlene joined Gabe at the table. "Here's a draft of the Rule Eleven motion." She slid a stapled legal motion across the table. "Do you buy any of that?" Always a good listener, she also occasionally donned an expensive hearing aid, at Gabe's request, when he wanted a witness to a conference or, like here, a second opinion.

"Actually, yes. I think every word she said was true. It's the shit she leaves out that worries me."

"So what do they fear?"

Gabe had a pretty good guess that the ammunition of which Phoenix spoke was not his cutting-edge legal skills. On the fear, he was sure of Phoenix's meaning.

"Her," he said.

FOURTEEN

MAY 4, 2009 –
OUTSIDE CAROLINE COUNTY, MONTANA

Ahmed glided into a parking space in front of The International House of Pancakes in Turnbull. Before he turned off Route 2, he saw the sign for Twin Rivers. Sixty miles. He swapped his helmet for his knit hat and glanced around under his sunglasses. He felt no apprehension. No stiff muscles or tension in his chest. Now, many miles from Adams and Yusef, the likelihood of coming under scrutiny for killing them had dramatically diminished. If he was lucky, the police had yet to find either body.

He strode into the restaurant and followed a skinny male teenager to a table. The place was nearly empty at four p.m. He removed his knit hat, his long coat, and his over-shirt, leaving only his black sleeveless T-shirt. He had been instructed to dress so. Starving from the long ride, he eagerly scanned the menu, which had pictures of the food next to the written listing. The pictures helped a lot because he did not know what each item meant. When the waiter came, this time a fat teenage female with a horrible complexion, he ordered a water, orange juice, eggs, and potatoes.

She smiled at him. "Seven eggs? Whoa, you must be hungry."

What did Adams used to say? "Damn straight. Been riding all the way from Bellingham, Washington. Headed to South Dakota." But Ahmed was dealing with a woman. "You have no idea how hungry I am, darlin'." Now she simpered. Her teeth were covered with metal wires. Truly hideous.

"Could you direct me to the bathroom?"

"Way in the back, to the right. I'll put in your order."

Ahmed had the map of the northwest United States memorized. More importantly, he had successfully provided misinformation to the girl about his direction of travel. There had been much lore at the camp about misinformation.

Misinformation, Omar said, should be part of every mission. Never pass up an opportunity to tell a convincing falsehood to the enemy, even a small one. If you are captured, this is an excellent opportunity to provide misinformation. If you are captured and it is suspected that you are a mujahid, the normal American rules will no longer apply. You will be imprisoned by secret police and tortured to betray your brothers and your mission. Lie about the magnitude of your mission. Tell them dozens of such missions are planned. Tell them the mujahid plan to attack all fifty states. In the end, tell them you went on jihad only because we threatened to kill your family. That is exactly what they want to hear.

Ahmed took his time in the small bathroom. He washed himself to the extent possible, and then knelt in prayer. It was truly sad, to have to pray in a filthy bathroom without a prayer rug.

When he returned, his eggs and potatoes were on the table.

The waitress handed him a newspaper. "Hey, thought you might want something to read, since, you know, you're alone and all." Ahmed smiled and took the paper, remembering that Omar had specifically instructed him to look at newspapers each day.

The press finds out about almost everything reports all of it. If any of your exploits are discovered, they will be reported in the newspapers. It will be good to know when the police learn of things.

As Ahmed ate, he flipped through the newspaper, not finding any news of Adams's or Yusef's deaths. The eggs were like normal eggs, but saltier. The fried potatoes were delicious, and Ahmed considered ordering more of them. He drank the orange juice in three gulps, feeling its nutrition seep through his stomach to his veins and muscles. *Stay strong. Stay healthy. Your body is God's vehicle.*

Ahmed looked around at the few customers. He had already begun to notice that while some young Americans appeared fit, most of them were either overweight, like the Cree Nation women, underweight, like Yusef, or just plain soft. Even the Americans who did appear physically healthy wore an expression of pasty ignorance on their faces. Especially in their eyes. They walked through life as if there was no war for truth raging across the planet. At one table sat a mother, father, and a young boy, perhaps ten years old. While the parents ate, the boy fiddled frantically with an electronic phone, ignoring his father's entreaties to put it away and finish his meal. Finally, the father took the device from his son, and Ahmed was astonished when the boy's voice rose in whining protest—loud enough to turn the heads of the other customers. The father sought to quiet him with whispers, but Ahmed heard the whispers—the boy could have his electronic phone back if he finished half his meal. Ahmed's eyes met the waitress's, who also stood near enough to observe the family. She smiled at Ahmed and rolled her eyes. Ahmed did not know the import of that expression, whether she mocked the father's weakness or thought him too harsh on his pathetic son.

Honor thy father and mother, Ahmed. Never question my word, especially in front of others. Ahmed's face burned, his jaw throbbed, and he remained on his hands and knees, head down. His father had delivered the blow as soon as they entered the house. When his father had told Akram Jamal at the market that he had just returned from work in Jalalabad, Ahmed had said, "Father, you haven't worked in Jalalabad since the summer." Now, Ahmed's father knelt by him. "Honor your father and mother," he said fiercely. When his father left the room, Ahmed had cried, still crouched on the floor. His mother gently rubbed the side of his face.

Ahmed glanced at the red electronic wall clock—5:20. He did not bother to survey the parking lot through the window, instead pretending to calmly read his newspaper. A couple walked in and sat at the table three away from his. He paid them little notice, immediately realizing neither of them could possibly be his contact. Both were over sixty and obese. The woman waddled like a duck, her huge bottom stretching beyond the sides of her chair. He listened to them order their meals, each requesting enough food for two.

The waitress brought him his bill, which he paid with a ten and a five.

"If it's not a problem, I'll stay and finish the newspaper," Ahmed said.

"'Course it's no problem," she said.

As he pretended to read, Ahmed heard the old couple laughing together, the woman's deep laugh filled the restaurant, much louder than the whines of the boy. He saw the side of her face and her broad smile as she listened to her husband relate some story or another. She kept laughing, even banging her hand on the table for emphasis.

Then Ahmed flinched, caught off-guard by the person standing next to and slightly behind him.

"Nice tat, dude. Old fucking school." The man referred to the skinny, grim, Western angel of death tattooed on Ahmed's shoulder. Below the tattoo was the American phrase, I woke up this morning and I got myself a beer. Ahmed hated the ghastly, evil symbol, but now it had served one if its purposes. His contact had recognized him.

The man sat down across from Ahmed and rested his hands on the table.

Ahmed, were it not for your faith, Omar said, I would suggest that you get a tattoo of something distinctly American, such as the American flag, or even a crucifix. But I cannot ask you to disgrace your body with such a symbol. Still, the tattoo is important. It is symbol of low status and a lack of education in America, and would never, ever, be expected of one of God's warriors. For that reason, you should bring such a symbol with you into the lion's den.

And so, on Ahmed's last trip away from camp, when Omar escorted him to the airport in Jalalabad, they had stopped at a brother's home. The brother, a man named Ali with a pretty young wife, grimaced when Omar described the tattoo he would engrave into Ahmed's upper right arm. Are you sure? the man had dared to ask. It was indeed rare to see someone question an order from Omar. But Omar replied good-naturedly. I know, I know, but it cannot be helped. That was a phrase Omar used often. It cannot be helped. Omar smiled grimly, a smile which reminded Ahmed that Omar himself had lived a life pained with such compromises. It has a dual purpose, Omar said. One is merely strategic. The other literal. You are, my friend, the angel of death to infidels.

A new feeling lurched inside Ahmed. His contact was not a mujahid, a mujahid pretending to be an Indian, or even a compromised Muslim like Yusef. His contact was impossible. The elderly white American wore a blue denim jacket and a cowboy hat. An American cowboy.

"We can talk here," the man said.

Ahmed said nothing. But the man kept talking. For several minutes he spoke. At the end of the speaking, Ahmed knew something important about his mission. Its target.

Ahmed spoke for the first time. "Who are you?"

The man pursed his lips, as if to consider a weighty matter, started to speak, then stopped. He fixed Ahmed with a hard stare, not as if to reflect anger, but rather to burn Ahmed into his memory. Ahmed did the same. The cowboy's thick mustache would not be forgotten.

"Good luck, Jeremy."

FIFTEEN
MAY 13, 2009 – TWIN RIVERS, MONTANA

Gabe took the cement stairs two at a time up to the broad double doors of his office. "Any news?"

Myrlene sat at the receptionist desk in a tight turtleneck sweater. "Where you been?"

"At the jail, just spent two hours with Bernard, his trial's in two weeks." Myrlene typed fast, looking down while Gabe stood in front of her. He held out his arms. "So?"

"Phil Jackson from Ernest, Passal, and Young in Helena called, wants to set up a meeting about Phoenix. Gillespie called, he's got something for you, wants to meet you this evening around seven if you'll swing by his place out in Western Caroline."

"Why there?"

"Don't know. Isn't that what he always does?"

"Tell him I can be there, but not until nine."

"I want to go," Myrlene said. "I'm in this case, right?"

"Sure."

"You file last night?" Myrlene asked.

"The packages have been delivered." Gabe had filed his motion to dismiss the lawsuit against Phoenix as well as Myrlene's motion for sanctions against the opponents, working until past midnight until he felt comfortable hitting FILE on the federal court's electronic filing system.

"So, Mr. Phil Jackson knows about the Rule Eleven?" Myrlene asked.

"Guess so. How'd he sound?"

"Friendly."

"I'll call Helena, but then I have to get back to the jail after the lunch lockdown. Bernard's seriously considering this plea deal, and he's methodical, wants to go over every piece of evidence six times."

"What's the deal again?"

"Plead to aggravated sexual battery, drop the rape charge. Two years."

Myrlene shook her head. "I can't believe somebody might go to jail for raping Belinda Murphy. Counseling maybe, but not jail."

Gabe laughed. "That's cruel."

"She's the biggest slut in Twin Rivers, and you fully know it. A stripper. A hooker. Hasn't she falsely accused a john of rape before?"

"This time she has a black eye and a fractured collarbone. Says Bernard raped her, and he told the cops he was too drunk to remember anything. They have a case."

"He was too drunk to remember to pay her," Myrlene said, settling on the truth of the case. "You think a jury will convict someone for a rape that happened at the Ram-it Inn?" Curly's motel behind the strip bar. Myrlene called up the stairs after him. "You see Grizzly Redford yet?"

"Gabe, thanks for calling back." Phil Jackson sounded over fifty and friendly indeed. And very confident. "Thought we should touch base on this thing."

"Me too." Gabe sat down.

"You know, I remember you, Gabe. I saw you win a motion in front of Ronson in 2000. The toxic tort thing in Seattle? I also knew your dad very well. A great guy. A great lawyer."

"Thanks, Phil, that means a lot."

"The whole community was surprised and saddened."

"We kind of knew it was coming."

Phil hesitated. "Well, anyway, he was a great guy. So what's with the motion for sanctions?"

"The suit has no merit on its face. It alleges physical danger to Montanans, which is totally speculative, and seeks discovery of private matters unrelated to the issues in the case. What am I supposed to think?"

"We don't agree they're unrelated."

"Really? What do the town's finances or Enos Terwilliger's suicide have to do with a terrorist attack in Montana?"

"You do criminal law now, don't you Gabe?"

"Yes."

"That's what I heard. But let me ask you, when was the last time you litigated a big case in a federal court?"

Gabe paused to shift gears. "Four years, as I'm sure you know."

"The funny thing about discovery in a civil case is that you never know what is material until after discovery." These fancy old lawyers were all the same. Their DNA required them to give condescending lectures.

"Fine, articulate to me what is relevant about your requests, and maybe I'll drop the sanctions motion."

Phil sighed."I don't have to give you a sneak preview of our response, you should know that."

"Phil, with all due respect, you're full of shit. Any lawyer would lay out their basic grounds for an argument to the other side. Especially in a civil case. You're trying to create unneeded litigation. Is that what you're gonna tell the judge? That we had to have a hearing because you won't talk to me?"

"Listen, Gabe, I believe the way they've been running that town is so messed up that trusting the town government with the safety and security of international terrorists presents a danger to Montanans. Maybe I'm wrong. We'll find out when we see the discovery. Terwilliger was the main citizen of Caroline County for forty years, and my clients are not the only people suspicious about his death."

"That's a stretch. I'd be glad to argue that in court. Financial missteps, of which I am unaware, have no relation to safety. That prison has been approved as safe by the Federal Bureau of Prisons."

"Yeah, after it wasn't."

"Also, Phil, I've been thinking, and I believe the funding sources of Citizens for a Safer Montana are relevant to this motion."

"Why?"

Gabe paused to savor that old buzz he'd been missing, the mix of anger and a higher energy. "Because I don't think your real clients give a rat's shit-smeared ass about the safety of Montana or a terrorist attack. I think they're worried about Phoenix Jamborsky running for Governor." Gabe was a little surprised he had said it—especially since he'd never heard anyone else, including Phoenix, make that direct claim.

"I have a suggestion for you, Gabe. No offense. I'm sure you've done your homework. But before we get too antagonistic, why don't you ask your client about Senator Bryant?"

"What does that have to do with anything?"

"Or about the autopsy report on Enos Terwilliger."

"Phil, I'm taking your response as an admission that your ginned-up suit is a vehicle to do a fishing expedition against Mayor Jamborsky and the town. I'm going to tell the court about it at the hearing."

"You can't, Gabe. Settlement negotiations are not admissible. That's a basic rule of evidence."

"This isn't a settlement negotiation."

"That's 'cause you haven't let me finish."

"Finish then."

"As we understand this to be a private settlement negotiation," Phil said, "I will make you an offer. If your client really wants to help Twin Rivers, she'll take it. We'll drop the injunction motion against the town, which gets rid of the discovery requests. Twin Rivers can have its prisoners. And its silly, overblown federal payout."

"If?"

"If Phoenix gives us a sworn affidavit concerning her knowledge of Beau Bryant."

"What?" Gabe said, raising his voice.

"Tell your client. She'll know."

"What about Bryant?"

"She'll know."

"You want her to provide you with evidence that will hurt Beau Bryant so somebody can bully him into not running for President. That's what this is about?"

Phil laughed. "Gabe, you really don't have this under control, do you? I suppose she trusts you, or you wouldn't be on this case. You should know that if you were to disclose this conversation to anyone, you'd be ruined."

Gabe paused, hands sweating, no longer having fun. "You didn't answer my question."

"We want her to provide us with the truth. That Beau Bryant is an ethical family man whom for four years she observed breaking his back for citizens of Montana. That he has helped her career out of loyalty, as he would do for any former staffer, and that anything else she has ever said or written about him that contradicts those things is false."

Gabe put his sweating hands on his computer keyboard but had nothing to type.

"This will be sealed, remember?" Phil said. "To see the light of day only…well, your client will understand."

Gabe did not answer.

"Talk to your client, Gabe. Right is right. Tell her I said that. And Gabe? I'm kind of surprised you're involved in something like this."

SIXTEEN

MAY 13, 2009 – TWIN RIVERS. MONTANA

Myrlene threw him his jacket. "You know we're an hour late for Gillespie, right? And the clerk's office in Helena called, they set the expedited hearing, at our request, for Thursday at ten." Two days away and three days before Twin Rivers Day. Just perfect.

Gabe's jeep cut smoothly through the thick gravel on the way to Gillespie's. Gabe well knew Gillespie's penchant for demanding meetings after normal work hours, and often at his own home. He worked on few cases, but when he did, he worked them constantly, sometimes e-mailing Gabe at three or four in the morning with a new thought. Gabe always pictured him at his desk—a big, tough old man typing on a dainty little laptop. Gillespie usually took handwritten notes while speaking to witnesses and liked typing them into his computer while relating the details aloud to Gabe on the phone. Gillespie lived in a high-end doublewide trailer on the eastern fringe of Caroline County. His cop pension provided him more than enough to live in town or any city in Montana, but he had, as he often reminded Gabe, moved to western Montana for the solitude and the rugged mountain scenery.

"Pasquali stopped by today." Myrlene parodied the sheriff's gruff but somehow poetic diction. "Darlin', please ask what's-his-name to give me a holler. Some people have their balls in a wad down at the jail, and he might be able to help me out."

"Strange." Pasquali was busy not only with keeping a handle on the training of so many new so-called law-enforcement officers in Caroline County, but also with the security for Twin Rivers Day. "I almost called him yesterday but didn't. I thought without giving away too much I could ask him about—"

"You can ask him now," Myrlene said in a tense whisper.

Down the road, his headlight beams caught a Twin Rivers police car and Pasquali's SUV parked in front of Gillespie's trailer. Gabe pulled up behind the county cars and shut off his headlights. The soft blue police lights covered the area in front of the trailer. Pasquali, followed by Deputy Glower, walked outside. Pasquali stripped off a pair of latex gloves. Myrlene's hands covered her mouth and unblinking eyes jumped from Gabe to Pasquali to the door of the trailer.

"Fucking tragic," Pasquali said under his breath as Gabe approached him. His heavy face drooped with sadness, as if in reaction to the removal of the buoyant force normally responsible for the old man's exuberance. "You comin' in?"

Gabe answered with his eyes.

"Stay on the plastic by the door." Pasquali pushed the door open for Gabe. Myrlene huddled behind him.

Gillespie's body sagged over his desk backwards, as if blown back onto it from a standing position in front of the desk. His head sagged off the end near his computer, his cowboy hat somehow still on. His boots dangled from the front. His arm jutted awkwardly out from his side. Gabe scanned the floor, first behind and then in front of the desk. Steps away he saw a black pistol. Pasquali squeezed past him and surveyed the scene from the far wall of the trailer.

"Shot?" Gabe asked.

"Yep," Pasquali said. "But this pistol's his, and it hasn't been fired. It wasn't a suicide."

They walked back outside. Deputy Glower, Myrlene, and Pasquali stood in a circle. Gabe placed an arm on Myrlene's back and felt her trembling through her thick winter coat.

"Deputy, I'd like to talk to Gabe alone if you don't mind," Pasquali said. Myrlene and the Glower exchanged an awkward glance and stepped away together, toward the cars. "Couple of things, Gabe." Pasquali pinched a huge wad of Copenhagen and looked thoughtfully past Gabe into the darkness. "I came by your shop today because it was brought to my attention that somebody filed a Freedom of Information Act request for an autopsy report. An old one. Enos Terwilliger's. And police reports about the death."

Gabe was patient. He knew Pasquali, whether in person or on the witness stand, gave up information slowly if at all. Pasquali packed the snuff into his mouth then wiped it with the back of his meaty hand.

"That same person also requested all booking information for one of our inmates, and booking information for that same inmate all across the state. At first I figured it was the folks from Helena, because the request was made at the state police office in Helena. You know, the lawsuit or something. But you know who made that request?"

"No," Gabe said.

Pasquali's eyes were not, as sometimes, squinted to the give the appearance of thoughtfulness. Rather, they were open and deep, probing, but softly. He was trying to figure something out he didn't already know, as opposed to trying to determine if someone else knew what he already knew.

"You did, Gabe."

Gabe looked away. He had not made any such request, and he could not tell where Pasquali was headed. Pasquali reached into his back pocket, pulled out a folded form, and handed it to Gabe. MONTANA STATE FOIA REQUEST.

The signature was not Gabe's, but Gillespie's neat and familiar cursive. Gillespie for Gabriel Lantagne, Esq. Something they had done on other cases. Not, in Gabe's view, unusual or uncommon.

Gabe shrugged.

"Do you know who the inmate was, Gabe?"

"No."

"Jonathon Scruggs."

Gabe remembered the name. The deciding vote.

"So what I'm wonderin' is," Pasquali said, "what do these two people have to do with each other? Scruggs and Enos Terwilliger? And why, taking you at your word you don't know, did Gillespie think these two issues relate to the case you got him working on?"

"What happened to Gillespie, Sheriff?"

"Don't know, but I'll do you one better than you're doin' me and tell you what I do know. One, the place has been searched, carefully. All of Gillespie's notes, and I mean all of 'em, even the ones he kept in the old filing cabinet, are gone."

Gabe had a thousand questions, and turned a moment to collect his thoughts about which he should ask. Or could ask. "Apparently, he made the request for me, but I didn't know about it."

"You didn't let me finish. The hard drive has been removed from that computer." Pasquali watched Gabe, who held his eyes. "And I came up here tonight for the same reason you did. Gillespie asked me to meet him here at 10. Seems he thought whatever you had him working on might require my attention. So I ask you, Gabe, given that the man is dead and all, the first murder in my county in several years, what did you have him working on?"

"I'm not prepared to discuss that," Gabe said. "Not without speaking to my client."

Headlights approached. The crime scene guy, Gabe surmised. But Pasquali recognized the car before he did. "Looks like you're gonna have that chance right now."

A car door slammed, and Phoenix emerged into the blue light, eyes wide. She was, uncharacteristically, clearly frightened. She gripped Gabe's arm, and Gabe could feel her shaking while Pasquali briefed her.

"Murdered?" she asked.

"We need to talk," Pasquali said.

Phoenix breathed deeply, shivering. "I need to talk to my lawyer first, Geno." Geno. Gabe had never before heard anyone call Pasquali by his first name.

"Fair enough. Gillespie's been all the way to Helena doing some investigatin', and I don't think I'm out of bounds to say it may have been more sensitive than he was used to back on the Crow reservation. Whether he died for it is what I need to know." Pasquali paused, like he so often did. For effect. "By the way, Gabe, Enos Terwilliger died by one gunshot wound to the head. He had several medications in him at the time, most notably a small amount of Vicodin and about double the legal alcohol limit— which for him meant he hardly had a buzz. None of this is a secret. Jonathon Scruggs was arrested on January 5, 2009. He made bail immediately, pled guilty in February, and was sentenced on April. He was released last week, May 9, 2009."

Another pause.

"So?" Gabe could picture the lanky college dropout who had cast the deciding vote for Phoenix plan only days before, but knew nothing about him or why Gillespie could believe him relevant to his assignment.

"So that's the information your fuckin' FOIA requests would have revealed. For future reference, you shoulda just asked me."

"I'm telling you, I didn't know about the FOIA requests. If Gillespie had a reason for the requests, I never heard it." Gabe looked away from Pasquali as he spoke, as that comment was not exactly true. He had asked Gillespie to nose around about Terwilliger. "Besides, that sort of semi-public information wouldn't provoke a murder."

"Not the requests, Gabe," Pasquali said, a throaty twinge of annoyance in his voice. "The reasons for them."

"Who knows about the requests?"

"Hell, anybody who wants to know. Gillespie made the request through Helena, and the Scruggs request went to every county in the state. As for Caroline County, you don't really believe I can control the gossip that flows out of the jail and the police department, do you?"

Gabe had handled hundreds of cases involving Pasquali and had questioned him in front of judges or juries countless times. Often the joker, Pasquali was serious now, and, as on the witness stand, he knew something he wasn't telling. Something he would not tell unless someone knew to ask for it directly. If then.

Pasquali waved his hand as if to back off a step."You may be right, Gabe. But I solve every murder that happens in this County, and this one will be no exception. I need to know what you do know."

"I need to talk to my client."

Gabe, Phoenix, and Myrlene walked towards the parked cars, leaving Pasquali and Glower by the open door to Gillespie's trailer.

"What the hell is going on?" Phoenix whispered harshly.

"Sounds like a question I planned to ask you."

"You hired Gillespie to look into shit about our case without telling me? Are you fucking serious? How can—"

"Listen, Phoenix." Gabe turned and gripped her arms. This was the first time he'd actually touched her beyond a professional handshake. Her arms were surprisingly soft, but they flexed slowly as Gabe spoke."You hired me to do a case, and learning about my client is part of the case. You need to trust me."

"I get that, Gabe, but you don't know enough to make moves like that without me."

"Whose fault is that?" Gabe said.

Phoenix turned away, and Gabe dropped his arms from hers.

"I'm staying at the ranch with Ayalette. Michael is away." There was unusual tension in her voice. "We need to talk. Like tonight, Gabe. Will you meet me there?" Phoenix's eyes quickly flared towards Myrlene but long enough to communicate that she wasn't invited.

"I expect you to not lie to your lawyer," Gabe said.

"And I expect to know what my fucking lawyer is doing before he does it." Her mock pleasantness carried such vitriol, Gabe stepped away from her.

Phoenix got in her car and drove away. Gabe and Myrlene stood in the darkness. Pasquali's and Glower's shadows silently watched the door to Gillespie's trailer.

SEVENTEEN
MAY 13, 2009 – TWIN RIVERS, MONTANA

Myrlene stared straight ahead on the drive back to her apartment. "I've, I guess I've…"

"Never seen a dead person before?"

"Never seen a murdered person before."

"He was also a friend."

"Gabe, this is really fucked up, if somebody killed him because of this—"

"We don't know why he was killed. Gillespie had a whole career full of cases and acquaintances all over Montana. Lots of people could have done it. A random person could have done it, a—"

"But they didn't. Somebody killed him today. And it has something to do with the case. Pasquali knows it."

"We'll see." Perhaps he should have been drenched with a feeling of heavy sadness. And confusion. Or fear. But he was not. He stopped in front of Myrlene's building, around the corner from the town square.

"Be careful with her, Gabe."

"She's just a client, Myrlene."

Myrlene gave him a long look, then shut the jeep door softly and walked away.

Phoenix stood gazing into the darkness through the wall-sized window. "Get a drink if you want. She said it distractedly, not as if to challenge. Or tempt. The autopilot of a good political host.

Over the last four years, whenever Gabe was directly offered the chance for a drink, he easily refused. His hard moments, his battles, were fought alone, usually at home, with the cold fingers of stress and guilt prodding at his heart because of a case, a woman, or just the general unease of wondering why things couldn't be just a little better. At those moments, he believed—in fact, knew—that even one gulp of liquor would banish the tension, leaving his heart in peace to pump strong. One downed glass of red. A chugged beer. A shot. That was at home. But in public, it had always been easy. He had even held a drink in his hand on many occasions while chatting at one function or another, both so as to not refuse the offer and to play a little head game with himself, like a right-handed boxer fighting left-handed against a weak opponent to make it more interesting.

Gabe walked to the bar and poured several shots of whiskey into a glass from the already open bottle. He could smell it. He thought of Pasquali's Sinatra quote: *I feel sorry for people who don't drink, when they wake up in the morning they know that's as good as they're gonna feel all day.* Holding it loosely and with confidence, Gabe carried the drink over to the chair near Phoenix and sat down with it. Just to make it more interesting.

"I wouldn't want anyone but you handling the case, Gabe. But I gotta know what you're doing."

"Agreed. But I gotta know the important facts. You're not letting me in all the way."

Phoenix turned, calm and thoughtful. The normal Phoenix, not the one from Gillespie's front yard. They sat in the matching burgundy leather chairs facing out the window but did not speak for a few minutes. "Can we smoke in here?" Gabe asked.

Phoenix answered by lighting a cigarette and winking. "How would I know? I don't live here." She stood and fetched a highball glass for an ashtray.

Gabe leaned back, placing his legs on the fancy wooden ottoman in front of him. The feeling he had around Phoenix was hard to name. The best way to describe it was *important.*

"Twin Rivers Day will be a national event, Gabe."

He did not respond, but noted where Phoenix's mind strayed as it eased itself. Not to the murder, and not even to her case. Twin Rivers Day was not just a town festival. It was, for her, a coronation. The launch of Phoenix Jamborsky.

Gabe related, in detail, the phone call with Phil Jackson.

"Shameless," was all Phoenix said.

"Your turn. You've told me about the town finances. Now let's have it. The senator."

Phoenix sat up and leaned forward, elbows on the knees of her jeans, and turned towards Gabe. Her bare feet gripped and ungripped the thick Western-patterned carpet as she rolled her cold drink on the sides of her face. She smiled, almost laughing. "I wasn't holding out on you. This is a personal matter without relevance to the injunction." Phoenix was suddenly the college girl, gossiping on the edge her bed, feet dangling, hands occupied by conversational lubricants.

Gabe raised the drink calmly, steadily, to his lips, taking only half a gulp. It swam gracefully down his throat, bounced happily in his stomach, and fanned out warmly through every nerve. *Better than he had felt all day.*

"The summer of ninety-two," Phoenix said. "I drove to DC with a girlfriend a few days after graduation without a paying job, only a commitment from Bryant's chief of staff, a guy named Bruno Hammersmitt, that I could sort mail for twenty hours a week for no pay. Christine and I rented a one-bedroom and got a hostess jobs at the Capitol Grill. What happened next was one of those little twists of fate you never can explain. Here I am, first day on the job, trying to remember whether table one-twenty-one is a two-top or a four-top, and Bryant walks in. Not with an entourage, but just with one guy. This was years before he was really well known. Way before anybody even whispered the word, President. But I knew about him. He was forty-four, two years into his first Senate term after having served two terms in the House. The youngest congressman elected from Montana in the twentieth century.

"As the night goes on, I catch him craning his neck around for the waitress. 'Can I help you, Senator,' I asked. And he turned, and—don't laugh, I realize how this sounds, but we had what can only be described as a major moment. Not a cheesy, sexual thing. It was more of an immediate sense of familiarity. Like the curious way some people hit it off immediately as friends. And I'm telling you, Beau is not the lecherous type, he just isn't. 'So you know me? That's refreshing.' At that point, Beau's actual waitress appeared. I stepped back, but my eyes locked with his for just a second. And really, Gabe, if you'd known me in college, you wouldn't have thought I was a slut, but as I turned my back on the table, I gave an almost embarrassing hair-bouncing look back over my shoulder.

"I didn't see Bryant for most of my first day at his office, but as I'm about to leave for the night, he walks into the mailroom and introduces himself to the three of us working in there. As he turned to leave, he said, 'Phoenix, can I speak to you for a moment?' Just like that. So we go to his office, and Bryant asks me why I hadn't mentioned the night before that I would be working for him. 'I'm sorry, Senator, blah, blah, blah,' and he starts asking me about my résumé, and that was it."

She paused for a moment, remembering, or thinking. "By Christmas, I was pissing people off. Bryant paid way too much attention to me, asked me to stay late to talk in his office, things like that. You got to remember, this was well before Monica Lewinsky. So Bryant called me in and he begins with, 'Hammersmitt thinks we've gotten too chummy.' I was twenty-four, wise in the ways of men my age, but with no guidance about how this was supposed to go. Bryant stood and says he's not sure he agrees with Hammersmitt. Clichéd as it is, the next thing I knew I was on my knees. I mean, all over him, tearing into his pants, clothes all over the place, and then we were doing it on the floor right by his desk. I worked there four years after that and didn't cut things off until the very end. I led a double life, I dated other people, one guy for a year, and somehow I kept it separate that I was sleeping with my boss the whole time. We would take a month or two off—and a few times, I was glad it was over—but then it would start again. Until I met Michael, it was never really over. That was ten years ago."

"Did you keep in touch?"

"Sure. He came to my wedding, and he's never stopped helping me. Some donations for the mayor's race. Advice. But I haven't been alone in a room with him since 1999."

"Until this week," Gabe said. Gabe finished his second whiskey, recognizing that each he had poured contained at least a triple. His cheeks felt flushed, but his mind was steady. "You blackmailed him into lying down on the Guantanamo issue."

She feigned an offended look. "I did not. He's always helped me."

"He's running for President. He wants your implicit promise this affair is buried forever. So he's giving you your little prison while technically opposing it."

"Beau doesn't believe I'd go public with this. Why would I? Don't believe for a second that Beau's in control of this suit. He… he wouldn't. These underlings are protecting him in their view, but they're not in contact with him about this. Don't forget, on its face, this suit is by a group of concerned hockey moms. That's all it will ever be, publicly."

"Maybe Beau trusts you, but some important supporters obviously do not."

"So that's all they want, huh? A sworn statement that nothing was going on with Beau? The sworn statement would never hold up anyway, you know."

"I know." Gabe eyes darted so very slightly towards the bar. Phoenix stood and retrieved the now half-empty bottle and refilled both glasses.

"But they want the statement in their pocket," Gabe said. "For the future maybe. In case things, you know, change. You could still expose the affair, but you'd be a fool. Like a Lewinsky. Flakey. In politics you'd be ruined."

"And there we come around to it," Phoenix said. "They think I'm going to declare for governor. For the 2010 race."

"2010? Next year?"

"They want Beau to support Martin, not me. I bet Jackson thinks a sworn statement from me saying Beau and I never had an affair will free Beau from supporting me."

"Are you running?"

"Hey, I've got the money, I'm getting the exposure. With Beau's help, and if the town rebounds this winter, my time is now."

"Damn, Phoenix." He felt himself slurring a little, but from experience, he believed he was a long way from others being able to tell. He lit a cigarette. *Oh, I've missed you*—the feeling of a cigarette while drunk.

Gabe looked at her seriously, wanting to get on with the business, over it, so he could relax. "This is the easy way out, right? Give 'em the affidavit."

"Not a chance. Look at it this way, Gabe. They can't win the case. Whether we can get it dismissed Thursday or in two months from now, they can't win. They have to make a deal."

"But they think the delay could cost Twin Rivers the contract. Guantanamo is supposed to close in months."

"So they figure, get the affidavit or block the prison. Either way, they feel I've been neutralized in some respect. There are two main things they want. One, Beau elected President. Two, and more importantly, the spoils of that election. For them and the other fat cats who've been sucking on Beau's tit for twenty years. Cushy jobs. Prestige. Power."

"So?" Gabe could tell he was getting distracted while Phoenix was all business—alive with the excitement of cooking a plan. Or, more likely, of relating a well-cooked plan.

"So they don't really give a shit about Martin becoming governor. I'm just as good for them. And that is what they have to understand. There are two ways to protect themselves from me. One is to destroy me, and I don't know what you see in front of you Gabe, but that's not gonna happen. Two, support me. What national politician in my position is going to out an affair that makes her look like a slutty ladder climber? If I win, it's all good. Do they want a lifelong ally moving into national politics, or a bitter woman scorned running off to the tabloids? I mean, really, these guys could use a lesson from Pasquali more than I could. Also, the one thing these bozos blatantly fail to appreciate is that there's a very good chance Beau will not become President. They have to understand I'm a better option for them than that clown Martin."

Better option for them for what?

"So where does this all leave us?" Gabe asked.

"It leaves us here: reject the offer, and tell Phil Jackson this—I'm not signing a false affidavit. Beau has my loyalty. We will get the prison contract, and we will get the case dismissed on Thursday. And if we don't..." Phoenix paused, as if considering the wisdom of some nearly spoken word. She gazed momentarily out the window, and then refilled both glasses. "And if we don't, I'm calling a press conference to disclose the affair, after which I will provide the press with an audiotape which proves it happened."

Gabe's mouth fell open, and he put a cigarette in it. "Jesus Christ, Phoenix."

"This is the game. It's how they play it." And then, like she believed her answer was not in keeping with whatever she believed to be the question, she added, "It's much harder for women, you know."

"I need to hear that tape."

"No. I promised myself that no one would ever hear that tape, barring the most extreme need. You only need to know I have it."

"What's on it?"

"Beau acknowledging the affair. Saying it meant a lot to him."

"You recorded him yesterday?!"

"I recorded him in 1999."

Whoa. "I can't do it that way, Phoenix. It's an ethical issue. I can't threaten them with a tape I've never heard. I can't even personally proffer that it exists. I have a career and a reputation. These are powerful people who knew my father. I'll beat them, but not by cheating. Frankly, I got to tell you, as your lawyer, if you won't produce the tape to me, I'm on notice that it doesn't exist. I could lose my license for representing that it does. These are big lawyers, Phoenix. I know a little something about how they roll."

Phoenix sighed. "I trust you. But can we be sure to win the hearing Thursday? It's not about your abilities, but Jackson has a point here. The discovery is arguably relevant to the capacity of Twin Rivers to properly manage the inmates, which arguably relates to public safety. It's a no-go, but they could keep the case alive, and we could lose the contract."

"There are no guarantees in the law. We could lose, we could win."

"But they'll go for my idea, Gabe! They will. They'll realize the safest bet is get me onto the team. Into the game. And you too."

"Me?"

"Pasquali likes you, you're a shoo-in for mayor. And then, who knows." She winked. Gabe gulped from his glass, breathing deeply. His body, right down to the veins and capillaries, still throbbed pleasantly as the liquor swirled through his system. Like the return of old friend.

"Just play me the tape."

"No."

Gabe sensed a twinge of pain. Like the tension of being caught between two good friends. *Man, is she good.* Phoenix refilled the glasses, leaned close to Gabe, and lifted hers to toast. Gabe watched her closely. "It's really hard to tell when you're lying," he said.

"I've never lied to you."

"Is there really a tape?"

Phoenix looked deep into Gabe's eyes from close up, her weight coming onto her bare feet, relaxing into squatting position in front of him."I'm trying to do something with my life, Gabe. Something important. I'm asking for your help."

Gabe looked away."Gillespie is dead. Killed, maybe because of me."

"Bullshit," Phoenix whispered, closer now. "He did a dangerous job for a living for good money. You had no idea. Pasquali will solve this. I bet we find out it had nothing to do with his work on this case."

Only one person in the room really knew whether the secrets Gillespie sought were dangerous or not, and she was saying they weren't. Gabe lifted his glass, and they toasted. He noticed small tear tracks on Phoenix's face, perhaps from earlier, because of Gillespie, or perhaps not. He could smell tobacco and whiskey mixed with a clean, wholesome smell he had often noticed when he was close to her. But he'd never been this close.

Because he was drunk, it took him a moment to notice that Phoenix's arms rested on his legs, her breasts soft on his knees. Suddenly they were on the floor, Gabe removing her shirt as she wriggled out of her jeans. He fumbled trying to kiss her but before even kissing, Phoenix undid his belt, reached into his pants with both hands and pulled him to her, levering her hips under him as she pulled. He slid into her easily and closed his eyes as they writhed maniacally in front of the window, thinking not of the mere act of sex but of being this close, this totally enveloped in her, this person he knew, did not know, admired, mistrusted, even feared. She gripped the back of his head. The floodlights reflected back into the dark house just enough for Gabe to see Phoenix's half-open eyes, as much prayerful as passionate. Gabe pulled out and came underneath Phoenix's lofted hips, seeing then that her underwear remained on, merely pushed to the side. Now on his knees, they studied each other for a moment.

Phoenix smiled and rested a hand on his leg. "I've been thinking about that for a while. You should believe that."

Gabe, drunk mind whirring, realized that for Phoenix, this was not a romantic moment, or even a lustful one destined to be replayed for pleasure as the years wore on. It was a consummation. A seal. Like a blood oath but sealed in another, more complex human exchange. It's harder for women, you know.

Gabe awoke to a friendly shake on the couch in the Terwilliger family room. His head throbbed and his mouth and lungs burned with the old but so familiar whiskey hangover.

"Hey, pal, aren't you a lawyer or something? It's nine a.m." Michael Terwilliger's friendly face was above him, and Ayalette stood nearby.

"Why are you sleeping at my house, Gabe?" she asked.

"He worked late with Mom and now he's late for work," Michael said. "Got coffee brewing if you need it. Phoenix had an early meeting. She left me a note saying to wake you up when I got home."

Ayalette happily padded behind Michael into the kitchen. "Get up, lazybones!"

Gabe drove home, showered, and got to the office by 10:30, where Myrlene, feet on the desk, was typing on a computer on her lap.

"Where have you been?" she asked. "Phil Jackson called twice, says he needs to know today about his offer."

Gabe walked straight past Myrlene up the stairs, his lungs and gut still burning with the morning-after liquor-cigarette combo he suddenly remembered so well. He sat down and picked up the phone. Strange year, and apt to get stranger.

EIGHTEEN

MAY 5, 2009 – TWIN RIVERS, MONTANA

Ahmed rode south on Route 17 into Caroline County. About fifteen minutes in, he slowed at a large, brown-slatted building with an obnoxious flashing sign standing between a gas station and a small motel. Pandora's Box. The Ramatin Motel. Texaco. He parked in front of Pandora's Box, which looked like a large restaurant or an Indian casino, plastered on his smile, and opened the door.

Loud American music filled Ahmed's ears as smoke hit his face. A long bar spanned the far left wall, and scattered tables filled the floor. Two men sat at a center table, and assorted lone men sat at tables along the wall behind him. His eyes adjusted from the bright afternoon sun to the dingy, smoky bar.

A woman approached him, smiling. "Table or stool?" From a distance she looked young. She wore short pants, a tight black button-down shirt, and a straw cowboy hat over stringy blond hair. Up close, Ahmed could see she was actually quite old, her wrinkles concealed by the dim light and a thick brownish-tan makeup.

"Looking for a job." Ahmed had no idea if the manner in which such an establishment hired someone was more formal than mere conversation, but thought it likely the standards were not particularly high.

"You musta heard we were looking. I'm Wilhelmina. You?"

"Jeremy." Ahmed spread his legs and sort of sank into his boots. It felt like a relaxed pose.

"You from Twin Rivers?" She beckoned him to follow her towards the bar.

"Back east." He didn't think she heard him. The loud music stopped as they neared the front of the restaurant.

"Just a second," Wilhelmina said. She picked up a microphone and turned back toward the tables. "Let's hear it for Jenny! Come on guys, it's tough out there, don't be stingy!" Wilhelmina's voice scratched abrasively through the near-empty room. A woman climbed down off the bar—young, with short-cropped brown hair. He stifled a gasp. The woman wore boots and a hat, but nothing else. Ahmed stepped back, his head darting to the side, looking to Wilhelmina. The naked woman passed him without a glance and disappeared behind a curtain into a hallway. Another young woman, this one with shoulder-length black hair and a robe, emerged from the same place. To Ahmed's chagrin, she stopped in front of him and, smiling, looked him up and down before mounting a short staircase to the bar.

"Now everyone, a warm welcome for Shannon!" Wilhelmina's loud voice seemed out of place in the smoky stillness of the restaurant. The music blared again, and Shannon began to dance on what Ahmed now realized was not a bar, but a stage. Eyes transfixed, he watched Shannon remove her robe and fling it into the air to the disjointed applause of the two men sitting near the stage. As Wilhelmina summoned him behind the curtain, Shannon turned and displayed her full naked profile.

"Yeah, she's hot, ain't she?" Wilhelmina ushered him down a hallway.

On a narrow street near the market, a man beat a woman. He slapped her repeatedly, yet she raised no defense, but merely shut her eyes and cried out with pain. Ahmed stopped dead, tears forming in his eyes. Ahmed's father squeezed his hand and pulled him quickly past the two. At home, they sat together on the floor. His brother Abu, just learning to run, bounced around the room, laughing.

His father spoke softly. Ahmed, that fool and some others you see speak harshly to their wives and train their daughters to accept such abuse. He was uneducated, probably believing he follows the word of God. But Ahmed, you see the way I treat your mother, and I assure you this is the way we have been taught.

The hallway led past rows of tall metal lockers and some wooden benches, then turned right into a small office dominated by a paper-littered desk. Wilhelmina spoke quickly, her high-pitched voice hard to understand when he could not see her face. But he was not listening anyway. He knew about nude dancing bars, and assumed they existed all over America. Whores who sinned against God by treating their bodies like meat to please a roomful of filthy, dishonorable men. Ahmed also thought of the two dancers he had seen, both as young as he, and already ruined by this decadent culture. Except in an American movie, he had never before seen a naked woman. Just now, he had seen two, and only feet away. Not only naked but wildly flaunting it.

Suddenly, Ahmed was face to face with another older woman, who sat behind the desk. She chewed gum with her mouth open, a cigarette burning in her fingers.

"Well, well, well, have a seat, roughneck. I hear you're looking for a job."

The woman who called herself Curly was the crudest human being with whom Ahmed had ever shared a conversation. Her language, often delving into a level of informality outside the scope of Ahmed's English, left him dizzy in the attempt to appear to understand it.

The quiet type. Just nod a lot. Change the subject if you need to. Mainly, just avoid long, detailed conversations, especially with intelligent Americans.

Ahmed could not yet discern whether Curly fell into the intelligent category, but adopted Karim's strategy anyway.

"Two hundred a week, and the dancers tip you out," Curly said. Ahmed had explained his situation to Curly—that he had traveled west to look for work but probably wouldn't be around for too long, he was eventually headed for California. He had forgotten even to mention the matter of his pay. "All cash. You're on your own with Uncle Sam. And remember our Golden Rule."

"Golden Rule?" It would certainly be something important.

"Eyes on the customers, hands off the ass." Curly wagged a warning finger in his direction. "Since you're vagabondin', will you be wantin' a room?"

"May I stay in the motel behind the restaurant?"

"You're cute," she said. "Twenty dollars a day, deducted from your pay at the end of the week."

Ahmed agreed. He cared nothing about the pay, and it seemed in keeping with his new job to reside at the motel. A bouncer.

"Wilhelmina checks the IDs, so don't worry about that," Curly said. "You just watch the customers. No hands on the girls, no extreme drunkenness. If there's a problem, you toss 'em out. If somebody's barred, I tell you, and you toss 'em out. It's a pretty tame crowd. Mostly, just stay alert and look tough—you shouldn't have a problem with that. And no getting drunk on the job."

"I don't drink," Ahmed said, then winced inside. He'd forgotten that American Indians always drink.

"In that case, you're already the best bouncer I ever had." Curly reached across the desk to shake his hand. He'd never shaken a woman's hand before. Her gaze was uncomfortably direct and her grip was firm and lasted a little too long. Then she stood and yelled out her office door. "Willa! Show Jeremy his room. He starts at six."

Ahmed stood by the door, back against the wall, so that he could see Wilhelmina checking the identification of those who entered Pandora's Box as well as keep an eye on the men at the tables watching the women. As for the women themselves, he could do without the distraction, a reminder of the weakness of man. He did notice the empty eyes of the women—four of them that night—who alternated between dancing naked on the stage and among the men, and even sitting on laps in exchange for a few dollar bills. *The girls can touch them, but they can't touch the girls. We don't allow it. If a girl calls for you, don't hesitate, react right away. But most of our fellas know the rules.*

Ahmed noted the sign by the door. No admittance under 21, and, ominously, No Firearms.

In the western states, and especially in the northwest, many Americans carry guns. They do so out of tradition. Most of them barely know how to operate the weapons, but never forget that any American man might have one. If engaging an American physically, incapacitate him quickly before he has any time to reach for his gun.

Now he had a job that might call for physical altercations. It seemed such altercations were legal if one of the men broke the rules of Pandora's Box. Even so, Ahmed examined each man, without staring too hard, for the telltale bulge of a pistol under clothes. Halfway through his first night on the job, he saw that the customers of Pandora's Box presented little danger to him: middle-aged men, most overweight, some with the drawn red face of drunkards. One table did contain a group of young men with short hair and fancier clothes, but they talked and moved like students or clerks, not soldiers. One man, obviously slightly drunk, stumbled up to Ahmed and asked his name.

"Jeremy Blain." Ahmed responded politely, but did not offer his hand, leaving his arms folded on his chest.

"You from roun' here?" The man wore a dirty billed cap and smelled strongly of smoke and sweet liquor.

"No, sir, Billings."

"Oh yeah? My sister lives in Billings." The man swayed slightly and fished around in his shirt pocket looking for something, checking the same empty pocket three or four times before giving up. "Damn lighter, I'm always losing 'em. Got a light?"

"No, sir." Ahmed was losing patience with the man, who was distracting him from watching the customers at the tables.

"Maybe you know her, Evelyn Winters, lives on Plantain?"

"Nah, man. Never heard of her." Billings was close enough that his knowledge of it could be called into question, and he knew absolutely nothing about it. At least now, he knew the name of a road. He would be from Plantain Road. The man reached into his pants pocket, removed a plastic lighter, lit his cigarette, and seemed to forget Jeremy was standing in front of him. Without a further word, he staggered back to his table.

As the night wore on, Jeremy began to nod at some the men as they walked past him to the restroom. Bare nods not designed to trigger conversation, but just the mildest acquaintance.

Strangers get noticed, friends get noticed, Omar said. Locals working at petty jobs do not get noticed. You want to be one of these people. Known but unnoticed.

Ahmed touched his face, a habit he had developed in the last five days, to check his beard. Capable of growing a full beard in several days, he had to pay careful attention. Perhaps would shave twice a day now that he was getting closer to the critical part of his mission.

"Hey you." Ahmed's thoughts were interrupted by the woman had had seen earlier, the one who'd looked him up and down. Shannon. "What's your story?"

"My…story?" Ahmed slid his eyes towards the tables, away from hers, which rested calmly on his. He forced himself to look at her, meeting her eyes for just a moment. Her eyes were dark, almost as black as her hair, both of which contrasted with her very pale skin. Ahmed stiffened, his chest tight. Shannon wore a thin wraparound skirt but no shirt. Her small breasts hung inches feet away from his folded arms. He stepped back, pressing himself against the wall. She had a youthful body, like a girl's, but something about her eyes was old, somehow wet with wisdom or maybe a sadness. Or maybe from drinking or drugs.

"I'm Shannon. Welcome to Pandora's." She said it as if to joke, although he didn't get it. Ahmed forced a smile. "I live here too," she said, "at least right now. Let me know if you have any questions about how things work around here." She smiled, turning her body slowly but keeping her eyes on his. She walked leisurely among the tables then disappeared behind the curtain.

As the night wore on, Ahmed became aware of another woman, one who did not dance on stage or remove clothes, but only brought drinks to the men at the tables and by the stage. Belinda, the men called her. Unlike many of the girls, who manifested an exuberance so boisterous it seemed entirely out of place in the grim surroundings, Belinda walked with small steps and slumped shoulders, eyes cast hollowly to the ground. Ahmed noticed another thing about Belinda. In between orders, she sat at the corner of the bar by herself, not watching the stage or the men, but reading—a book, not a newspaper or magazine. She appeared able to remove herself from the situation, to travel beyond the smoky room into her thick old book.

By the end of the night, Ahmed was exhausted. Each of the dancing women besides Shannon gave him twenty dollars. Shannon gave him thirty. She wore a shirt now, and Ahmed did not flinch away when she leaned close to give him the money. "The tip-out should be fifteen percent, those bitches will screw you."

Back in his room, at two in the morning, Ahmed prayed. *God forgives all indulgences during jihad, Ahmed.*

He prayed for an unusually long time, lost in meditation for the first time in many weeks—for the first time since he arrived in Canada. He was so deep in his thoughts and prayers that he did not realize at first that someone tapped on the door to his room. First softly, then louder.

His heart froze.

Police in America use the theory of overwhelming force, Karim said. If they plan in advance to arrest you, they'll come with dozens of men. In that case, fight to the death and take many of them with you. But you'll never escape. That fight will be your jihad, and as noble as any other.

Ahmed felt a pride in how calm he felt. No frantic movements. At peace. He reached under his mattress, grabbed his loaded pistol, and slid it into the back of his waistband. Wearing only his denim pants, he quickly donned a short-sleeved shirt and boots. He then opened his large backpack, expertly jammed a magazine into his automatic rifle, and propped it by the door, out of sight from the outside but within his easy reach. His movements, unlike during the encounter with Yusef, felt like those of a patient animal, like those of a mujahid.

Bang, bang, bang on the door. Ahmed thanked God for his life, placed his right hand around the grip of his pistol, and opened the door with his left.

"You an early riser or something?" Shannon stood alone in the doorway. She wore the same white shirt from earlier and a pair of baggy pants. Despite the cold, she wore simple flat sandals, one foot balanced on the other. She swung a half-full bottle of brown liquor by her side. Ahmed's eyes quickly covered the area. No danger. He met Shannon's eyes, which were bright and awake despite the hour. Her cheeks were red against her pale complexion. The liquor bottle dangled from one of her fingers, its shadow moving large behind her in the empty parking lot.

NINETEEN
MAY 14, 2009 – TWIN RIVERS, MONTANA

"That's really disappointing, Gabe," Phil Jackson said. "This whole thing's gonna just drag and drag, and I guarantee you, that won't play out to your client's benefit."

"You've heard our response." Gabe's morning hangover always reminded him of metal on metal, as if his life force, the healthy lubrication of living, had been sucked away from overuse the night before, not to return until midday or perhaps until replenished by the night's first drink.

"You mind if I give you some advice, Gabe?"

Annoyance welled up inside, clanging loudly, bouncing around his intestines and ringing in his ears. "Feel free."

"In the end, what we do is supposed to be about justice, not just the game. All we're asking for here is the truth. Your father was tough but he always understood that."

Annoyance turned to rage. "How about I give you some advice? One, never mention my father to me again. I never heard him mention you. Two, don't lecture your opponent on ethics when you've practically admitted you filed a frivolous lawsuit to extract a phony affidavit from my client. On an unrelated matter, I might add. You got it?"

"Gabe, you don't understand—"

"No, I really do understand." Gabe raised his voice into the phone.

"Listen, son, before you get emotional, just remember you're a lawyer to your client, not a friend. The mayor is only your client, and it's part of your job not to believe everything she says. Don't you see that what I'm trying to do here is protect the reputation of an honest man? I couldn't care less if Phoenix wants to run for higher office. But she has to learn—"

"You have to learn! I'm a lawyer working on a case, and you've broken the rules of ethics, maybe even the law, by filing this suit in the first place."

Phil did not respond at first, and Gabe could sense the calculation like a ticking clock.

"You obviously interpreted our last conversation in a way you shouldn't have," Phil said. "If you misunderstood me, I'm sorry. Let's move forward."

"I agree. Move to dismiss the case."

"You won't prevail tomorrow, Gabe. Discovery will go ahead. We'll get our deposition of Michael Terwilliger and the financial records."

"I'm beginning to think discovery's not such a bad idea," Gabe said.

"Really?"

"Really. Maybe *you* shouldn't believe everything *your* client tells you. Maybe we should get you some of that discovery you want, and maybe some you don't."

Phil paused again, longer this time. "Maybe we should both settle down and talk about this before court, Gabe. Maybe it would help both our clients."

"See you tomorrow." Gabe hung up.

Myrlene was leaning against the wall by the stairwell, shaking her head. "Is that how you used to do things? Back when you were a hotshot lawyer?" Gabe sensed an undisguised annoyance he had never seen in her before. "Pasquali's downstairs. Said to take your time, but he needs to talk." Myrlene slouched with her arms crossed and her legs wrapped one behind the other. She looked so very young. For the first time in the months of their affair, if that's what it was, Gabe felt aged compared to Myrlene. She stared at the floor like a teenager.

"Send him up," Gabe said.

"My problem here is that people just don't get shot like this in Caroline County, Gabe. As long as I've been Sheriff, only one person has been murdered in Caroline County in any way except three. One, domestic. which includes love triangles. Two, drunks fighting. Three, insurance fraud."

Gabe smiled at Pasquali's friendly jab. He had represented Morris Clutchfield for killing his father, allegedly for insurance money. Clutchfield had been acquitted. "That was an assisted suicide."

"I'm counting it." He seemed strangely un-Pasquali-like. Uncomfortable, perhaps. Or even more un-Pasquali-like, worried. "But Gillespie fits none of 'em. That tough old bird had no wife, no relatives, and no close friends that I know about. He didn't frequent bars, use drugs, have any debts that I can find, and everybody back in Crow-ville loved him. All he did was read books, tend his goofy little garden, and work for you."

"For me?"

"He lived on a federal pension, and with his lifestyle, he didn't need much money. You hired him sixteen times for investigations in the last three years, and he had only one or two other jobs during that whole period. I figure he worked 'cause he liked it, probably liked you."

Gabe had not spent more than a few minutes digesting Gillespie's death, or the gnawing realization—rather, the virtual certainty—that Gillespie was murdered because he was investigating Weasel Junction. "What can I do to help?"

"Whoever killed him entered his home and had at least some conversation with the man. The two sat down briefly, Gillespie behind his desk, the perp in the rickety chair in front of it. From this I'm surmising they knew each other."

"Not necessarily," Gabe said.

"No, but think about Gillespie. He lives way out east, he's not listed, and his private investigator ad at the courthouse lists only his cell number. So he's got nothing to steal, the files are worthless as far as money goes, and the cases he's worked on for you are all bullshit. Bullshit meaning nobody would care about them anymore."

"What does that tell you?"

"That whoever killed him knew him, wanted the files, and wanted them—not to get at what's in them, but to make sure nobody else ever got to what's in them."

"If they're all bullshit, Gabe said, "then who would care?"

"They're all bullshit except possibly one. Your current case. Which I know to be the big showdown this week in Helena. Yeah, of course I know. You gotta win the case this week. I get it. But Gabe, I need to know what you had him doin' and why, and especially why you think he was investigatin' Scruggs or asking about Enos. These are what are commonly called clues."

"You know that's privileged. At least for now. Maybe if the case ends tomorrow—"

"This is a murder case. I know Phoenix and Egan and you and whoever else are fixing to make Twin Rivers the next Rio de Janeiro, and I'm helping when I can, but people don't get killed like this here, son. Not on my watch. We might cut corners, but not this one. Now I believe you had Gillespie looking into somebody in Caroline County, and this Scruggs dude in particular, but I'm not going at Scruggs until I understand more."

"Where is he?"

"He's around."

"Are you sure?"

"I got my eye on him. I'll know if he leaves the county."

"I didn't have Gillespie doing anything related to Scruggs. I asked him to indirectly investigate Enos Terwilliger's death."

Gabe thought he saw surprise in the wily Sheriff's eyes, but who could tell?

"Does Phoenix know that?"

"She does now, not before."

Pasquali picked up his hat, turned to leave, but stopped as if to ponder. His huge profile displayed unusual tension, the hard-thinking squint Gabe was starting to recognize."I don't know what information you need to win that case on Thursday, but I can't imagine it has anything to do with that motherfuckin' topic."

"I don't know either," Gabe said. "But somebody does. I'm entitled to investigate the case and even my client. Sometimes we protect them from themselves, huh, Sheriff?"

Pasquali smiled wryly, his form of gentle condescension."Look, Gabe, either get the case dismissed or don't. But play it straight. If we don't get the contract, so be it. Why do you kids always think you gotta control everything every damn second?"

A strange remark from the man most people believed controlled the whole county, but Gabe understood. He walked around his desk to face Pasquali, who slowly tucked his hat onto his massive head, straightening the brim. Their eyes met.

"Enos Terwilliger, huh?" Pasquali said. "Let me give you a little history lesson. A short one. One your client shoulda given you before getting you into this case."

Gabe waited.

"This is a nice place to live. I've given my life to it. I've seen some changes, but not many. Not compared to other places. Now Weasel Junction is gone and Twin Rivers is here. But Enos Terwilliger is exactly the topic you can't ask about around here. Do your thing. Win or lose. But leave that fucking shit alone." Pasquali raised his eyebrows. Back to normal. "Good luck tomorrow, hotshot." He bounced nimbly down the stairs.

Gabe watched for Pasquali out the window, but he did not appear from under the awning covering the front steps for some time. When he did, he glanced up at the window with his standard, friendly smile. Pasquali climbed into his truck, U-turned, and drove off, away from the town center.

"What do we need to do?" Gabe turned, and saw that Myrlene now occupied the chair in front of his desk, computer in her lap. "The hearing, Gabe. We need to prepare. Like now. Will her highness be joining us?"

Gabe pulled himself back to the world of lawyering, of calm thinking and planning. "She's in Missoula. Some meeting. She'll meet us in Helena tomorrow."

They worked, as always, reading, talking, typing. Every federal case—trial court, appeals court, and US Supreme Court—on early dismissal of injunctions. Irreparable harm. Frivolous allegations.

Around eight o'clock, Gabe said, "We've got this. It's ready."

"At least it won't be your fault if you lose. What we're asking for is an extraordinary remedy. Most judges just let the case play out."

"Most cases are nothing like this one," Gabe said.

"We'll see." She gave him a real Myrlene smile, both cute and wise, but more than anything, just honest.

Gabe walked to his jeep and waited by the door while Myrlene unlocked her car, just a few spots away. Their eyes met, but it was too dark for Gabe to see a meaning in hers. The moment lasted just a second too long.

"Big argument tomorrow, makes sense for you to rest," she said. "Pick me up in the morning?"

Gabe just nodded in the dark.

Feet up on his balcony, Gabe held an outline of his argument. Reviewing. Rehearsing. Imagining the back-and-forth in the courtroom with Phil Jackson. If the court played it fair, they could actually win. It was only 9 p.m. He had plenty of time to wind down and still get to bed early.

At two-thirty a.m. he hoisted himself out of his chair and walked inside, leaving two empty wine bottles and packed ashtray in a row on the dirty glass table.

TWENTY

MAY 15, 2009 – UNITED STATES DISTRICT COURTHOUSE, HELENA, MONTANA

Gabe and Myrlene parked in front of the Federal Courthouse in Helena an hour early, and Gabe realized instantly that Phoenix was already there. A TV truck and half a dozen reporters swarmed around the courthouse's main entrance. "No pre-hearing quotes," she'd said. "Not from you or from me. Only on the way out. After the win."

The reporters ignored Gabe anyway, and he walked through the metal detector as Myrlene and the marshals wrangled their two leather-bound boxes through the screening point.

Upstairs, Gabe perceived the lay of the land quickly. Jackson and group of dark-suited lawyers stood in a circle at the end of the long corridor beyond the courtrooms. Phoenix sat alone on a wooden bench in front of Courtroom 2, managing to appear both sympathetic and confident in her prim pantsuit.

Down the hall, Phil spoke briefly to his colleagues, and then began to approach. In the seconds before he got close, Phoenix shot a glance at Myrlene, who perceptively stepped away. "I trust you, Gabe," Phoenix whispered, close to his ear. "Don't forget about the tape."

"There is no tape," Gabe said.

Phoenix's eyes widened in what, yes, mock incredulity, a brief glimmer of the Phoenix from the other night. But today she wasn't a scattered, complex, and confused young woman, nor the folksy deer-hunting friend he had known for the last year and a half. She was Phoenix the small-town politician—older, serious, no-nonsense, motherly. "Just win," she said, and looked away.

"However you do it, just win. If you can't, that's fine, but if you won't, that's not." The second before Phil arrived, she fixed a look on Gabe that required an answer.

"I got it," Gabe said, eyes on Phil.

"Ms. Mayor." Phil shook Phoenix's hand and then Gabe's. "Gabe, a brief word. We're first on the docket. It's our last chance to…well, to chat. I don't want you to be caught by surprise in there. In the witness room, maybe?"

Gabe motioned for Phoenix to stay put and followed Phil down the hall to a small room meant precisely for such discussions. The room contained a table and six chairs, but both men stood, leaning back against opposite walls.

"You're not recording this, are you?" Phil asked.

"Please."

"I wasn't happy about our conversation the other day," Phil said. "This is just a case, after all."

"But there you go. You see, it's not. You guys are trying to throw your weight around to threaten a woman with a legitimate right to be in politics in this state, and using this bullshit injunction to do it. You know she's gone out on a national limb with this contract, and you want to make her look bad. Period. You know you can't win."

"Oh, Gabe," Phil said. "I have a client, you have a client. Are you telling me that it is impossible that terrorists will attack in Montana because of Guantanamo prisoners?" He smiled mockingly.

"That's not the point. Lots of things carry a threat. Factories carry a threat, biological labs carry a threat. Being a US state these days carries a threat. That's not grounds for an injunction, and you know it."

"At the risk of incurring your wrath, Gabe, I am going to mention your father again. I did know him. Had many cases against him. Usually he won. The state usually does. But one thing he, we, always knew was that the middle way worked. Resolution. He knew, Gabe, that the law is not about being right. It's not the touchdown, it's—"

"It's the game," Gabe finished, an accidental acknowledgment. It was a phrase his father had used, a phrase being bastardized by Phil. "You don't manipulate the system. That's not the game."

"I appreciate your endearing naiveté. Maybe you are…maybe—"

"Like my father," Gabe said, this time finishing a sentence Phil had not meant to begin.

"Let's get to the point." Phil stood erect now and pointed at Gabe. "You can have your fucking prison, and Phoenix can prance around under the national spotlight. God help her if something happens, but screw it. But she can't have it for free. Get me that goddamn statement, about her and the senator, and walk the fuck out of here. Case closed."

Gabe sighed. His mind drifted back to the argument. To winning. "She can't trust you to keep any of this private," Gabe said. "The sworn statement itself will destroy her career—the fact that you needed to ask for it. You'll use it say she falsely claimed an affair, that—"

"Jesus, Gabe. Do you think I want this conversation going beyond this room? My client is an organization comprised of legitimate activists concerned about the safety of the state. Think about it. Citizens for a Safer Montana has more than seven hundred members. You think they want the issue traded away for some political bullshit? Half of them voted for the President, for Christ's sakes."

"Does Bryant even know about this?"

"I'm not answering that, but it's enough for you to know that he isn't driving this. Bryant's the real thing. We're talking about the goddamn presidency, Gabe. Get on board. He'll take this state a long way. Even Phoenix. But she's out of control—"

"You're out of control," Gabe said. His hangover had ebbed, but as Phil spoke, it flowed. Metal against metal. "And this is not the way my father did things. Neither do I. Selling out clients for politics. And to get a false affidavit. If your injunction is worth a shit, then beat me today, and—"

"All right, Gabe. I hate it to come to this, but if this hearing goes forward, win or lose, I'm going to bury Phoenix Jamborsky. Bury her." Gabe glared at Phil, but felt his hands tremble, something he had not felt in a long time. And never outside a courtroom. "We'll out her, and do it now," Phil said. "She's falsely claiming an affair with the senator. Blackmail, really, to get her shitty prison and his endorsement for governor. Beau's people know it's better for him to take that hit now, but believe me, when it's over, when the dust settles, the senator will be standing tall, and Phoenix will be a forgotten joke. Talk to your client, Gabe. She's dangerous, but she'll see the wisdom here." Phil moved closer and pointed in Gabe's face. "We don't want it this way either. She chose this way."

Gabe stepped to him. "Fuck you, Phil," he said quietly. "You talk to your client. The affair happened, and we have a tape to prove it."

Phil stepped back, straightened to his full height, and contemplated Gabe. Gabe could see the litigator in him, the smooth operator, the well-polished shyster that wowed juries and flattered judges. Now his full perceptive power, gained from years of reading others' hearts—witnesses, jurors, clients, and opponents—focused itself on Gabe.

"She recorded the senator admitting an affair, and you, Gabriel Lantagne, have that tape, is that what you're telling me?"

Gabe instinctively realized that to avert his gaze even slightly would end the game. "I'm telling you the tape proves it, Phil. And that the tape goes nowhere, ever, unless you decide differently. You win today, and it's item number one turned over in discovery. Transcribed too. Public record. Now end this case."

"Let's hear it," Phil said quickly.

"Not a chance." Gabe still met Phil's gaze, but Phil looked away, just a dart of the eyes. Yes. A doubt. And now Gabe clearly saw it, the mirror-like glint in Phil's eyes. Like a snake oil salesman who in the end knows his true station, and that it is below the honest man. The admiration of the poseur for the real thing. Looking down, Phil folded his arms, and Gabe saw in him a raw honest moment. A question. Maybe a disappointment. Phil had not gotten where he was today by believing all of his clients either.

"Give me a moment," Phil said.

And while Gabe waited, alone in the small witness room, he realized another thing about Phil: the consummate angle-player had actually believed his own side of the story this time. Until now.

"Your honor, after extensive discussion among counsel, Citizens for a Safer Montana moves to non-suit the motion for a permanent injunction." Phil's suave baritone filled the courtroom, rendering his announcement to untrained ears as a claim of victory.

Judge Freeman raised his thick eyebrows and perused some papers on his desk.

"Will you be re-filing?"

"Not sure, Judge. We hope to reach an accommodation that will safeguard our concerns."

Judge Freeman shrugged. "Motion granted."

Gabe picked up his briefcase as Phoenix softly gripped the inside of his arm.

"Mr. Lantagne?" Judge Freeman stood up, preparing to leave the bench. "I knew your father very well. Great lawyer. He's missed."

"Thank you, Judge." Gabe turned towards the gallery as Freeman disappeared behind two wooden doors. Myrlene, in the front row of the gallery, extended her arms, miming, "What the hell just happened?"

TWENTY-ONE
MAY 5, 2009 – TWIN RIVERS, MONTANA

As long as the woman is not a Muslim, Omar said.

In Ahmed's village, there had been attractive girls seeking husbands, but once he had chosen his path, he could not be a proper husband. In the camp, there were the old women who cooked meals and mended clothing. And there was Rada, a teenager who had come to the camp with her grandmother after her parents had been killed by police. The same police, it was said, had ravaged her repeatedly. In Rada's manner, Ahmed sensed only a terrified coldness as she delivered bowls of rice to the trainees at the tables. But strangely, though they had spoken only briefly, and about superficial matters, Rada was probably Ahmed's closest female acquaintance besides his mother.

Ahmed stepped back from the door, aware that a rude rebuff of the girl named Shannon might be perceived as odd, even suspicious. She was of the disposition to offer herself to men for their pleasure, and certainly American men rarely turned her down. Ahmed somehow succeeded in stashing the two weapons under the bed before Shannon pushed the door open and stepped uninvited into his room.

"Not exactly the Ritz Carlton, huh?" she said. Ahmed noticed a mild slur in her speech, though not having heard her speak much before, he had no idea if she were drunk. She looked very much awake as she cheerfully plopped down on the corner of his bed. "What a shithole, you know?" Without requiring a response, Shannon pointed authoritatively to the white plastic-encased cups on the table. Ahmed awkwardly picked up a cup and offered it to her. She snatched the cup, plied away the plastic delicately with a practiced hand, and filled the cup three-quarters of the way with the liquor. Then she held the bottle out to him, making an exaggerated pouring gesture. Ahmed fumbled with the other cup, managing to tear the plastic, but also the cup.

"Gimme." Shannon leaned forward and took the cup from his hand. She finished unwrapping it and then skillfully trimmed the top half of the cup away, creating a smaller one below the tear. Ahmed perched on the wooden chair by the small desk, trying to appear relaxed, but not wanting to be too close the girl who appeared bent on drinking with him. She foisted the makeshift cup of liquor into his hand.

"I'm very tired," Ahmed said. Perhaps the girl would see tiredness as a reason he would not drink much.

"Oh, Jeremy," Shannon said, right after drinking half her cup of liquor. She leaned back on one elbow, feet bouncing in front of her while her toes barely gripped the dirty sandals. "I don't live like this—really, I don't. I have a house, and almost a college degree. But that's life, right? I doubt this is your final stop in life either. So where are you from? I hear you're headed to California, is that true? How long will you be gracing us with your presence? Curly's not so bad, and as a place like this goes, it's pretty good. Almost free housing, even."

The girl talked and talked, not truly expecting a reply from him, but simply running over her questions with more information about herself. The strong, silent type. An easy role to play with Shannon. Perhaps she would become so drunk she would not want him to have sex with her. And on she went, as Ahmed watched the clock behind her. From two, to three, to four. She had moved into the Ramatin only a week ago and was its only permanent resident. Good information to have. Her husband— "I'll call him my ex-husband"—beat her so badly one night that she ran away. To show Ahmed a tiny bruise on her leg, she pulled her baggy pants down past her hips, brazenly displaying a light blue undergarment as well as the smallest sliver of hair protruding from each side. She quickly pulled them up, but not before Ahmed gasped.

"I know, it's a bad bruise. I'm over him. He doesn't know where I am, and if he found out, boy, you wouldn't want to see his reaction."

The quick and honest motion with which Shannon displayed her treasure to him was the devil's way to tempt and torment him, a fact to which he attributed the stirring in himself.

You will not be sinning against God if you have a woman in America, Omar said.

Ahmed breathed deeply, praying to himself as Shannon went on and on. She related the details of her sad life—her schooling, her father in prison, her marriage. But as she talked, Ahmed relaxed in the knowledge that she would not be demanding any detailed conversation from him.

"I figure I'll hide out here a week or so. Then I'll go to town. I might see Gracie, but I sure hope not. He doesn't go to town much. Have you heard about the town meeting? And the Twin Rivers Day celebration? A guy I know, a regular here, is a cop. He told me it's a secret, so don't tell anyone, but I hear the mayor is going to give everyone in town thousands of dollars if we get the terrorist contract. Then I'll get out of this shithole. Curly says the Sheriff's closing Pandora's that night so all girls can vote. I vote yes, hell yes, we need the money. I could use one of those prison jobs myself. Maybe I'll get to meet the mayor. Maybe she can get me a job. Maybe…"

Ahmed's ears perked up. He had never expected to hear anything from Shannon that bore upon his mission. The old cowboy at the pancake house had provided Ahmed his target. Now Allah, through this drunk girl, had provided him his venue. Twin Rivers Day. Barely two weeks. Ahmed smiled for real, but inside.

As the clock approached four-thirty in the morning, Shannon slowed down. The bottle of whiskey lay empty on the carpet. Ahmed could hardly understand her words now. She sloppily knocked the empty cup off the bed, leaned back, and began to snore loudly. Ahmed walked to the bathroom, dumping his untouched liquor in the sink. He rolled half of the blanket on the bed over the drunk girl without disturbing her. Then he turned off the light, lay on the floor, and slept, the light sleep of a mujahid, a sleep where the slightest noise would wake him. He knew it was stupid, allowing the girl to sleep in the room with his cash and weapons, but she was harmless. Besides, it would not hurt his jihad for those at the strip bar to believe he had spent the night with her. Tomorrow, he would pray and purify himself. He did not have to work until 5:30 p.m.

Ahmed awoke to the rustling of movement some hours later. Shannon was standing, staring blankly around. He pretended to be asleep, watching her through slitted eyes. She picked up her cup as well as the bottle and placed them softly in the small plastic trashcan. She then looked at him, smiled slightly, and left the room, shutting the door quietly behind her and disappearing into the early morning light.

Ahmed kept going up. He jumped or rolled under fallen trees and skillfully dodged his way through prickly brush. Refusing to give his lungs a rest, he cranked his legs only harder as the air got thinner. Upon Shannon's departure, he had packed some necessities into a small backpack and ridden his motorcycle up the high winding road above town until he found a small parking lot from which a trail began. But he needed no trail. During training he had learned to find his way back past his own markings, so here he quickly left the marked trail, knowing only that he would continue up until he was tired. He carried his automatic rifle, as he had done towards the end of this training. He took small steps, back straight, unless he needed to bend or twist. Higher and higher, until the forest became thinner. The hard trudging reminded him of his training. He also thought of his family. Of Abu mainly. And especially of his father's concerns about Abu.

Abu is not like you, Ahmed. He, God willing, can have a good life, but I worry for him. He has a soft soul. He is meek and trusting. His mind is superior, but he has the soul of a woman. He takes after his mother, like you do after me. He is one for books and quiet living and will need protection from the meanness of life. Ahmed agreed with his father. Abu, only four years younger, acted far younger than that. As a young boy he had chased insects and laughed at silly things like a girl. Abu had no friends in the village and never spoke at school, even though he, like Ahmed, attended nearly every day.

Ahmed rested on a huge rock and looked back down onto the valley, at the far corner of which lay the town of Twin Rivers. The rest was a wide wilderness, as wild as his homeland, as the camp, if not as remote. Lungs heaving, he sought communion with God while he calmed his thoughts. On the trek back down, he took his time, breathing the cold mountain air through his nose as he retraced his route. Back through the trees, away from the snow, and finally to a quiet, flat section of woods a few hundred yards from his motorcycle. The sun told him it was early afternoon.

He opened his pack, drank some water, lay out his prayer rug, and donned his topi.. Until now, he had been nervous to wear it, even while praying in bathrooms or motel rooms. Now, he did not care. Close to his mission, he was stronger, and detection remote. In mid-prayer, a gunshot startled him to his feet—and to a sight he could barely fathom. A huge brown bear sped towards him. Ahmed shouldered his rifle, aimed it, and unloaded a long burst into the animal, which dropped awkwardly onto its side, roaring.

The shots and the growls echoed over the valley. A snapping noise turned him towards another surprise, this time behind him and slightly below. On the trail. A white man with a rifle. Ahmed trained his weapon at the man. The man's eyes and posture exuded competence, but also terror.

Then it was Ahmed's turn to be scared. Far below, a police car pulled into the parking lot. Its arrival turned the hunter away from Ahmed. Ahmed didn't know how many policemen were in the car, nor could their disappearance go unnoticed. He turned and bounded silently up the ridge again and then around to the west and down.

Since he had entered America, Ahmed had not seen another motorcycle with a sidecar. Its presence in the same parking lot as the police car might well be remembered. Ahmed cursed himself for his indulgence with the training and the praying. And especially with the rifle. *Be at peace, Ahmed. Be at peace.*

An hour later, Ahmed lay on his bed, using the remote control to flip television channels. In this way he calmed himself, telling himself not to worry about the bear, the hunter, or the police car. He watched American news on CNN, including, to his great interest, a story about Twin Rivers, the prisoners from Cuba, and the town mayor. Shannon was right, Jamborsky was indeed a woman.

Your contact will provide you with your target and final supplies, Omar said, but the method and manner of your mission will be decided by you. However you accomplish it, your status in the pantheon of God's warriors is assured. Eternal bliss guaranteed. I envy you, Ahmed. I truly envy you. Omar spoke from a seated position in his wise, quiet way.

The clock next to Ahmed's head clicked to five-fifteen. Time for work. He prayed and then dressed, donning the sleeveless shirt that displayed his tattoo. Before leaving, he shaved as closely as he could. Shannon would probably not be at work tonight. She had been too drunk the night before.

But Shannon was at work, on stage in fact, when Ahmed took his place by the door. A couple of men from the previous night recognized him. "Hi, pardner," one said.

"Another day, another dollar," Ahmed replied, a phrase he had just heard on CNN. Life in America. Days and dollars, but no God. Shannon bounced on the stage then swung herself to the top of the long golden pole, able to cling to it with only her legs as she glided down. He noted her tightly muscled stomach. Even her skinny arms were strong. She was like a wiry skeleton with sexuality. Ahmed laughed to himself: Americans called this work, standing around protecting whores from drunks. Shannon left the stage and disappeared into the back. Another song started and new girl climbed onto the stage to strip. Ahmed went into his mind. To think of other things. His little village. Abu. He hoped Abu still attended school—but of course he did, his mother would have it no other way.

"Jeremy! Jeremy! Out back, now!" Curly screamed at him from the curtained door, breaking Ahmed out of his daze. The rough old woman, who always spoke loudly and cursed, was scared.

Ahmed moved briskly between the tables and through the curtain, unable to guess what demanded his attention in the back but realizing the crude wrinkled woman was, in fact, his boss, and he was supposed to be pretending to do a job. He strode through the open back door, where a crowd of strippers stood staring, hands over their mouths.

Shannon stood frozen against the brick wall in the full harsh light from the solitary bulb by the door. Shirt still off, she shivered, gripping herself, red face streaked with tears. Directly in front of her stood a young man with a pistol. It took Ahmed only a second to assess the man's intent through his posture, his trembling, and his wide, staring eyes that aimed everywhere and nowhere. This man was crazy and would use the weapon. Ahmed was surprised that the man's bearing reminded him of something from his training—a Russian prisoner he had once seen at the camp. The Russian was beaten, defeated, just a shell of a person by then, but his reaction was not resignation but rage. Instead of calmly praying in the cage, awaiting his fate with dignity like other prisoners, he cursed constantly and loudly at all who passed, trying to gouge eyes and tear throats with his spindly fingers. To take someone with him. Like the Russian, the man aiming the pistol at Shannon trembled with rage, not fear.

Just don't let anybody bother the girls. Essentially his only job duty.

Ahmed calmed himself and stepped into the light, stopping less than ten feet from the man with the gun.

"Stay the fuck out of it!" the man screamed. "This is between ME"—he pounded his chest hard—"and the slut." It was unlikely that the man, probably her husband, could hit Shannon with a bullet even if he fired from such close range. He reeked of moral and, more importantly, mental weakness.

The man lowered the gun a few degrees and looked at right at Ahmed. "BACK OFF, pal!" There were tears in his eyes and he pounded his chest again.

Ahmed's training kicked in; he felt complete calmness. He sensed all that was behind him even while focusing intently on the enemy before him. The fool obviously thought he had a safe distance between himself and Ahmed. Ahmed rested on his heels, careful not to appear to be considering a move.

Curly spoke from behind Ahmed. "Come on, Gracie, we can talk this through, put down the gun, she's freezing to death."

The man turned toward Curly's voice, but before the gun swung ten degrees away from Shannon, Ahmed's face was an inch from his. The gun fired, but into the air, as Ahmed snapped the man's forearm—the one holding the gun. The bone punched though the skin, white and then covered with spurting blood. Ahmed now held the gun and carefully placed it into the man's mouth as he crumbled. Foot on the man's chest, Ahmed held the trigger. He looked into the man's eyes, which seemed to spin in his head, uncomprehending.

Americans are very afraid of death and violence, Omar said. Even those who kill in self-defense, even those who kill worthless vermin such as a rapist or murderer, are prosecuted for it. The government tells its citizens to believe in the sanctity of human life, but places no value on ours. On yours. On your mother's, brother's, or any of the lives of the old people and children in your village. The leaders in America would kill everyone in your village to gain a hundred votes in a close election. But the normal citizens in America do not react well to violence or killing.

Ahmed remembered Omar's words but believed that even in America such a mongrel must have lawfully surrendered his right to live. How could it be any other way? But standing in a circle of horrified onlookers, he paused before pulling the trigger. He looked again into the man's eyes. He wanted to see the hatred, to reassure himself. But he did not. What he saw, under the harsh light and with voices screaming all around him, was deep pain and suffering. Not exactly insanity, but a desperate, soul-wrenching loneliness. Just like that in the eyes of the condemned Russian.

Then, even above the loud, mostly female voices, Ahmed heard a sound he was trained to know. The cock of a gun's hammer.

"That's enough, son. You've done well. Now drop it and step away." A stranger's rough voice cut through the shrill din all around

Ahmed. Ahmed looked up and saw an obese man wearing a hat. He could not see the man's features in the shadows outside the circle of light, but knew from the man's stance that he aimed a pistol and knew how to use it.

Ahmed sat at a table inside the strip bar sipping a cold glass of water. He tried his best to look calm, but under the full lights in a room with four policeman, his heart beat ferociously. The girls sat all together around a table, relating their version of events with hysteria and a relished enthusiasm.

One of the girls, whom Ahmed believed too fat to even be a nude dancer, mimed her version to the young, nervous policeman, who wrote on a pad as he watched the reenactment. "And then Jeremy was like, suddenly in his face, and you heard crack, crack! And Gracie screamed and went to the ground, and I thought Jeremy would shoot the little creep. I mean, I'm glad he didn't, but the fucker had it comin' if you ask me." Other girls interrupted, adding details.

Suddenly, the room quieted. The old policeman, the one who had urged Ahmed to drop the gun, entered from the back. "Y'all get on home. Evening's festivities are over."

More than any other person Ahmed had yet seen in America, the man, though old and overweight, carried himself with the nonchalant confidence of someone who knew about fighting. He approached Ahmed's table, pulled out a chair, and sat down. He removed his hat, and Curly set down a small glass of liquor in front of him. The old man's eyes met Ahmed's, not judging, exactly, but searching.

Because of your physical skill, people in America will be stupid enough to believe you're not smart, Karim said. This idiocy can be used to great advantage. Do nothing to dispel this notion when speaking to Americans. Play dumb, as they say.

Behind the casual manner, the policeman clearly employed the same strategy.

"Where'd you learn how to handle yourself, son?"

Speaking to the policeman, Ahmed learned that he had not only not committed a crime but had perfectly executed his job as a bouncer. He quietly prepared himself when the policeman looked at his driving license, but after the writing down the information on a skinny pad of paper, he returned it.

"You gotta be the best damn bouncer Caroline County has ever seen. Ever thought about police work? You change your mind about California, look me up." The man laughed, a deep-throated bellow that filled the whole bar. He patted Ahmed roughly on the shoulder then stood. "Closing time!"

Ahmed walked out the front door behind the old policeman in a single file line that included the other policemen and the girls. Outside, a series of bright flashes hit his face. Temporarily blinded, he squinted hard into the darkness but kept walking. If the light presented a threat, he was dead.

"Ahh, lay off the man, Martha Ann," the policeman said. "You got to stop listening to that police band. Nothing to see here." He ushered the old woman away, but she clicked and clicked, flashing the light at Ahmed again and again.

"This is a story, Sheriff, a real story, baby."

"Don't mind her," the policeman told Ahmed. "You'll be a hero for a few days. Maybe you'll get laid." He laughed. "But then I expect that's not much of a problem for you anyway."

Ahmed did not understand everything the policeman meant but he understood that his picture would be in an American newspaper. As the police drove away, each of the three cars following the sheriff's in turn, the lights in Pandora's went out. A loud lock clicked. The parking lot stood empty and almost perfectly dark, the only noise a cold winter breeze high up the in the trees. Ahmed stood alone under the stars, shivering in his sleeveless shirt, wondering why the same image kept running through his head—Abu and his mother on the road. Abu had not known that Ahmed was never coming back.

Although he didn't feel tired, Ahmed had nowhere to go but his room. He prayed, and then turned on the television. He flipped channels, but found nothing but gratuitously violent or silly films. He had seen enough of those. He turned off the television and lay in his bed in the dark. "Nothing to see here," the old policeman had said. At some point he fell asleep, but it was only the half-sleep of agitation, not the warm, contented sleep of the confident soldier.

Nothing to see here. Ahmed awoke on his sleeping pad and immediately heard loud snoring from the trainee next to him. Trainees were under strict instructions about when to eat, when to train, when to pray, and when to sleep, and so far, Ahmed had never violated those instructions. Omar commanded all the trainees, and all rules applied to all. No one was special.

Yet Ahmed was so restless he could not remain in the tent. The snoring spoke of tension in the mind of the young trainee from Chechnya, and lying awake listening to it did nothing for Ahmed's peace of mind. So, for the first time in his eleven months at the camp, he broke a rule.

The sentinels posted by Omar patrolled only the far perimeter of the camp. Even the ones lucky enough to be supplied with infrared goggles never turned the devices into the camp. And so Ahmed walked, the silent walk he had mastered over the last eleven months. Past other trainee huts. Past the wooden tables where they ate. Along the far side of the rifle range, around the pond where the foothills began. One hour, then two passed while he walked. He never stopped, never changed pace. He worked to train his eyes to see important signals, even mere shadows, in the dimmest light. The half moon shone from the horizon. He walked until he believed his legs were satisfied.

Coming back along the back of camp near one of the most commonly used training paths up the mountain, he passed within ten yards of Omar's hut. He veered to grant it a wider berth. He did not fear detection by Omar. He was mere weeks away from his jihad, and despite the equality among the brothers in the camp, he knew he had graduated beyond petty scolding. Yet he saw no purpose in risking waking Omar, who could be awakened by the slightest noise, even a change in the breeze.

Suddenly Ahmed stopped. He heard noises from Omar's hut, a quiet rustling that nevertheless drifted from the windows to Ahmed's ears, which, calmed by the long noiseless walk, missed nothing. Omar had heard him and would emerge in seconds with his rifle. Ahmed stood stock still, prepared to hurl a friendly whisper at Omar. He was not afraid; a soldier could handle a mild rebuke for late-night hike. But Omar did not emerge from the hut nor call out to ask who passed. Ahmed decided to stay frozen until the rustling stopped. But it did not stop. The mild breeze slowed and then quickened while Ahmed stood, his senses bent upon Omar's window and away from the area around him. As he focused, he lost perception of all but Omar's window. He enjoyed training his mind to direct perceptive abilities to one spot, then expanding them back to the whole, like the zoom function on the infrared machines.

Ready to sleep again, Ahmed was about to walk away, when the rustling sound increased, accompanied by another sound, an impossible sound. Ahmed stood for a second longer, then ran. Even his stealthiest running made noise in the quiet night, but nothing that would be heard by Omar, whose own ears were nearer to the noise about him. Ahmed slid back into the tent and began his soft breathing exercises to calm his heart.

The noises coming from Omar's hut were the muffled but high-pitched chirps of a woman. It was not possible, yet true, that Omar was with a woman in his hut. As Ahmed drifted off, he also realized another truth: Omar was not with a woman, but with Rada, the quivering teenage orphan.

Ahmed jolted upright, awake and sweating. His left hand gripped the pistol next to him. Shannon's bony body slithered from a stooping position over the bed to a curled position next to him.

"Didn't mean to scare you," she said. "All the keys open all the doors." She was dressed. The skin on her face, which now rested against his neck, felt feverishly hot on top of his cold sweat. And yet Ahmed lay still.

Her arm rested on his chest, and her legs next to his, but she made no further movement. "Thank you for staying with me tonight," she said softly with a slurred tiredness. Ahmed slid the gun up under the pillow next to him and shut his eyes. With nowhere else to put it, he slid his right arm out from between him and Shannon and rested it on the bed above her head and around her body, not touching her. Shannon's hand traced its way down Ahmed's shirt to the edge of his baggy underpants. Just as the bare tip of her finger inserted itself under the elastic, he touched her hand, moving it away softly with his own quivering fingers. It would be her way to believe she had to pleasure men in exchange for security. Moments later, he could feel the soft rhythm of her breathing as she slept. He closed his eyes but doubted he could sleep with a woman next to him. He was surprised when the morning light woke him and Shannon was already gone.

TWENTY-TWO
MAY 15, 2009 – HELENA, MONTANA

"Twin Rivers is proud to step up and do its duty to our nation, and we are not afraid." Phoenix spoke before a squirrel's nest of microphones in front of the Helena Federal Courthouse. "The Citizens for a Safer Montana had every right to bring their case, to ensure that all proper safety measures would be taken. We have now come to agreement that Twin Rivers can do its duty without unnecessary risk to Montanans. We will be employing up to ninety law enforcement personnel to guard against those seeking to do our country harm, a fact which will render Caroline County the most heavily patrolled county per capita in the United States. The federal funding will also render our prison the most secure in America."

Behind the reporters, a gaggle of poorly funded protestors tried to get some attention, but the camera trucks circled Phoenix. Gabe and Myrlene stood behind her, on camera but silent.

As Phoenix stepped from the tightly clustered group of reporters, she positioned herself between Gabe and Myrlene and began to walk. Microphones jumped into Gabe's face as they moved through the crowd.

"You're Richard Lantagne's son. Did this affect the case? Are you a criminal attorney by trade? What would your father think of terrorists in Montana?"

Gabe stopped to make a comment but noted Phoenix's stiff body language of disapproval. "My father would think that justice had been done. Twin Rivers was also his hometown. He would be proud it's doing its duty to the country."

"Not bad," Phoenix said, as the three of them escaped the crowd of reporters towards the parking garage.

"So, what's next?" Gabe said.

"I've got a meeting across town," Phoenix said, "then I'm headed back to work on TR Day. You sure you don't want to give that speech?"

"I'm sure."

Myrlene was quiet, apparently trying to get away from Phoenix as soon as possible by exempting herself from the conversation. Phoenix turned to her, smiled, and touched Myrlene's shoulder. "Thanks for all your work, Myrlene. You're going places."

Myrlene delivered an authentic-looking smile and did not flinch from Phoenix's touch in any perceivable way—perceivable to anyone besides Gabe, anyway. Phoenix walked to her car, and Gabe and Myrlene turned toward theirs. But Phoenix called Gabe back, and approached him closely, looking him in the eye from a foot away, Myrlene now out of earshot. "I need to see you later, once I get back to Twin Rivers. There may be a development."

"Call me," Gabe said.

She reached her arm to his chest and tucked a folded piece of paper into his shirt pocket.

Gabe did not read the note until he sat in front of his desk back in Twin Rivers, with Myrlene downstairs checking phone messages. The crisp folded paper wasn't a note, but a check for one hundred thousand dollars.

Gabe parked on River Street in front of Phoenix's apartment, a three-bedroom suite above some boutique-ish shops. The lights were on. Upstairs, she invited him in. Without asking, he made a drink from the bottles sitting on a small kitchen pass-through.

He gestured with the glass to take in the apartment. "Not bad."

"Had to move somewhere," she said. "It would be so much easier to live at the ranch. Ayalette, you know. But I guess you can't have your cake and eat it too."

Gabe very much doubted Phoenix really believed that.

"I'm giving you an award on Saturday, speech or not," she said. "For dedicated representation of the town of Twin Rivers, to a man who I believe will someday be mayor, Gabriel Lantagne." She flourished her arm in a royal gesture towards Gabe. She'd been drinking, but maybe not much. She wore an old pair of jeans and the top to the same business suit she had worn in court. "Soon too. The governor's race is next year, so I'll announce in a few months."

Months?

"I'm starting to doubt I'll have much competition in the primary. At least that's what I heard today."

"From whom?"

"Let's go for a ride," she said. "If we're going to move forward, I need to show you something."

"Why not just tell me?"

But Phoenix was already by the door, boots on. She packed some things from a closet near the door into a worn leather purse.

"Quiet now, Michael and Ayalette will be asleep." *One in the morning? No kidding.*

They pulled into the Angel Sky, and Gabe parked quietly on the gravel, far from the house. Instead of climbing the stairs to the front door, Gabe followed Phoenix along the side of the house and down the hill, where she punched a code into an electronic gate. Further down the hill, a trail began to wind far around the house to a stable. As they got closer, Gabe could hear a horses inside.

"You ride?" Phoenix asked.

"What kind of Montana boy doesn't? What are you up to?"

"You'll see. You delivered for me. It's time you learned about this town."

As they saddled the horses, a mild sense of dread filled Gabe, not the dread of danger, but a familiar feeling of guilty regret, the letdown after compromising himself to feed his desperate need for something he'd never quite had. Something his father had always had, Phoenix had, even Pasquali had. Uniqueness? That distinguishing quality that made people great.

They trotted alongside each other on a dark trail. Phoenix held a flashlight, but the horses clearly knew where they were headed. Phoenix chatted, thoughts seeming to wander. Ten minutes. Twenty minutes. The trail never changed through the flat valley.

"You know the story of Terwilliger's Ride?" she asked.

Everyone who grew up in Weasel Junction knew the story of Terwilliger's Ride. 1876. Amos Terwilliger. The old cowboy and gambler who founded the Triple Ace Ranch, about a third of which was now the Angel Sky. In those days, the criminal justice system in Weasel Junction lacked certain modern-day notions of due process, and so it was that the town sheriff decided to hang two horse thieves—one man, one woman—who had been caught headed out of town on two Triple Ace brands and confessed to horse theft. The man was a known ne'er-do-well, and the woman a half-breed Flathead Indian who lived and worked on the ranch. Apparently, nobody gave old Terwilliger a heads-up about the hangings, though the horses were his. It wasn't until the early morning of the impending hangings that a ranch hand woke Amos with the news. The sun had just begun to creep over the flat plain to the east, and the hangings were scheduled for dawn.

Terwilliger, who was over seventy, jumped on a horse, tore out the back plain of the Triple Ace, and rode the eleven miles to town as fast as he could. He galloped into town only to find that he was too late. The man and woman were swinging from the gallows at the end of River Street. Horrified, Amos had a heart attack right there and died.

"Of course," Gabe said.

"Well, this is it," Phoenix said.

"This is what?"

"This is Terwilliger's Ride. This path. It winds eleven miles from the site of Amos's house to the beginning of River Street."

They rode in silence for a while.

"But only Terwilligers know the real story of Terwilliger's ride." Typical Phoenix, even in idle chatter she had to maintain her privileged insider status. She, of course, was no longer a Terwilliger.

"All right, I'll bite, what's the real story?"

The trail suddenly entered a thickly wooded area then dipped into a valley, snaking through the trees.

"The real story is that the young Flathead woman was Terwilliger's lover. She stole the horses to run away with a degenerate gambler from town. Amos loved her but was so consumed by passionate rage at her betrayal that he authorized the hangings. The next day, the night before the hanging, he tossed and turned and finally realized that his love for her was so strong he wanted her to live, even with the other man. He would stop the hanging, give them the horses, and let them go in peace. With that decided, he was able to sleep, figuring he'd get up early and get to town way before the noon hanging."

"I thought it was a dawn hanging."

"He heard from a ranch hand about the change in schedule—just before dawn."

They left the trees and again trotted in the dark on a path, surrounded, as far as Gabe could tell, only by flat plain.

"Jealousy..." Phoenix said. Why had she wanted to tell him about Amos—Enos's grandfather, Michael's great grandfather? "...is so fucking arrogant," she finished.

Without warning, Phoenix diverted from Terwilliger's Ride and took a ninety-degree turn into the grass and down a hill. Hundreds of yards from the thicket of trees, Phoenix slowed her horse to a slow walk and Gabe fell in next to her. They'd descended for several minutes when Gabe heard an engine approaching. Suddenly a light pierced the darkness, blinding Gabe for a moment until a middle-aged Mexican man appeared next to them on an ATV. Manuel Foreva, top hand at the Angel Sky.

"Ms. Phoenix?" Surprised, his eyes questioning.

"Manuel. Good evening."

"To you as well." Manuel, who had seen Gabe both at the ranch and in town, looked him up and down suspiciously. Manuel wore a holstered pistol.

"Yeah, Manuel," Phoenix said. "We're going to the barn."

"The big barn?" Manuel asked, as if skeptical, on some level, of Phoenix's authority in that regard.

"I'm sure." Without further hesitation, she led Gabe past Manuel, who putted slowly behind them, revving the engine loudly and erratically as if to reflect his displeasure.

They passed several small barns before descending a steeper hill. Soon the terrain flattened and they approached a massive structure, larger and more sun-bleached than any barn Gabe had ever seen. Three stories high and covering half an acre, it loomed over its surroundings. Though huge, it rested on the floor of the valley and was thus invisible from the trail only a quarter mile above them. They dismounted and tied the horses to a post.

"You ask, you get," Phoenix said. Gabe was about to ask why she was only now showing him whatever she was about to show him, but he didn't have to. There was a legal term for the relationship they now had after he'd lied for her to Phil Jackson. Coconspirators. The law attributed one coconspirator's knowledge to the other. Perhaps reality did too.

Phoenix swung open the barn door, and they entered a small room with a hay-covered floor. Once Gabe's eyes adjusted, he saw that the main barn was separated from the entryway by a stone wall that went all the way to the ceiling.

"Manuel?"

Manuel grunted but stepped forward with key. When the door metal door opened, the three of them stepped inside. Gabe immediately felt the heat and beaming light, which seemed to come from all directions.

"Holy shit," Gabe said.

Phoenix smiled. "Yeah."

"How long?"

"Since the seventies. They started outside. Switched to grow-houses in the mid-eighties. War on drugs, you know. Profits tripled."

"Who knows?"

"This is only the second biggest in Caroline County."

"Egan?"

"And Thompson. It's been scaling down since I became mayor."

"How much?"

"It varies. Maybe two thousand pounds a month these days. Used to be much more."

"How can it be?" Gabe thought back over his life growing up in Weasel Junction.

"I meant it when I said this town can keep a secret, Gabe. Anyway, welcome to what we Weasel Junction insiders call The Trade."

Pasquali. Michael. Egan. Thompson.

"You gotta give Enos and company credit," Phoenix said. "They knew what they were doing."

"Who else knew?" Knows. Knew.

Phoenix looked at Gabe with a hint a of pity in her expression.

"My father?"

Phoenix walked partway down one of the neatly cropped rows of bulging, budding pot plants.

"All they did is help the town. Which is all I'm doing now by ending it. In 2009, you can't run a town in secret. Not anymore. That's what I've been telling the rancher boys since I got here."

"And in 2010 you can't run for governor if you're one of the biggest drug dealers in Montana."

"Me?" She'd used this mock indignation on him before. "I'm divorced, my friend. And if anything, I'm responsible for curbing—and after TR Day, ending—Weasel Junction's addiction to marijuana money."

"The graduated tax?"

"Every word true. You never asked me where the money came from." Phoenix paused momentarily to massage a marijuana bud with her fingers. "I can't say it's not a little sad. But you'll be the mayor of a clean rich town. Believe me, your father would have been glad to see this cleaned up. But this was where he was from. His place. What was he gonna do? Not have a career? Rat out everybody who ever helped him the second he got to Helena?"

Phoenix was also talking about herself.

Reversing Terwilliger's Ride, they made it back to the top of the Angel Sky in good time, considering the darkness. Gabe maneuvered the jeep put of the long driveway without headlights, and then drove Phoenix home in silence.

"A nightcap?" she said.

The dawn crept through Phoenix's closed blinds, waking Gabe, who looked over at Phoenix. She was already awake.

"So why tell me now?" he asked. "About The Trade?"

Phoenix smiled. "You know why."

Gabe looked at the ceiling. A sense of longing—for what?—returned. He felt as if all the booze, food, cigarettes, sex, all of everything, could stream into his body without ever filling the mildly unpleasant emptiness.

"I've got to get up," Phoenix said. "Lots to do for TR Day."

Gabe stood and fished around on the floor for his clothes in the dull, filtered dawn. His stomach heaved slightly, signaling only a manageable hangover.

Before he left, they shared a cigarette in the living room. Perched cross- legged on a barstool, Phoenix wore only a robe, which hung open, exposing her casual nakedness. Faint stains of her own lipstick smeared the center of her chest, the residue of transfer from her to him and back. It was then that Phoenix chose to mention another detail. As Gabe drove away, he marveled at the audacity of Phoenix Jamborsky. Apparently, TR Day had a surprise new speaker. A man who would announce Phoenix as *someone I hope to see as the next Governor of Montana.* Gabe actually felt sorry for the guy, as hard as it is to feel sorry for a US Senator.

God, Bryant had to hate her. A real candidate for President, and he had to back down on terrorists coming to Montana. Certainly, at least, Bryant and Phoenix now shared an interest in stopping anything from going wrong. Another win for her.

After a quick shower at home, Gabe pulled up to his office, where Myrlene and Pasquali were sitting together on the front steps. Myrlene's skinny body shivered in the early-morning cold, her trembling, gloved hand holding a lit cigarette. Both of them focused on the porch between them, where they had *The Weasel Junction Wallflower* spread wide.

"Congratulations," Myrlene said glumly.

"For what?" Gabe said.

"For your award. The first annual Richard Lantagne Citizenship Award goes to you. This is the Twin Rivers Day edition. Looks like you, some high school kid, and some dude who beat the shit out of stripper's husband will all get awards tomorrow. Let's see, how do they put it? 'The award named for Weasel Junction's favorite son goes appropriately to his son, the man some believe destined to lead the town.'"

Gabe glanced down at the three pictures on the front page: himself, the kid from Twin Rivers High in a football uniform, and a bald, terrifying muscle-head walking out of the titty bar next to Pasquali.

"I told her I didn't want an award. She never said she was creating an award in my father's name."

"The mayor's been creating just about whatever she wants lately," Pasquali said. "That's her business. But I got two pieces of our business today: Gillespie's murder, and, less importantly, the security for Phoenix's glamour-fest. I hope you don't mind, but I've recruited your assistant here to help with crowd control tomorrow. She'll be checking IDs at entry point two while my man frisks everybody. Nobody's getting into the staging area without ID and a frisk."

"Why her?"

"Because we're a little short in the intelligence department at the moment, Gabe." His response showed an uncharacteristic hesitation, perhaps apprehension.

"Are you actually worried about this shit? Terrorists?"

"Not terrorists," Pasquali said. "Crazies. I've already seen it this morning. The freaks are arriving. The town hasn't seen a nationally publicized event like this, not ever. Phoenix only just told me this morning that Bryant is coming. Just fucking great. At least he has his own security team—though they guard only him. We are fully responsible for security around the stage and the whole festival ground."

The festival ground was actually just the town square, a couple of hundred square yards between the end of River Street and the beginning of downtown. Four glorified blocks.

"So no cars are comin' near the stage, all bags will be searched, and we got cameras," Pasquali said.

"Cameras?"

"To cover most of the square. Of course, like most of the shit around this town, they don't actually function, but they put on a decent show. Plus I'll be walking around sizing people up. That's as good as any freakin' camera."

"I can help," Gabe said.

"You'll be on stage."

"No, I really won't." Gabe wasn't sure why he said it, or if he meant it. The award was fine, but for Phoenix not to mention the part about his father when it was clearly already planned?

"Suit yourself, you know most of the lowlifes in Caroline County, so you can mix with the crowd. I'll get you a walkie and a sidearm. Now on to more important business, tell him what you told me, Darlin'."

"Jonathan Scruggs," she said. "A few friends of mine have seen him around since his release. He's been hitting all the bars and indulging heavily."

Gabe wasn't sure how he felt about Myrlene engaging in active investigation for Pasquali, if that what she was doing. Especially if one believed that this inquiry was related to Gillespie's death.

"I didn't ask her to do it," Pasquali said.

"I saw Scruggs last night at Ramhead's. I went alone." Myrlene hesitated and shot a dark look at Gabe. "We talked. I thought if I got to know him, I might learn something. We had a few drinks, and each time he bought a drink for me, he ordered a beer and a shot for himself. Each time he peeled a hundred from a pretty thick wad and told Bartlow to keep the change, acting the big shot, and he got so drunk, Bartlow was sick of him even with the huge tips."

Pasquali raised his eyebrows at Gabe. Gabe met his hard gaze. "Plenty of ways to make a wad of cash in Twin Rivers."

"But last time I checked," Pasquali said, "that fool don't know about any of 'em."

"Right before I left him," Myrlene said, "he was mumbling something about how he might leave town soon. Said he should head out to Hollywood—with all the acting he'd done lately, he could land himself an academy award. He was really wasted. I think he fell asleep in his truck outside the bar."

"I'm going up to the Angel Sky later," Pasquali said. "Gonna interview some of the hands about Scruggs. I plan to find out before TR day if somebody, including Michael Terwilliger, has, shall we say, engaged Scruggs's services to help wind up town business. If not, that means he got his cash from somewhere else. I need to know where. And what it may have to do with Gillespie."

Myrlene's blank stare revealed that she had no idea about The Trade. Pasquali's plan made some sense, but did not strike him as the sort of ingenious police work Pasquali would bother to mention. Gabe held Pasquali's eyes.

"Why not just approach Scruggs?"

"I got my eye on Scruggs, but spooking him today would be the worst thing to do. I gotta see what he does. Will you come with me up to the ranch."

"Why?" Gabe said.

"Because your client, the mayor, owns half of the Angel Sky ranch. I wouldn't doubt it if Terwilliger views you as his lawyer too. This being Friday, payday, I expect the hands will be around at the end of the workday. Leastways, that's how they used to do it. Terwilliger doesn't run the ranch at that level, but we may need his permission to go up on the property and ask around. If we run into Foreva, and you're with me, he'll think we're on some kind of legal business as opposed to a murder investigation."

Gabe thought about it. "I'll call Phoenix and Michael. Doesn't sound like a problem."

"All right, then," Pasquali said, but his hard look conveyed something more.

Back in the office, Myrlene sat at Gabe's desk while he picked up the phone to call Phoenix. He considered Myrlene briefly. She seemed so young, so naïve, so, well, so much like someone he shouldn't be involved with.

"Today? With TR Day tomorrow?" Phoenix said. "This can't wait a day?"

Gabe could picture her with the phone cradled on her shoulder as she bustled through other tasks, barely listening.

"You know Pasquali. He's working a murder case."

"Okay, fine, you guys have my permission to talk to the hands at the ranch. I'll tell Michael. For what it's worth, I've never heard of this Scruggs character, and I doubt Michael has either. Michael doesn't hire random outsiders, none of us do. And if Pasquali needs to do it today, whatever, that's his bailiwick, although I think he needs to get his priorities straight. Tomorrow is the biggest day in this town's history. In our history. I know you get that, but Geno clearly does not. Anyway, I need you to come over now. There's somebody I want you to meet."

TWENTY-THREE

MAY 16, 2009 – TWIN RIVERS MONTANA

Gabe checked his watch on the way to City Hall. Ten-twenty a.m., and a hell of a day ahead of him. A quick visit to see what Phoenix wanted and he'd head back to the office, then Pasquali and the ranch followed by God-knows-what prep for TR Day.

Gabe hustled up the stairs and breezed into the mayor's office. Before he said a word, the receptionist buzzed Phoenix. "Mr. Lantagne has arrived."

Despite the small-town feel of the City Hall building itself, Phoenix had upgraded the mayoral chamber to meet her aspiring standards. A new oak desk complemented the old wooden furnishings and the marble fireplace. Before her desk sat two high-backed leather chairs, and Gabe could see the top of a graying head over the back of one of them. He approached Phoenix, hand extended, assuming that the presence of a third party rendered this meeting formal. "Good morning, Ms. Mayor."

"Gabe," she said, "I'd like you to meet Senator Bryant." Bryant leaned forward and gave Gabe a warm, firm handshake.

Gabe sat in the other chair. "Please, don't let me interrupt."

"Not at all," Bryant said. "I was just leaving. Came to town for tomorrow's event. Haven't spent a night in Weasel Junction since, well, since the night of Mayor Jamborsky's wedding." He turned back to Phoenix. "So we're finished, I suppose, Ms. Mayor. But you should know I wrote an op-ed piece for the Washington Post to run tomorrow coinciding with my appearance at TR Day. I urge the President—and you—to reconsider. For safety's sake. But beyond that, I'm done with the matter. I support all Montanans, if not all their ideas. Now that you've accepted the contract, we'll endeavor together to protect our state and Weasel Junction."

Phoenix smiled. "Twin Rivers."

Bryant broke his stately demeanor with a sarcastic smirk that seemed jarringly out of character. Bryant was sixty years old, but despite his silver hair, he could have been ten years younger. His eyes studied Gabe in a way that was neither warm nor hostile. Interested. Maybe curious. Surely he knew that Gabe had played a role in the dismissal of Citizens v. Jamborsky, and probably even in the matter of the secret tape and the affair that had come to bear so recently on the question. Bryant was probably in town only because Phoenix had put the screws to him about two endorsements, her beloved TR day and her political future. And in her wily way she had secured the endorsement that mattered most—the governor's race.

Gabe searched Bryant's calm look, and in it he found no anger, no judgment, not even a shred of disdain. What he thought he did see was a look of sadness, of sympathy perhaps. Even seated, Bryant was a formidable man, not only because of power, but because he exuded a cautious, placid wisdom that placed one, perhaps falsely, at ease. Gabe could not resist staring at the man a second too long and, in doing so, received the very slightest smile. An acknowledgement of something? Bryant would wave to everybody at Twin Rivers Day, but if something went wrong with Phoenix's prison, it was the President's ass and hers. Not his. Bryant then shifted his gaze from Gabe to Phoenix and his calm smile changed to a dark jab. And in that moment Gabe realized what the Senator had meant by his little simpatico smile. Phoenix may have out-angled Bryant but at least it was over. Gabe's Phoenix Jamborsky ordeal was only just beginning.

Bryant stood, nodding to a man in the back corner of the room whom Gabe had not seen. A tall man with his arms folded. Ron Westerman. Westerman opened the door for Bryant, who looked at Gabe once more. "I'm sure you get this all the time, but I knew your father. You know why he was the best attorney general this state has ever had?"

Gabe had little time to think, but the right answer popped through his lips anyway, an answer which confirmed his own opinion of his father, and of himself, and made an ever so small but insightful comment on Bryant's own situation. "Honesty."

"Nope," Bryant said. "Honesty's part of it, but let's face it, that doesn't get you there. This is politics, after all, and being mostly honest is about all you can hope for. The reason he was the greatest attorney general the state has ever had is because of judgment, especially judgment about those with whom he surrounded himself. You can't help where you're from, but you can help where you go. A great prosecutor doesn't bring to trial every case he can win. He has a sense for the proper balance and sets his course on it. It's called judgment—of events, of the mood of the populace, and, perhaps most of all, of how decisions will affect the future. The long run. It should always be about the long run. Richard Lantagne was a great Montanan—a great American even—because he understood that."

Gabe waited, sensing the Senator had not finished.

Bryant's eyes gleamed under a bit of wet melancholy. "Good luck with that." He then walked out, leaving Gabe alone with Phoenix.

All clients minimized. Most doled out the truth slowly, feeling a need to give out information, even to their own lawyer, only on a need-to-know basis. In this way, Phoenix was no different than other clients. She was the mayor of a town and perhaps a future governor, not a criminal defendant, but as with criminal clients, it wasn't just a half-truth here and a silence there. The lying never stopped. Her reality was a well so deep, you could wait and wait while the stone fell, and in the end not be sure if you even heard the faintest echo of a splash.

"Was there really even an affair?" Gabe asked.

Phoenix returned his gaze without flinching. And it was Phoenix the schoolgirl, the gossipy one drinking barefoot by the window, eyes wide with the cute craziness of it. "I sure did try."

"Do you tell the truth about anything?"

"I'm sorry, Gabe. You really didn't expect to learn all about the town in one day, did you?"

"You're my client."

"Was your client. Now I'm your political benefactor, like Beau is mine. It doesn't matter why, Gabe, it just is."

"Why would Bryant feel threatened by a bluff about a tape."

Phoenix sighed. "It had nothing to do with a tape. It had to do with how far I'm willing to go. They were wrong about me. I was right. Now we move on. The future."

Gabe did not respond.

"It's harder for women," Phoenix said.

"You blackmailed him with a phony affair."

"No." Phoenix's eyes blazed now, and she walked around the desk. "I proved I was tough enough for the game. You think Beauregard Bryant would endorse me for governor, make me a lifelong ally, if I were just a Lewinsky? Think about it."

Gabe's head pounded. That familiar feeling. No food, body pulling itself out of hangover mode.

Phoenix's eyes and posture softened. "Part of my mission here has always been to save this town from The Trade. Do you know what would happen to dozens of people, honest people, not to mention the totally innocent families who built their lives here, if we don't transition to a new and lucrative, not to mention legal, scheme around here? I'm not denying my ambition, but don't deny my desire to help people. The Terwilliger plan has outlasted its time. It's a miracle it hasn't already blown up."

Now she was back to the Phoenix he knew. Or one of them. Bryant didn't trust her. Pasquali didn't trust her. Yet they worked with her anyway. Gabe marveled at her ability to push and pull, to briefly sever the invisible cord connecting them so that its mending felt all the better.

"Let me give you the award tomorrow, Gabe. Announce you as a hopeful for mayor. You've earned it. You want it. Don't think your father got where he was by only examining everybody else's morals."

Gabe was so sick of people mentioning his father he didn't even react to it. "I don't need the award. I'll think about the endorsement if that time ever comes."

"Be on stage at least?"

"Maybe."

"Okay, those on stage need to arrive at 10:30, through the back of River Street, to skip security. Beau and I will sit in the center, with Ayalette on my right, then the football guy, then the bouncer. You'll be next to Beau."

"I gotta go, Phoenix. I'm really busy today. I got a jail visit, client calls, Pasquali."

"If you're going to the ranch later and you see Michael, don't tell him Ayalette's coming to TR Day, he insisted she not miss her riding lesson. Screw that. Her trainer's on this payroll too." She winked and pointed to herself. "My daughter's gonna hear the first time her mother's name and *governor* are said in the same public sentence." Suddenly distracted, Phoenix began shuffling papers around her desk as she peered at the blinking lights on her phone indicating three calls. Then, after a moment's hesitation, she looked back up at Gabe. "You know, sometimes owning half a ranch is more of a pain in the ass than it's worth. Whatever Pasquali's up to at Angel Sky, I seriously doubt he's telling you or anyone the motives behind it. Oh, and one last thing." She glanced again at the blinking lights on the phone. "The best place to hide a lie is a pile of truths."

TWENTY-FOUR
MAY 14, 2009 – TWIN RIVERS, MONTANA

Ahmed's eyes watched the dancers on the stage and the men at the tables, but his mind wandered increasingly to the minute details of his mission. Training himself for it. Going over every step again and again so as to repeat important lessons.

The explosives training came last, and was taught to Ahmed and three others by a one-armed, limping Bosnian named Zlatin. Behind Zlatin's back, Karim made an obscene joke about explosives experts, something about how the inventor of dynamite had blown himself up, and never trust an explosives expert with all his parts. It was typical of Karim's undignified way. Zlatin was a real mujahid who had fought for years beside his brothers in Bosnia, most of whom were now dead. Zlatin could not fight anymore, so he now devoted himself to teaching others. His soft, thoughtful ways contrasted with Karim's loud, Scottish blathering. Karim could not fathom the soul of such a hero. And yet Karim took part in the explosives training and appeared knowledgeable about the remote cellular fuses and other modern technology he had purchased and brought to the camp.

They started out by learning the different types of explosives. Primary explosives were generally not used for bombs, but for detonators. Lead azide, lead styphnate, mercury fulminate, and others. Ahmed learned to create a detonator from these and even simpler materials. Low explosives—like fireworks—came next. They also did not serve to create big explosions, but they burned fast, serving as a propellant. Ahmed learned to create a small bomb from hunks of metal, even thumbtacks, and gunpowder taken from bullets. Such a bomb might do to a kill a person, but not for a real explosion. Zlatin spent a lot of time teaching high explosives. These were the materials which caused stunning explosions far in excess of their mass. Nitroglycerin, RDX, TNT. Only a well-financed and well-manned mission made use of such materials. The Chechens relished this portion of the training, for they would have some semblance of a funded army when they returned home to fight the Russians. But Ahmed, a lone soldier, paid most attention to blasting agents. Blasting agents are not generally used in military weapons, Zlatin said, but mostly in mining. They blast, and blast well, in a small area but are not as useful for fighting. They will blow a very small group of men to bits or put a hole in the side of a standard building, but will do little damage to a marching force or a fortified position, especially since they cannot easily be launched. Dynamite, the world's favorite blasting agent, was Ahmed's focus. Zlatin knew of Ahmed's special mission and trained him individually with dynamite and other ad-hoc explosives like fertilizer. A sole mission, a martyr's mission, a symbolic mission, does not require a huge explosion, Zlatin said. It is the location of the explosion that matters.

Ahmed learned the weights and measures of dynamite and how to predict the size of a blast area. They spent the last few days of the training alone, creating small fertilizer bombs from diesel fuel, ammonium nitrate fertilizer, and a primitive yet effective detonator that Zlatin could create from simple aluminum and two cellular phones, one rigged to signal the other to detonate the bomb even from kilometers away.

Karim annoyed Ahmed, and perhaps even Zlatin, by constantly playing around with his fancy cellular fuses. He hid behind a tree while blasting off several bombs Ahmed had made. Ahmed and Zlatin stood in the open watching Karim's explosions. I love this shit, Karim said. Can remote detonation happen from across the world? Ahmed asked. Zlatin touched his lips and looked up, as *he often did while considering. It could be done, but the timing and other factors render it almost impossible. Without being in a position to see the event in real time, it is hard to imagine how the person controlling the remote detonation could coordinate with the soldier in the field. Without remote detonation, the soldier himself is the only hope. If the detonation malfunctions, or if the soldier is seized and restrained, the bombing mission will fail.*

Ahmed knew of bombings in Israel where a soldier had momentarily hesitated at the apex of a mission, had lacked faith at the critical moment. In some cases, remote detonation had saved the mission and martyred the hero. He asked Zlatin about such situations. In those cases, the detonation was triggered from mere blocks away, he said. Why do you ask about this? You will be alone, and in any event will not hesitate. On the last day of the explosives straining, Ahmed created three small dynamite bombs. All detonated with the predicted blast radii, blowing apart the ground, a tree, an in one case the carcasses of two dead goats. Three sticks, Zlatin said. I believe you are right, Ahmed.

His twelfth straight night on the job. Twin Rivers Day approached. His rescue of Shannon from her husband had been followed by a flurry of congratulations from the dancers and bar patrons, many of whom constantly sent drinks over to him, none of which he touched. Eventually Wilhelmina stopped bringing the drinks and started giving Ahmed the extra money at the end of the night. Most notably, his job became easier. The girls were all friendlier to him now.

Even the loner Belinda approached a day or two after his altercation with the crazy man everyone referred to as Gracie. "I just thought I should let you know, Gracie don't seem like much, but his family's got some money. They bailed him out of jail, and he's on house arrest out in West Caroline. He ain't supposed to leave the house or come near Shannon, but you never know with that fool. Just thought you should know." Ahmed smiled to himself. Belinda obviously believed he and Shannon were engaged in a sexual relationship.

He also noticed that the men who came to the bar gave him a wide, respectful berth. "These boys are scared shitless of you now, Jeremy," Curly cackled. "I ain't seen such exemplary behavior in here in all my fifteen years."

At the end of one night, Curly called him into her office and informed him that she would be increasing his pay to three hundred dollars a week. "I even picked up two new dancers this week, hot ones. One of 'em mentioned our class-A security as a reason to work here. Hah! I knew you was a good one."

Ahmed pretended to be grateful. Curly would never know he cared nothing for the salary.

Each night since his encounter with Gracie, he retired to his room after work. And each night Shannon—hazy, tired, and smelling of liquor—appeared and slept next to him. He had decided to allow it. It cemented the public perception that he was involved with Shannon. All the dancers believed it to be so. One, a brazen Indian girl, had tried to put her hands down his pants while he stood in the hallway after work one night. When Ahmed resisted, she gave him a look of mild annoyance and then yelled out for other dancers to hear, "Yeah, he must be taken."

As for Shannon, she never tried to engage him in sexual relations again. Two things Shannon did speak of as she drifted off to sleep with Ahmed lying next to her were Twin Rivers Day and Mayor Jamborsky. "That fifteen thousand dollars will change my life."

Two days before Twin Rivers Day, Curly called Ahmed into her office and gave him the phone. "For you, Mr. Popular. Now you got the damn mayor's office calling."

Ahmed took the phone and listened.

Back out at the bar, his mind raced. This was not bad news. In fact, the more he thought about it, the more he realized it might make his mission easier. Not just easier. More successful. Successful beyond Omar's wildest dreams.

But where in the world would he get an American business suit?

TWENTY-FIVE

MAY 16, 2009 — TWIN RIVERS, MONTANA

Gabe rushed up the stairs to his office, where Myrlene read a magazine with her feet on her desk.

"You see Redford yet?" she asked.

"Just came for the file," Gabe said. "On the way now."

"No, you're not," she said. "Pasquali just called. Said he needs you right now. At the Hunt Club."

"Hold the fort," Gabe said.

She looked down, frowned, and turned the page of her magazine.

Gabe parked on the gravel by the door to the Hunt Club. He'd never been invited, alone, to Pasquali's Club. In his mind, the Club had always been for Weasel Junction insiders, a place marked by years and years of the exclusive confidences of the town's real leaders. He wondered if his father had been on this very stoop, bracing himself to stroll into a room full of secrets that could bury the town and his own career.

Pasquali sat slouched on the leather sofa watching the news on the huge wall-mounted television. Without asking, Gabe proceeded to the bar and made a neat whiskey. He sat down in a lush leather chair near Pasquali.

"Thompson was right. This is gonna be a goat-ropin' wankathon," Pasquali said.

CNN's cameras showed a mostly empty Twin Rivers town square, a few workman still hammering away at the railing along the back of the stage. Large American flags hung on each side of the stage, and a Twin Rivers seal Gabe had never seen before screamed town pride from the front of the speaking podium.

And tomorrow, the town's mayor will announce a federal contract...

Pasquali hit the mute button."They don't know the half of it." He set down his drink and rested his hands on his massive belly. A laptop lay on the coffee table in front of him. For the first time, Pasquali looked tired to Gabe. "So, Mr. Lantagne, I need somebody I can trust around here, and I don't know if that person is you."

Gabe leaned forward, straining for the correct response.

Pasquali said, "I know everybody's got their balls in a wad about Twin Rivers Day, awards, stimulus packages, senators, governors, and whatnot, but that's never been my thing. But I'll tell you what I do care about it: a man was murdered in this town not five days ago and nobody seems to give a shit."

"I give a shit, Sheriff. But what can I do?"

Pasquali picked up his laptop. "Somebody killed Gillespie the very day he sought information on two people. One, Enos Terwilliger. Two, Jonathon Scruggs. Plainly, those two things bore some relation in his mind, and you haven't been too helpful in this regard."

"Ask away," Gabe said. "But I'm telling you, I have no idea. Whatever Gillespie found out, he made the connection on his own. I suppose he was planning to tell me that night."

"You're not understanding me, Gabe." Pasquali said. "I've always known, at least in part. Your extracurricular activities must have your head in the clouds, because you haven't been asking the right questions, and you usually do. At Gillespie's, I told you the FOIA request demanded jail information on Scruggs, and I informed you that he'd been bonded out of jail on that embezzlement charge. And you asked me no questions about that, Counselor."

Gabe took a sip of his whiskey. "Okay, who bonded him out?"

Pasquali leaned forward and placed a look of blistering scrutiny on Gabe as seconds passed. The small laptop seemed out of place in the hands of a country cop, but Pasquali fancied his gadgets—his TV, his iPhone, his little video camera.

"Egan?" Gabe said.

"Not Egan. Egan's got himself so well insulated he's the one person who could survive the outing of Twin Rivers." Pasquali opened one of a stack of files in front of him. "I've been tracking Scruggs's phone calls in real time over the last four days, and I've reviewed his last month's worth of old calls. Nothing special at the beginning of the month. His mother, some LA numbers he calls regularly—one of 'em's a talent agency—calls to some other knuckleheads from around town."

How did Pasquali know which numbers belonged to knuckleheads as opposed to anyone else in town? But this was Pasquali, after all, the same man who was reputed to have deleted jail records to help a Caroline County man beat a criminal case in Missoula. Town lore also said he'd doctored death certificates to help Caroline County residents get life insurance payouts. Gabe had no idea if the old stories were true, but if he had any sense of Pasquali's loyalties, they were not to his badge, and certainly not to the system, but to Weasel Junction. For him, justice happened behind closed doors. Like Phoenix, Pasquali traded on his own brand of smoke and mirrors, and in this way his infamous Hunt Club matched him well—a simple, worn exterior hiding a modern, well-equipped core.

"This is odd," Pasquali said. "Scruggs calls a UK number, Glasgow area, at 6:45 a.m. That got me looking further back, and Scruggs has been making and receiving calls from that number about once a month since January. Almost like clockwork. Always right at the beginning of the month. Now this here particular call comes, but in the middle of the month.

My records only cover this year, so I don't know how far back it goes yet."

"Family?"

Pasquali gave a skeptical look, clicked some buttons on the laptop, then turned it toward Gabe. It displayed a MapQuest image of Caroline County, complete with landmarks and street names. A small pushpin traveled Route 2 North. "This is Scruggs today at 5:42 in the morning."

"GPS? You're tracking him?"

Pasquali punched keys on his computer. Gabe was hardly surprised, either that Pasquali had access to this technology or that he would use it on Caroline County citizens. Gabe watched the pushpin wind its way up Route 2.

"So Scruggs wakes up at four-thirty in the morning in his car outside Ramhead's, then drives through town where he stops at the town square for seven minutes, then drives up Route 2 where he makes a phone call to Scotland at the Texaco next to the titty bar. He stays there for twelve minutes, then drives his truck along the dirt road below Mountain Road, where I lose the signal and haven't yet gotten it back."

Pasquali waited. Gabe again struggled to find the right question and came up empty.

"So why does an overeducated, hung-over good-for-nothing get up early," Pasquali said, "go into town to a place where nothing is open, then to gas station twelve miles away which also isn't open, then drive into the middle of nowhere and just stop?"

"I'm still not seeing it."

"You better be giving me all you got, boy." Pasquali's normal way was to cover his hardness with a cool, funny exterior. Gabe had not heard such sternness from the man before. Gabe met his stare.

"I got a question for you, Gabe, and your answer to this question is going to determine a lot of things. Most immediately, whether I trust you."

Gabe leaned back and sipped his whiskey. What was the old man talking about? Pasquali moved the computer from his lap and with amazing deftness reached towards Gabe, yanked the drink out of his hand, and sent it flying back over his own shoulder where it shattered against the wall under the animal heads. He barked at Gabe in a cold harsh whisper. "Where is your head, boy! You're Gabriel Lantagne. Now listen to my fucking question. What have you and Phoenix been up to since that night we found Gillespie, and I mean specifically."

Gabe stood, maintaining eye contact with Pasquali for just a second. Then he crossed the room. CNN silently flickered behind him. Pasquali watched Gabe patiently for his answer—the role reversal lost on neither. Gabe, who usually cross-examined the Sheriff. As to Pasquali's precise concern, Gabe had no idea, but the notion that Pasquali might believe that Phoenix knew something about Gillespie's murder jumped to his mind. Knew something, or even worse, had something to do with it. And then he realized that Pasquali was wondering the same thing about him.

"Since that night," Gabe said, "Phoenix and I have spent two nights together, one at the ranch, and then last night at her apartment. In between, she took me to the Angel Sky and showed me the barn, which you already figured out. I last saw her at her office, where she had a meeting with Senator Bryant."

Pasquali smiled. "You're a good man, Gabe."

In a flash, Gabe realized Pasquali already knew where he had been. At least where his jeep had been. He had wanted to see if Gabe would lie about it.

"You're tracking me too? And Phoenix?"

"Especially Phoenix. Only person of interest I haven't been able to tag is Terwilliger. The truck he usually drives is too far onto the Angel Sky property. That's one reason I kind of figured I could use your help. We go together, he won't be as suspicious. I can plant the device while he tells you about a new calf birth or some shit, whatever the fuck that dude talks about."

Gabe had never heard Pasquali, or any other person for that matter, cast even the slightest aspersion on Michael Terwilliger. Michael, the gentlemanly cowboy, was Caroline County.

"I've never had much use for the son," Pasquali said. "He can't live up to his old man. Now Enos, that guy was a walking piece of history. It's a shame he's gone. Enos would have a handle on this situation, let me tell you."

"Fine, but why do you need to track Michael?" Gabe said.

"You remember when he hung around after the town hall meeting while I was countin' the votes? When I read off the names of the voters from jail, and Thompson challenged Scruggs's ballot?"

"Yes."

"Of course I knew Scruggs was a county resident, but I wasn't gonna step out of my neutral role just then. Remember, I pocketed his vote until Glower fetched him from the jail so Floyd could do his thing."

"Yeah, so?"

"Michael was standing right there, right before the lights went out and Ayalette ran over, and he heard us talking about who knew Scruggs."

"We know Scruggs never worked at the Angel Sky."

"Exactly. Never worked a day at the Angel Sky before or since," Pasquali said. "No relation to Terwilliger that I can see."

"Right."

"And both Michael and Phoenix were standing there listening to us argue about Scruggs, and neither one of 'em said a word.

"What would they have said?"

"Manuel Foreva bonded Scruggs out of jail in January. And Foreva doesn't leave the ranch unless a Terwilliger tells him to."

TWENTY-SIX

MAY 16, 2009, 6:00 A.M. – TWIN RIVERS, MONTANA

Ahmed awoke early. Shannon snored beside him. It was horribly foolish to leave her sleeping in the room with his guns and cash, but Shannon had never shown any interest in delving into Ahmed's personal matters. She was content, it seemed, to wink at him at work and sleep next to him at night. He had been perfectly lucky, really, that Shannon was not of the temperament to ask questions. Before leaving the room, he watched her sleep for a moment. What a pretty girl, what a sad soul.

Ahmed wore his long black coat to hide his pistol. The first time in America he'd encountered police—on the snowmobile—his pistol felt as large as a cannon. That was not two weeks ago, yet now he strode without fear. He stepped slowly through the motel parking lot, across the back lot of Pandora's, and approached the Texaco station, which was closed. His contact must have known it opened at 7:00 and so planned to meet him at exactly 6:45. Ahmed stood alone, hands in his pants pockets, and waited.

Ahmed saw from a distance that the person who pulled his truck into the gas station was not the distinguished older man from the Pancake House but a young man with long blond hair. When the man parked and walked towards him, Ahmed noted his disheveled clothes. As the man got closer, Ahmed smelled the same sickeningly sweet, stale alcohol that had often emanated from Karim. The morning-after smell.

Ahmed nodded to the man.

"I did as I was told," he said. "It's in the truck."

Ahmed nodded again, perturbed by the man's sloppy demeanor. He followed the man to the truck, climbed in, and inspected the materials. He turned his back on the man without fear. When he pulled the plastic sheet away, he saw what he expected to see. Way too much of it.

"Only three?" the man asked, as if it were Ahmed's fault that he did not take all of the dynamite from the truck.

Ahmed looked at him scornfully.

"I thought you would take all of it..." Then, in the way that a fool's conversation skips from one topic to another, he said, "One more thing."

The man fumbled in his coat and pulled out a small package. Ahmed took the unopened envelope that had been through the American mailing system. The man then stepped away and dialed a phone number. A week earlier, Ahmed likely would have pummeled or even killed the man for engaging in such a sudden, unpredictable act without its purpose being known to him. But now, a day from his mission, things had changed. The matter was in God's hands, and Ahmed's heart had ceased to bother with fear. The man whispered into the phone, and then handed it to Ahmed. Ahmed was surprised the man expected him speak to some unknown person on the phone, but seeing no other way in the matter, he took the phone.

"Blain," Ahmed said into the phone. He listened, then handed the phone back to Scruggs.

Ahmed then turned away, his stomach churning and his temples pulsating. He looked up and down the road feeling anger and something else. Something buried away, or at least normally reserved for dark, quiet times. He faced the empty road and saw that no cars approached from either direction. The voice on the phone had shocked him. The month since he had heard it seemed years.

Congratulations, soldier. You're so close to your mission and to heaven. Your mother and your brother Abu will be proud to know of your success, and they will receive the full benefit of your actions. Omar saw them yesterday in your village. He stayed at a distance but told me to tell you they're doing well. We'll be watching them very, very closely. God willing, your mission will succeed. If not, perhaps Abu will come to camp and study with us? And I'm sure your mother could find a home here as well.

Ahmed felt his lungs contracting, unable to capture enough air. The snarling Scottish accent had given him additional instructions.

The fool standing in front of you knows nothing. He's the lackey of our friend in Montana and of no use once he's made his delivery. He'll give you not only dynamite but a cellular fuse. Use this fuse with your device. It will work better than one of Zlatin's makeshift contraptions. As for our delivery boy, kill him now. Be with God, soldier.

Ahmed said a quick prayer, turned, and faced his contact, breathing deeply and rapidly to soothe his screaming heart.

Ahmed drove along the narrow gravelly road, a high ridge on his left. On the ridge, he knew Route 2—called Mountain Road as it approached Twin Rivers—would carry substantial traffic soon. Not county residents, but commercial trucks passing through from the South, most of whom would never bother to stop in the town, even for gas, but highway signs posted the location of Texaco, the motel, and Pandora's Box. Ahmed drove as fast as appeared safe on the poorly maintained road, all the while scanning for a proper place. He knew that however far he went, he would have to run back to the motel without being seen.

Finally, he veered off the road and through a grassy field, hoping a hidden bog would not incapacitate the truck within view of the road. He then jerked a hard left and squeezed through a group of straggly trees, the truck banging loudly on many of them. Descending into a steep ravine, the truck stopped with a heavy jolt as its front end jammed between two trees. Ahmed got out and scanned the area. Trees and the steep ascent of the ravine blocked any view from the gravel road or Mountain Road on the top of the towering ridge.

As Ahmed opened one of the back passenger doors, his contact's eyes pleaded with him from above the hastily contrived muzzle.

There are many types of kidnappings, Omar said. Sometimes the mission will be planned, such as the abduction of a political figure, a journalist, an infidel spy, or a tourist. The methods for such must be well planned and involve multiple soldiers working from safe locations. The purpose, plainly, is not to injure or kill for its own sake, but to make a point. However, there may be other situations where a mujahid needs to abduct an enemy for a tactical reason—for example, when killing the person is not appropriate or prudent. In such cases, the soldier is forced to act quickly and improvise. Almost any clothes can serve to bind and silence even a strong man for hours

They practiced for days and learned how to incapacitate a person without creating permanent injury or death and to quickly bind hands, feet, and mouths. If one shoves a sock or a wad of cloth into an abducted man's mouth to silence him, he may panic and swallow it, choking himself to death, Omar said. Thus, if one must use such a method, make sure the object you use is a large one, with a broad surface area that cannot fit beyond the wide opening of the mouth.

The contact's bulging cheeks heaved with his heavy breathing; Ahmed would have to unbind the gag unless he wanted the man to die soon. He climbed partway into the back of the truck and pulled out his pistol. What had Scarface said to terrify his enemies? Ahmed screwed up his face, fixed his contact with a harsh glare, and aimed the gun at his face.

"Say hello to my little friend."

The man's eyes widened. Ahmad held the gun softly a few inches from his contact's head and put an index finger in front of his mouth. The man stared at him in panic before suddenly understanding and nodding frantically.

Ahmed tore the tight sliver of cloth, actually the bottom of his shirt, from his contact's face and pulled the rest of the wadded-up shirt out of his mouth. The man wheezed and coughed, gasping for breath, but did not deliberately trigger his vocal chords as far as Ahmed could tell.

"Leave town tonight," Ahmed said. "If you do not, I will find you and I will kill you…you fuckin' cockroach."

Ahmed ran hard, remembering the mountain trails at the camp. His heavy boots slowed him, but as his legs pumped, his lungs felt stronger and stronger. After about half an hour he used his arms to scramble up the ravine and, luckily, he crossed Mountain Road at a moment when no trucks roared around the corner. Fifteen minutes through the woods and he came up several hundred yards from Texaco. From there, it felt safe to walk along the road. The cool morning air felt good on his sweating skin. He crossed the Texaco parking lot towards the motel. Just as he got near his room, Shannon's door opened, and she leaned out, smirking at his heavy boots.

"Ever heard of running shoes?" She laughed. "If we're going shopping, let's get moving. I'm on at six." Without awaiting a response, she disappeared into her room.

Ahmed entered his room, retrieved his topi from the backpack, and went to the bathroom. He prayed in the small tile room. Running had made him feel strong. Which was a good thing. A good thing to be strong, and with God, for your last full day on earth.

TWENTY-SEVEN

MAY 16, 2009, 2:30 P.M. –
TWIN RIVERS, MONTANA

People had called Booker Wilson crazy fifteen years ago when he opened an upscale men's clothing store on River Street. He had the money to open the store anywhere he wanted, and the choice of Weasel Junction seemed absurd. The town had no discernible commerce, and the only people who wore suits were the lawyers at the courthouse. But by diversifying a little, adding some Western flair, and taking advantage of the tax-free environment, Booker's store now graced one of the most beautiful little town centers in Montana. No one would guess that River Street, the heart of Weasel Junction with its shops, theatre, and lovely town fountain, was surrounded by, well, pretty much nothing.

But things had changed, and fast. The town's wealth seemed to evaporate right around the time Mayor Pritchard was defeated by Michael Terwilliger's ex-wife, which was also right around the time old Terwilliger killed himself. And as bad things came in threes, the town started going to hell. Booker had voted against the mayor's cockamamie plan to bring terrorists to Weasel Junction, but he had to admit that fifteen thousand would help a lot. He would invest it in some kind of apparel that a glorified prison guard might want to wear. Anyway, he supposed times had changed, and he certainly didn't mind that Twin Rivers Day would bring a passel of out-of-towners, not to mention everyone in Caroline County, down to River Street the next day.

For now, though, business was dead. He sat on a stool behind the cash register, watching CNN. In fact, he could see a CNN truck outside his front door, already setting up for the big event.

A couple walked in, a thin young girl leading a stocky young man with a shaved head, maybe a Native American. The girl wore a long black coat which dragged behind her like a robe. It hung open, displaying her torn jeans and tight white T-shirt. What Booker noticed most was her pretty smile as she chatted to the stoic tough guy by her side.

The girl approached Booker, enthusiastically spinning and gesturing to her friend. "We're looking for a suit."

The man directed them first to the small rack containing the most expensive suits he stocked, all one thousand plus—a rack very few Twin Rivers residents perused for very long. He didn't want to discourage them exactly, only to alert them that this was not a cheap store. He could easily direct them to the trendy thrift store down the street.

But the girl examined the suits with a seeming expertise, quickly selecting a twelve-hundred-dollar Italian pinstripe.

"Yes," she said with finality. "But we need it tailored today."

Booker laughed, looking around and extending his arms. "Do I look busy?"

The young man paid at the register with a wad of folded hundreds but appeared very confused about the tailoring process. Booker beckoned towards the back. "Follow me, follow me."

Minutes later, Booker realized the only real tailoring required, aside from cuffing the trousers, was to let out the jacket's back and shoulders to accommodate the customer's muscular build. The young man stood in front of the three-way mirror, looking at himself in the suit. Finally, he cracked a smile.

"It suits you, you can admit it." Booker brushed the jacket's shoulders. "You look good."

The girl picked out some shoes for her companion, also expensive. The couple left the store, her arm entwined in his.

You can't go on first impressions with young people, but what a nice, attractive couple. Weasel Junction needed more like them.

TWENTY-EIGHT

MAY 16, 2009, 4:30 P.M. –
TWIN RIVERS, MONTANA

Gabe was surprised that Pasquali asked him to drive. He'd never seen Pasquali ride in a passenger in a car or travel otherwise than as the driver of his signature Suburban. The frivolity of the convertible jeep and the abdication of control seemed very un-Pasquali. Gabe thought back over the events of the last few days—hiring Gillespie, the murder, his night with Phoenix at the Angel Sky, the hearing, the barn. And finally, Beau Bryant and the detail-laden affair that never was.

"Hey, Sheriff?"

"You can call me Geno when nobody else is around." Pasquali held his hat in his lap as the wind blew over them.

"Why'd you call Phoenix up to Gillespie's that night if you didn't yet know the murder had anything to do with her case? Since when is the mayor called to crime scenes?"

Pasquali turned to face Gabe. "And I call myself a cop." He laughed, banging his fist on the dashboard. "I didn't call her up there. I assumed you did!"

Without a further word, Gabe pulled over and shut off the jeep, and the men looked at each other. "Phoenix couldn't have had anything to do with this, Geno."

"You never know what a person will do," Pasquali said. "She's running for governor, and if Gillespie was onto something, nothing can be ruled out. Michael Terwilliger cares about one thing—the ranch. And that's a topic not even I know everything about."

"Are you telling me everything you do know? About Enos Terwilliger? His death?"

"You know about The Trade now, which was why I originally believed somebody was hot to bury the topic of Terwilliger—and Scruggs, for that matter, if he was hooked up with it, which of course I still believe, or else why would Michael bail him out? But then I wondered why Michael didn't vouch for him that night behind the church. Everyone standing there that night knew about The Trade except you. So that leaves me with Michael acting secretively about Scruggs for no reason. Then we got Gillespie, who gets killed for asking around about Scruggs and Enos's cause of death."

"You investigated Enos's murder, didn't you?"

"Phoenix called 911 from her cell. She'd heard the shot from the house, but by the time she found the body, two ranch hands were already there. Manuel Foreva was one of 'em. Michael was a hundred miles away at the time. And Gabe, I grilled those two up one side and down the other. Both insisted that Enos was already dead, gun by his side, when they came up on the body—long before Phoenix made it down to the stream. I even polygraphed the younger fella and scared him so bad he quit the ranch and never came back. But he passed."

"Did you polygraph Manuel?"

"No," Pasquali said. "Manuel Foreva has lived at the Angel Sky since birth, his great-grandfather worked for Elijah Terwilliger. That's pre-Angel Sky. I know the man, and Manuel Foreva is not one to lie to cover up the murder of a Terwilliger."

"Okay, so Enos killed himself. The official version is correct. No cover-up, no nothing."

"There is one thing I haven't told you, and you can take this for what you think it's worth. Enos had a crazy streak, but knowing the man, I just don't see him killing himself. It was that night I realized The Trade had to end, 'cause as deep as I reach inside myself, I can't be sure I didn't let Enos's death go too easy for fear of the shit-storm that would have followed if the state police showed up at the Angel Sky. Lies beget lies."

"So why does it matter? And if it does, why does it matter tonight?"

Pasquali thought for a long moment before speaking. "You're a defense attorney. You know it's never about one thing, it's about, what do you guys call it, the *totality of the circumstances*. And here we have TR Day, the prisoner contract. Scruggs's spending money, Gillespie, and Terwilliger playing dumb on knowing Scruggs. And you know what else?"

Gabe waited.

"January. Phoenix announced that she wanted the prisoners in January. The same month Foreva bonded out Scruggs."

"And the same month Scruggs started getting calls from abroad," Gabe said.

"Nice catch." Pasquali folded his meaty arms and shut his eyes."We can't close the circle any better than that, at least not yet. Scruggs is coming nowhere near TR Day, that's settled, but I still wanna find out if Michael knows something we don't about Gillespie, Phoenix too, and why the hell this shit-storm has to coincide with the biggest gathering in this town's history. I got to consider even remote possibilities. Every angle, no matter how unlikely. Disasters, my friend, begin with the unexpected."

"In that case, I got an idea," Gabe said. "Several, actually."

"What are we gonna do?" Pasquali pulled out his can of Copenhagen and focused on the task of opening it with his fingernail. Gabe sensed no condescension in the question but another emotion, which surprised him. Relief. To have someone on his side. Someone else who might actually be able to do something.

"Nothing," Gabe said, "until tomorrow. But for now, you need to go over to the jail and assert some of your legendary influence."

"What?" Pasquali said.

"Let me worry about Michael Terwilliger, I'll explain tomorrow. We gotta get focused on TR Day security, since that's obviously our immediate concern. You talk about the unexpected; you're gonna love this."

Pasquali listened to Gabe's idea, then laughed. "Hah! Not bad. The Weasel Junction way. You ever consider sheriffin' instead of politics, you let me know. I'm getting old, case you haven't noticed."

Gabe's phone rang. He looked at the caller ID and then held the phone up to Pasquali so the sheriff could see that the incoming call was from Phoenix's cell phone. He spun the jeep around, back towards Twin Rivers.

As Pasquali climbed out of the jeep at the Hunt Club, Gabe realized he had a question that could not possibly be answered on a Friday night. Except maybe by Pasquali. "Geno, have you seen the divorce decree and settlement order for Michael and Phoenix?"

Pasquali frowned."I'm offended. What kind of a redneck operation do you think I'm runnin' here? When I miss something, Gabe, it's cause I want to miss it. I pulled that and all their other fuckin' records at the courthouse four days ago. The deed to the ranch, tax information, everything."

"Tell me about it."

Fifteen minutes later, Gabe and Pasquali, in separate vehicles, turned opposite directions on the town road, Gabe towards City Hall, and Pasquali towards the Twin Rivers jail.

TWENTY-NINE

MAY 16, 2009, 4:50 P.M. – TWIN RIVERS, MONTANA

Ahmed strolled along River Street with Shannon, the fancy shopping bag held by its plastic handles with one hand, his new suit in its sleek black carrying case over his shoulder with the other. He followed Shannon's pace as they crossed River Street to the shops on the other side. She walked close to him, bumping him occasionally. Ahmed tried to mimic the walking of the other men perusing the shops. Some hurried, but most walked slowly, taking time to gawk at the television trucks setting up near the stage at the end of River Street. Which was perfect, because Ahmed himself wanted to study the details of the entire square, the stage, and the low, metal security fence which was still being constructed. He scrutinized the rooftops: it would be difficult for a sniper to hide on them because most were just flat metal. The two-story shop windows provided little cover, as one could see well into them from the street. Only the imposing brick structure at the end of River Street, behind the stage, possessed the qualities important to concealing a sniper. He would meet the mayor the next morning at the back of City Hall, from where he and some others would proceed through the building to the public stage.

"It's so refreshing to know he can't hurt me now," Shannon said out of nowhere, smiling up at Ahmed. She must mean because Ahmed was with her and not because of the silly notion of the home confinement her husband had received as punishment for trying to kill her—which was no punishment at all for a worthless drunk. If news got out of such ridiculous punishments, Americans would surely commit more crimes in order to earn the right to be lazy. What a country.

Shannon put her arm behind Ahmed and steered him from River Street down a side road towards his motorcycle. "Did you hear that Senator Bryant will be on stage tomorrow? I bet you get to meet him!" She squeezed his arm. Ahmed was not overly familiar with American political leadership positions, but from Shannon's tone, senator was above mayor.

Ahmed had learned in the last two weeks that Shannon did not care if he never spoke, which was one of the reasons she was an ideal companion. In fact, he had hardly spoken since their arrival in town; of course, he never really knew what to say to Shannon.

"Thank you," he suddenly said.

Shannon turned, stopping him with a light touch. "For what?"

"Helping me buy the suit."

They cruised up Route 2 as dusk fell, a soft pink sky ahead of them.

"Big Sky!" Shannon yelled from the sidecar, pointing ahead, her finger crossing the expanse above and all around them.

Ahmed had no idea what her words meant beyond the fact that no person, no matter how oblivious, could fail to notice the beauty of God's earth at such moments. As the motorcycle rounded the bend just south of Texaco, Ahmed thanked God for his life.

THIRTY

Gabe opened the door to the mayor's office. The receptionist was already gone. Classical music drifted through the lobby from Phoenix's office—the much-used opera version of Beethoven's Ninth. It reminded him of driving along an empty highway in the Italian Alps. Or maybe a detergent commercial.

Gabe took loud steps towards Phoenix's office but entered the open door without knocking, sensing that Phoenix knew someone was there, knew it was him, and was waiting.

Feet on the desk, she was reclining in her plush mayoral chair and looking right at Gabe. She lowered the CD volume with a small handheld remote.

"We're ready," she said. "Speech's done. Beau's arriving at 11:30 to the back side of River. What I need to know is whether you'll be on stage. I'm prepped if you are, prepped if you're not, but I thought you might want to review my comments about you if you'll be accepting the first annual Richard Lantagne Citizen Award."

Phoenix maintained her relaxed demeanor, allowing a long silence to pass while Gabe approached and sat in one of the high-backed chairs in front of her desk—the same chair occupied by Senator Bryant hours before.

"The Richard Lantagne Award," he repeated flatly.

"There's also an annual Egan Crowne Scholarship for the football player, and an Amos Terwilliger Heroism Award—not annual, only when deserved. That's for the strip-bar guy. So will you be on stage or not? Being up there with Beau can't hurt your chances at the mayor's race, you know. But if you're out, you're out."

"You might have asked me before naming an award for my father."

Phoenix sighed. "Two things come to mind. One is that I do things, I don't ask permission to do things. That's why I'll be such a great governor. The other is that with all due respect to a helluva lawyer, a good guy, and a decent lay,"—she smiled now, the private Phoenix having fun—"you don't own the rights to your father's name. He was Weasel Junction's favorite son. Shit, I knew that before I moved here. There's scotch on the side bar."

"No, thanks." Phoenix squinted briefly at his refusal of the drink. She looked deeply relaxed. Contented. This was the way she celebrated her victories. Her moments of satisfaction after beating everyone else yet again. She celebrated alone. So did he.

"I've been talking to Pasquali about this Gillespie thing," Gabe said, "and I think you should consider the possibility that whoever killed him has further plans."

"That's Pasquali's job and I'm sure he can handle it."

"I mean plans for Twin Rivers Day."

"Like what?" Phoenix said. "Gabe, a terrorist didn't kill Gillespie. Nobody we don't know will be inside the town-square barricade tomorrow, not without a proper search. We have thirty armed men on staff."

"Trainees who haven't even been paid, yet alone trained."

"The contract was certified at 4:30 today." Phoenix said. "Our first check's in the mail. And by week's end, there won't be a living stalk of pot in Caroline County. We did it, Gabe. I know it wasn't pretty, and I respect the fact that you don't like everything about how it went down, but I need people I can trust. For the future. In the end, please see that what I've done, what we've done, has helped the town. Will save the town."

"And helped yourself."

"Of course. But I've got to get there. You have to get there before you can make change. Progress. It's a dirty business." Phoenix smiled sadly. "Not everyone is Richard Lantagne. Maybe you are, but I'm not. It doesn't mean I won't help people."

Again a silence, seemingly comfortable for Phoenix but not for Gabe. *Who makes their son sign a prenuptial agreement? Sometimes owning half a ranch is a pain in the ass.*

"Got a question for you," he said.

"Attorney-client." She remained reclined, eyes toward the ceiling.

"How did you end up owning half of the Angel Sky?"

No reaction. "Aaah. Good old Montana. Women are treated well in divorces here. But I don't like your suggestion. I married Michael because he was the most beautiful man I'd ever laid eyes on. I still feel for him. Of course, those kinds of feelings aren't always enough."

"No," Gabe said. "Enos made Michael sign a prenup. You told me that yourself. Keep it in the family, remember? The rancher boys' golden rule."

"I don't see what this matters, but he loves his daughter, and—"

"He could have kept Ayalette's full rights in the ranch intact without giving you anything. That would be keeping it in the family."

Phoenix's eyes flashed, and if Gabe had seen that look before, it had been only once, in the booth in Helena with Ron Westerman when he had threatened her. "Gabe, this has been an insane week, and it's not over. Tomorrow will be a great day for both of us, and I don't see what my family's troubles have to do with anything. Michael is a generous soul, and allowing me a portion of the ranch provided security so that I would stay in Weasel Junction."

"Bullshit. He could have set you up in town without giving you half the ranch—fifty percent of the biggest fucking private ranch in western Montana, and he did it in a way that could deprive

Ayalette of her inheritance. You're free and clear, and could bequest or even sell your interest in the ranch to anyone, anytime. I'm asking why."

Phoenix smirked and leaned back, sipping her drink. "So along with the sheriff, my attorney has been investigating me? You're engaging in Pasquali-envy, my friend. This is nothing, and what business is it of yours anyway?"

"Manuel Foreva bonded Scruggs out of jail," Gabe said. "Anybody who knows about the Angel Sky would automatically wonder if Michael ordered it. Or if you did. Gillespie may have been killed for investigating this exact fact. And yet you and Michael act as if you've never even heard of Scruggs. I also talked to Pasquali about Enos's death, and it was very interesting. I need to hear from you what happened. I'm trying to protect you and protect the town. Think about it. If it weren't for The Trade, Pasquali would have brought in the state police on the Gillespie murder, and when The Trade's gone, he'll do just that. Enos kills himself, and right after that, you get divorced, your prenup is dissolved, and you walk away a multi-millionaire. You can't believe these questions will never be asked. And you know what else? While you're at it, I want you to tell me who called you to go to Gillespie's the night he was killed, because it sure as hell wasn't me. If you know something about Gillespie, anything, if the Gillespie murder had to do with The Trade, or Michael, or Enos, and you helped to cover it up, you will not only never be governor, you'll go to fucking jail, just like Westerman threatened. I'm your lawyer. Tell me. Now. Your excitement about Twin Rivers Day is blinding you to the immediacy of this problem."

When he finished his grand bluff about learning details from Pasquali—fat chance she'd ever believe the circumspect sheriff would invite him that far into the town—Gabe braced himself for the blast. He was shocked that he wasn't facing Phoenix's icy stare or phony smile. Instead, in her frozen, almost skeletal mask of tears, he saw that she believed Pasquali had told Gabe all he knew. Whatever that was.

"Attorney-client," Gabe said, hoping the legal bond of trust meant something more to her than the promise of a friend, because its strength turned not on the warmth of the human soul but the cold assertion of a right.

A small whimper escaped Phoenix and her drink fell from her hand. Either she was suffering the most soul-wrenching form of sadness, or she was a sociopath. After a few minutes, her rapid shallow breaths slowed and her chest stopped heaving. She seemed to be steeling herself to speak. When she did, her voice came across low and steady. Controlled. A glimmer of the efficient manager in her, reaching out from the drowning depths.

"I hardly remember how it started," she said. "Enos was so like Michael yet so much different. Before long, he couldn't stay away from me."

Gabe sat, ear to the well, and the stone fell deeper and deeper into the black silence.

THIRTY-ONE

MAY 16, 2009, 10:00 P.M. – TWIN RIVERS CITY JAIL, MONTANA

Grizzly Redford lay flat on his bunk, fully awake though the dawn had just poked in through the narrow window slats. Jeff Jeffords, the man on the bunk above him, serving time on his third drunk-driving charge, ripped a huge fart in his sleep. Somehow, Grizzly's cellmate had managed to sleep all through the night and half the day, as if his hangover was so bad it lasted clean through his two-week sentence. Grizzly, on the other hand, slept short and light in jail. Instead, he read. Everything he could get his hands on. *The Bible*, though he wasn't too religious, *Time Magazine*, though he did not follow politics, and *People*, though he couldn't give a rat's ass about Hollywood celebrities. *Field and Stream* he digested thoroughly, and of course, *The Weasel Junction Wallflower*.

Pasquali was decent enough for a cop. Grizzly couldn't claim the old sheriff had ever done him wrong. His lawyer was a different story. Grizzly had called his office from the jail phone every day since his conviction, eight straight days, and never been put through. Gabe was good and had helped him in the past, but this was bullshit.

The thing that bothered Grizzly the most was that he had told the truth in court. Sure, he should have told Gabe about the Arab dude from the beginning, but law was a tricky business, and he liked to play his cards close to the vest. Fuck it. At this point, he just wanted out of jail with as little damage done to his hunting rights as possible. But then there was TR Day, and Grizzly was nagged by the worry that something big was going to happen. Something bad. It just didn't feel right, such a huge celebration, the cash everyone in town would soon receive, and all with that Taliban motherfucker from the woods still out there.

Suddenly his cell door banged open, and Pasquali stood in the doorway, leaning against the wall, his gut, as usual, hanging over his belt, a thoughtful smile on his face.

Grizzly stood. "My lawyer finally show up?"

"Lantagne's not here," Pasquali said. "But he did you one better than a legal visit. Much better. And you best not let him down."

Grizzly just stared at the fat old Sheriff.

"You're being released on bond. In exchange for one day of work release."

"Work release? I ain't got a job, and you know it, Sheriff."

"Now you do."

Grizzly shuffled down the hall behind Pasquali, hardly able to believe his luck. When they got to the booking area, Deputy Glower handed him a bag filled with his possessions, including his street clothes.

"You're on special security detail for TR Day," Pasquali said.

When Grizzly heard the details, he was shocked.

"You damn well better be as good a marksman as you claim, my friend. You damn well better. And if you do anything but follow my express orders, you're going straight to federal court for that grizzly, you got me?"

Grizzly's hands shook as he wriggled out of his jail jumpsuit and quickly dressed in his hunting outfit, the one he'd worn when he was arrested. Then he stood straight before Pasquali and Glower, a feeling stirring in him that he had not enjoyed in many, many years. Not since the Army.

"I got you, Sheriff." Grizzly loved the clipped crispness in his own words. "I won't let you down."

THIRTY-TWO

MAY 16, 2009, 10:15 P.M. – TWIN RIVERS, MONTANA

Ahmed knelt in the center of his room. On this mission, his prayers had often been rushed. Not like back in his village, or even at the camp, where, among Muslims, he could take proper time to pray and meditate. He practiced clearing his head, taking steady breaths from his diaphragm. Thoughts interrupted from every direction, but he let them go. Ahmed's father had taught him to meditate. He had initially cursed his inability to control his own mind. Even at fourteen he could control his body better than most men—in sports, in fighting, in juggling balls to please his little brother. He could run through and around the village with Abu on his back, skinny little Abu who liked mostly to read on the front porch. Ahmed could run as if unburdened even with Abu squeezing his neck and squealing. But his mind was as undisciplined as any stray dog.

Thoughts will always intrude, his father said. Just let them drift away as they will. Imagine a bubble. Let the thoughts float away like soap bubbles. Let them come, just do not grasp them. As time goes by, they will come less, and then stop.

Ahmed let thoughts of the last month bubble away. Of Canada and Adams and Yusef and the fat woman at the Pancake House and Shannon. And those thoughts drifted off, along with the thoughts of the camp, and of Omar and Karim and the training. And of his village, and his father and mother and Abu and the police who walked roughly out the door gripping his father's arms.

Some can meditate so deeply that they float above their bodies, his father said, able to see the world, including themselves, as God sees them. They are in the presence of God. Feeling his awesomeness, his grandeur. They may feel the urge to hide themselves, but if they sit still in the moment, they have an experience that changes them forever. Have you experienced this, Ahmed asked. His father laughed. Of course not, do I look like a monk? It is enough of a job to worry about this village without adding enlightenment to my problems. His father laughed, his hearty, joyful laugh that served to balance his deadly serious side.

Ahmed's mind had gripped the memory of his father instead of letting it bubble away. But he kept sitting and kept breathing, and the bubbles floated away and burst until hardly any came.

Ahmed started with a shiver. He looked at the clock. One-thirty in the morning. Three hours since he sat to meditate, and he felt a calm invigoration more still and yet more active than he had ever known. He prepped for morning and then lay in bed in the soft light of one far bulb. He had always believed that his decision to leave his village for the training camp had been the most clear-headed, conscious, and directed decision of his life—the moment when he had been closest to God. As his relaxed muscles melted into the sheets, he realized that God had spoken to him once again. He felt a deep sense of peace, the absolute absence of fear or anxiety. This bliss must be what Shannon feels from consuming drugs and alcohol. How fortunate for him that his peace came instead from knowing God's will. From truly, finally, understanding what God wished for him. And the rewards that would follow.

When Shannon entered the room, Ahmed pretended to be fully asleep. She rubbed his bare stomach and heated his neck with her alcoholic breath.

THIRTY-THREE

MAY 16, 2009, 10:30 P.M. –
TWIN RIVERS, MONTANA

"When I moved into the ranch house, you got to understand how it was." Phoenix's eyes were still glassy, but a new drink sat on her lap. "I'm thirty-five years old, independent, never been married, never even really lived in Montana since high school, and here I am living in this splendiferous mansion, and with no job. Enos's room was on the far side of the house and our suite was on the other, but still, you're like surrounded by this entire Terwilliger thing. I've already told you, Michael rides the ranch. It's forty-seven miles at its widest point, with camps all over the place. He'd be gone two, three days at a time and then come riding in. So soon enough it's Enos and me having dinner, and then Enos and I having drinks. I think I was angry at Michael for the whole setup, but I can't blame him. I swear, Gabe, I don't understand this piece of myself. It's like, one day I'm the bride of this beautiful man, and I mean physically but also, inside. He may be a bore but he's a good person. And the next day I'm sucking his father off in the living room, practically begging him to stick it in me right there. It was like Enos knew where on the ranch Michael would be, and once the staff left, it's the two of us in the house. This is when we started talking about me running for City Council and the whole thing about eliminating The Trade. I mean, the guy was mentoring me. And then we would go to his room and he would fuck me."

Phoenix stood and walked across the room for another drink. Her gait and blank stare testified that these disclosures were both torturous and liberating, whether or not precisely true.

And yet, a part of Phoenix, a dark part, delivered the story as something less than shameful. Something, in fact, of a boast. Does a person need to reach such depths to earn moments of occasional perfection, to differ oneself from the army of blanched-out souls like himself?

"This went on for two years, believe it or not, until that day when Manuel called the house and asked me to ride down to the stream. Enos was dead. Michael sat on the stream bank. 'I don't know what to do,' Manuel said."

"I thought Michael was out of town."

"That was our story. All Michael said to me, and all he has ever said to me concerning my affair or his father's death, was, 'You had to know this would happen.' Of course Michael is a fool and wanted to turn himself in and take the consequences. I wouldn't have it. I protected him, got Manuel and Elian on the right page, and we moved on. Frankly, I was a little worried about Manuel, always have been. He was Enos's guy, you know, Enos's generation of the Terwilliger-Foreva saga. Manuel, like just about everyone else around here, revered Enos and felt ambivalent about Michael. But I think he realized we were all royally fucked, not to mention the whole town, if a state police investigation swarmed down on the ranch. Plus, let's face it, everybody likes Michael. Respects, maybe not. But likes, always."

"And Pasquali?"

"I'm sure he didn't buy everything, but he has no clue about Michael. Michael was miles into Angel Sky country before Geno showed up. But think about it, what was even he gonna do? See, this is part of the whole reason I always wanted to end The Trade. It's all rosy on the outside but every major player holds the key to the future for all of the others. Or the key to a jail cell. Pasquali hates that part of it as much as I do, which is the main reason he joined my team to end the Trade."

"And the ranch? The prenup?"

Phoenix met his eyes and then smiled like a naughty but scolded child. "A Western politician needs a ranch, Gabe."

Kerplunk.

Gabe realized he would never, could never, understand the magnitude of Phoenix's crimes because the level of premeditation would be locked away forever in her heart, perhaps even from her.

Hi, are you Gabe Lantagne? I met your father on his last campaign...

But as with other clients he had known—compulsive and skillful liars who could fool an experienced judge, lawyer, or cop with their layers of obfuscation—Phoenix actually telegraphed the truth when she told it. He believed her. And, after all, it made sense.

Manuel Foreva would never cover up the murder of a Terwilliger. Unless it was committed by a Terwilliger. If Phoenix had killed Enos on Angel Sky property, the staff would have taken her down. For that reason—among others, he hoped—she never would have done it. Enos wasn't killed by steely calculation. He was killed by red-hot rage.

Gabe's phone buzzed. Pasquali. He stood.

Phoenix appeared less upset now and actually smiled weakly under her red-rimmed eyes. "Attorney-client."

Gabe turned to leave. But Phoenix spoke again.

"As far as Manuel bailing that guy out, I know nothing about it, but I assure you if Michael had anything to do with it, he had a good reason. I'm telling you, Gabe, Michael doesn't have a malicious bone in his body."

By telling him about Enos's murder under the attorney-client privilege, Phoenix had won yet another victory. He could now never reveal the truth without giving up his career. For her, that made him the perfect friend.

Gabe returned Pasquali's call as he hurried down the City Hall stairs, the completed wooden TR Day stage looming above him.

"You're gonna want to see this shit." Pasquali said.

THIRTY-FOUR

MAY 16, 2009, 11:50 P.M. – TWIN RIVERS, MONTANA

Gabe followed Pasquali's directions and parked his jeep behind the Suburban on the gravel road beneath Mountain Road. He could see the light through the trees and down the ravine. Probably Pasquali's flashlight. His steps were loud in the perfectly quiet night. Pasquali stood near the back of a truck, its tailgate opened, flashlight scanning the inside. The bashed-up vehicle was wedged between two trees, tires flat. Pasquali did not turn.

"Holy shit," Gabe said.

"Scruggs's truck."

Gabe studied the neatly bunched bundles of dynamite. Six bundles, with an ominous tangle of wires and electronics on top.

"I think it's a remote fuse or trigger," Pasquali said. "It's not a timer. It looks cellular."

"Geno, let's get the fuck out of here, it could go any minute."

"I don't think so." Pasquali said. "I think this shit is going to be triggered tomorrow. Why here, I have no idea. Are you seeing what I'm seeing?"

"I just see dynamite," Gabe said. "Enlighten me."

"There are five bundles of six, and one bundle of three."

Nothing.

"Dynamite is sold in dozens."

"Three sticks missing," Gabe said. "Where's Scruggs?"

"No idea. He's not here, but this is sure as shit his truck."

"How are we gonna defuse this thing?" Gabe asked. "Without bringing in the state police, that is?"

Pasquali paused, and, as he often did in such moments, packed his lower lip with snuff. "We're not. We're not gonna do anything of the sort."

"Huh?"

Gabe heard a noise behind them, and Deputy Glower appeared at the top of the ravine. Pasquali briefed him.

"Take shifts. Nobody gets near this truck. Watch it from the top of the ravine. Between eleven and one tomorrow, we'll need three deputies on this detail, evenly spread at a distance to make sure nobody approaches this truck. And I want video on it—with the feed straight through to my phone."

"What's gonna happen between eleven and one?" Glower asked, his Adam's apple quivering on his thin neck.

"Twin Rivers Day, Sherlock."

"You telling the mayor about this?" Gabe asked.

Pasquali did not reply.

Gabe and Pasquali walked towards the cars, flashlights illuminating the ground before them, cold darkness all around.

"Where are you going?" Gabe asked.

"Home to sleep. You should do the same."

"What about Scruggs? Aren't you gonna look for him?"

"He's either dead or long gone."

Gabe parked in front of his office and was surprised to see that Myrlene was actually there, sitting on the steps next to a bottle of beer, smoking a cigarette. He approached slowly, communicating surprise with his eyes. Without speaking, he sat next to her on the porch, and they both watched the street for a moment.

"Want a beer?" she said.

"I don't drink. What the hell are you doing here after midnight?"

Myrlene stood up and walked inside. Gabe followed. He made

a move to flick on the downstairs light but Myrlene touched his hand, indicating she wanted it to stay dark. Gabe winced. He'd been meaning to tell her they should stop their affair, and he was in no particular mood to have that conversation tonight.

In the muted street light coming through the front blinds, Gabe could see someone lying on the couch. He approached and bent close. He saw the scraggly, scratched-up, sleeping face of Jonathon Scruggs.

"He showed up this afternoon. You've been ignoring my calls and texts. He said he knew you were the best lawyer in town and that he needed one badly. Said he didn't know where else to go and he can't go home. Says a Cuban gangster abducted him and plans to kill him. He thinks the Cuban is going to blow up something in Twin Rivers."

"Call Pasquali." Gabe knelt close to Scruggs, listening to his rough boozy breath.

"He's all over the place," Pasquali said. He had just returned from Glower's car, where he had placed a handcuffed and dejected Jonathon Scruggs. Pasquali sat on Myrlene's desk. Myrlene and Gabe leaned back on the couch.

"He obviously doesn't know his dynamite has been rigged to blow up his own truck in the same spot the supposed gangster let him go. The story about a Cuban gangster is bullshit, but he believes it from the way the guy talked or some shit. But he did have some valuable info."

"What?" Gabe said.

"It's garbled. You know he's drunk, kind of beat up, and had duct tape residue on his face and hands, so I believe that part. Says when he got locked up in January, some dude, turned out to be Manuel Foreva, turned up to bail him out. Foreva said he worked for a British dude who was willing to hire Scruggs over the phone to do various tasks. Foreva would deliver Scruggs cash for the little jobs he did for the dude. Mostly, Scruggs provided the information about the town through text messages and texted photographs—the jail, the police, the town folk. Basic stuff. Last week the Brit called Scruggs and offered him thirty grand to deliver some dynamite to a guy, who turned out to be this Cuban. At the exchange yesterday, the gangster abducted him and stole his truck."

"What does Foreva know?"

"Can't tell." Pasquali held up his palms, shaking his head as if to denote the absurdity of the whole thing.

"It's sure not good old Weasel Junction anymore," Myrlene said.

"So what now?" Gabe asked.

"I'm keeping Scruggs in protective custody until we sort this out, at least until after TR Day," Pasquali said. "First off, nobody gets anywhere near TR Day unless we know the person. No strangers. Period. Only credentialed press and Caroline County residents, all of whom will be searched at the checkpoints. Second, Michael Terwilliger and Manuel Foreva do not get near TR Day. Those two are priority one until we figure this out. I'll have a man with Scruggs at the jail to show him pictures e-mailed from us of anybody at TR Day who matches the description of this Cuban guy. I tell you, if Terwilliger had anything to do with Gillespie or this dynamite shit, he's fucked." He shot a glance at Gabe. "All of it, come what may."

Pasquali continued on with Glower and Myrlene about TR Day security until Gabe interrupted him. "Terwilliger won't be at TR Day. And I don't think he's behind anything. But I know how to find out."

"How?" Pasquali asked.

"To start with, the ranch isn't the only thing he cares about." Myrlene made coffee while they talked.

"I've used stupider ideas." Pasquali smirked and picked up his hat, placing it carefully on his head. "Security detail begins at eight." He walked out. Gabe looked at the clock: 4:10 a.m.

Myrlene and Gabe stayed on the couch in silence for a few moments. Then Myrlene said, "You know, far be it for me to make such a suggestion, but why wouldn't Pasquali call in the state police or the FBI? I understand this town likes to keep things in the family, but isn't this a little beyond, well, extreme?"

Gabe sighed. "It's a long story."

"You in a hurry?'

So Gabe told her. Twin Rivers was home to America's biggest pot growers and had been for thirty years. Myrlene was, after all, a member of his law office and the one person on earth with whom he could lawfully share Phoenix's secrets.

THIRTY-FIVE

MAY 17, 2009, 9:00 A.M. – TWIN RIVERS DAY, TWIN RIVERS, MONTANA

The high-powered scope on the rifle lying beside him was better than anything Grizzly Redford had ever used, even back in the army. On top of City Hall, he leaned, seated, against the towering red-brick pillar. From his vantage point, by rotating around the pillar, he could see three hundred sixty degrees. He scanned the crowd in front of City Hall with binoculars. His steady hands told the story of his previous nine days of sobriety. His steady mind, he believed, came from doing something *important*.

Use the binoculars. Under no circumstances are you to aim this rifle unless ordered to do so. You see your man, or anything suspicious, call me on the walkie, and await instructions.

Grizzly took a deep breath, confident that he would follow Pasquali's instructions perfectly. He examined face after smiling face with the binoculars.

THIRTY-SIX

MAY 17, 2009, 9:20 A.M. – TWIN RIVERS DAY, TWIN RIVERS, MONTANA

Ahmed coasted down Mountain Road towards the town so as not to splatter his suit with dirt or dust from the road. It was indeed apparent that Twin Rivers Day would draw a crowd. There were more cars on the road than usual, especially for a Sunday so early in the morning. Ahmed swung onto River Street and quickly saw that a barricade as well as the crowd would prevent him from driving far; besides, he didn't like being seen on the distinctive motorcycle. He parked at the end of a row of cars on a side street and walked down another side street in the direction of the City Hall building at the end of the street. He knew he looked businesslike, worse even than the scurrying businessmen in Islamabad. As he crossed the street, he imitated the walk of an American businessman, laughing to himself. The bottom of his black overcoat trailed behind him. It was like a cape, fluttering in the wind to make him bigger than he was.

Ahmed rounded the corner, making a left as the crowd thinned, and saw a policeman checking identification and searching people as they funneled inside the metal fence. He passed them, scanning the back of City Hall for his appointed arrival location. *Be at Peace.* A short man at the door waved frantically in his direction, and Ahmed soon realized the man was beckoning him. He made eye contact and smiled.

"Come on, come on, Jeremy Blain, right? We're gathering at ten." The man wore a silly small tie, the kind like a ribbon on his neck, and gestured, even spoke, like a woman. He extended his skinny, somewhat feminine hand. Ahmed stepped forward confidently even though two armed policeman flanked the door.

"I'm Oliver Crawford, the Mayor's assistant. The award winners are gathering down the hall waiting on the mayor. I'll be instructing you on the ceremony."

Ahmed shook the man's hand and followed him through the door without glancing at the policemen. When he got inside, his heart relaxed. There were no policemen inside at all. No metal detectors, none of the trappings of official presence and scrutiny he had spent weeks fearing.

He entered a small windowed room that looked out at the back of the stage and the mounting crowd in front of it.

"Make yourself comfortable, Jeremy. This is Gregory Hunter and his family. He's receiving the town scholarship. A great football player, I hear." The boy was big and muscular, but carried himself with the movements of a young dog before it learned the shape of its body. No one to fear. The parents shook his hand politely. An obese mother and a sagging father, whose body foretold his son's future.

The homosexual then began to instruct them on how to accept their awards. Ahmed just stood quietly, looking out the window at the stage. The clock on the wall said 10:10.

Perhaps his previous, positive experience with the fat sheriff had softened his instincts. Or it could have been that the man, despite his bulk, carried himself with such a casual manner that he did not betray his intentions through heavy steps or edgy movements. However it happened, Ahmed suddenly found himself staring down the barrel of the sheriff's pistol. The football boy's mother screamed. Another policemen quickly ushered the family out of the room. Ahmed considered the possibility that he could kill the Sheriff without being shot, but decided against it. The fat man and his gun were too far away. Instead, he turned from the policemen, and looked out the window, relaxing his muscles.

"Easy, Jeremy," the sheriff said. "This could all be just a big misunderstanding."

A third policeman relayed a whispered message to the sheriff and delivered it very carefully so as not to disrupt the man's concentration. The sheriff issued several orders without removing his eyes from Ahmed's. Ahmed could not hear the precise nature of each order, but he did hear 'Ramatin.'

To Ahmed's surprise, the Sheriff ordered the other policeman out of the room. Now the small room contained only the two of them. Ahmed wondered if the Sheriff perceived the full extent of the danger before him.

"Start by slowly opening up that coat," the policeman said. Ahmed opened coat jacket slowly with his left hand

"Take the coat off, move slow, and put it gently on the table," the fat man said. The gun did not shake or waver from pointing straight at Ahmed's lower chest, the perfect place to aim a gun— unlike the head, the target of an untrained soldier.

Ahmed obeyed. Taking two unhurried steps, the sheriff placed himself into a position where he could feel the coat without substantially changing his distance from Ahmed. "Next, the jacket."

Ahmed repeated the procedure with his suit coat.

"Now raise your left hand above your head and pull out your shirt with your right, show me your bare chest and stomach." Plainly, the sheriff had perceived that Ahmed was left-handed, but likely did not know he could use both hands, arms, and feet equally well. Ahmed did as he was instructed, maintaining eye contact with the man.

"All right, very, very slowly, empty your pants pockets on the table, then unbutton your pants, and let them fall."

The man was not attempting to humiliate him, but checking for explosive devices or weapons without having to come too close to him. Ahmed again did as he was told, laying down a wad of dollar bills on the table along with his driver's license. He dropped his pants, the belt buckle hitting the ground with a metallic clink.

"Turn around slowly and keep the left arm up and the belly exposed."

Ahmed turned, and when he again faced the man, he saw that the gun was lowered.

"All right, fix yourself, and have a seat."

Ahmed righted his pants and shirt, replaced his jacket, and sat down at the opposite side of the table so that the table was between him and the fat man, who still stood, gun at his side.

"Boy, I got you for buying dynamite, kidnapping, threats to bomb, threats to kill, and rigging a truck to blow sky-high. Unless you want me to arrest you and call the FBI, I suggest you tell me who the fuck you are, where you're from, and what the hell you want from us here in Weasel Junction."

Ahmed paused for some time, not to consider his reply, but rather to reflect on the fact that he had planned to die today, and probably still would.

"My name is Ahmed Ilyas Khan. I am visiting from Pakistan. I need to go home."

THIRTY-SEVEN

MAY 17, 2009, 10:10 A.M. – TWIN RIVERS DAY, TWIN RIVERS, MONTANA

Gabe, stationed by Egan at the main barricade checkpoint, held his walkie close to his ear. He began running towards the back of City Hall before Grizzly even finished speaking. He was vaguely aware of Pasquali's response. *Hold tight, Redford. Hold tight.* Gabe's legs cranked, but he was forced to take the indirect path— far around the barricade—all the while dodging through the crowd.

"Pasquali's in the last room on your left, alone with the suspect," Glower said, as Gabe, out of breath, arrived at the back door to City Hall, pistol in one hand, walkie in the other. "Redford called him in from the roof, and then Scruggs ID'd his newspaper photo as the Cuban. Ed and Doug are searching his room up the motel as we speak."

"Where's Phoenix?" Gabe scanned the back parking lot of City Hall and noted it was roped off and empty. Scattered revelers filed along the ropes and headed for the manned entrances around the front, but for the most part the back lot stood quiet.

"Not here yet."

"Does she know?"

"The sheriff said need-to-know," Glower said, "and he decides who needs to know."

"Egan?"

"He's running the show out front with a couple of deputies."

"I'm going in." Gabe started to move past Glower, who raised his eyebrows in what appeared to be intimidated skepticism until Pasquali's voice barked through his lapel intercom.

"Send Lantagne in. No one else."

Gabe had never before laid eyes on Jeremy Blain, the heroic if unassuming bouncer. But the young man sitting across the small conference table from Pasquali did look like his Wallflower picture even with the addition of a thousand-dollar pinstripe suit. His overcoat lay neatly across the table. He didn't appear distressed or anxious, rather sort of bored. Gabe sensed no tension, either in expressions or movements, between the thick-shouldered young man with the shaved head and Pasquali. Pasquali's cuffs remained on his belt. The man rested his chin on a palm. His eyes moved slowly from Pasquali to Gabe as Gabe approached the table.

"All right now, tell this man what you just told me, starting with who you are," Pasquali said.

The man breathed a small sigh, as if to consider, but not as if he doubted himself, rather to signify an unpredictable though petty event.

"My name is Ahmed Ilyas Khan. I'm visiting from Pakistan, and I need to go home."

Gabe looked at Pasquali, eyes widening.

"He's clean," Pasquali said. "And so's his motel room."

Gabe sat next to Pasquali and listened to the five-minute narration from Jeremy Blain or whatever his name was, who spoke slowly and with very controlled English.

"Wait here," Pasquali said to Blain, and Gabe followed Pasquali out of the room.

Eyes half shut and arms folded, the old man slumped against the closed door. Gabe could see his mind cranking, the whirs and machinations working overtime. *Your problem is, you don't know nothing about politics.* Maybe Pasquali had been partly right, but in the end, Pasquali, Phoenix, and Michael were easy to read when Gabe stayed with the basics. Pasquali cared about Weasel Junction. Phoenix, herself. And Michael, Ayalette.

Gabe took out his phone and looked at Pasquali.

"Do it," Pasquali said. As if on cue, Phoenix and Ayalette entered the back door of City Hall, both beaming. They held hands and walked slowly, Phoenix's heels clicking on the slick stone tiles. Ayalette waved, looking like a cowgirl in her hat and riding boots.

Thankfully, Michael answered the phone on the third ring. "Hey, Gabe." He sounded as good-natured as ever. "Aren't you busy with all the bigwigs downtown? What is it, Earth Day or something?" He laughed.

"Actually, yeah, sorry to bother you. Here's the problem…"

Phoenix and Ayalette were halfway down the hall now, Ayalette skipping and pulling her mother faster towards Gabe and Pasquali.

"Phoenix is busy, we're waiting to go onstage, and Ayalette is freezing, all she has is her riding shirt, so can you get somebody to run a jacket down here, something that fits her—you know it's on TV and all." Gabe awaited a gasp. At least a pause. Something.

"Ha!" Michael laughed. "Typical. I thought Lettie agreed she shouldn't miss training. Typical. Like mother, like daughter. Sure, I'll send Manuel down with a jacket."

"Thanks." Gabe hung up.

Pasquali winced. For whatever reason, he must have wanted Michael to be guilty. Which made sense, of course. Pasquali was a master of the small-town game, and such a master won on the simple moves. But Pasquali had a weakness, in some ways a monumental one; he really didn't understand the world outside Weasel Junction. Like who might actually benefit from Phoenix's fiery death on national television.

"Well, are we ready?" Phoenix stopped, feet together, holding her arms out to the side. *Check me out.*

"I imagine so," Pasquali said, thereby adding another vow of silence to his ever-growing list—this one between him and Gabe.

"Good," she said. "You know, it's a damn good thing Twin Rivers sticks together because we sure can't count on anyone else."

"Huh?" Gabe said.

"Beau just cancelled. His security team is on the way back to Helena. Something about a Foreign Affairs Committee call. And you know, he's full of it. He was calling all the way from his Helena office. Which meant he left TR last night. Which means he never planned to come at all." Phoenix shrugged.

Gabe wanted to look at Pasquali but did not. The man didn't deserve an *I told you so.*

"How's the crowd?" Phoenix asked.

"Huge," her assistant said, appearing excitedly from down the hall.

Gabe and Pasquali went back inside the room where Ahmed Ilyas Khan waited. This time, Gabe did all the talking.

When they were done, Pasquali stood up and swung open the door. "Come on out, Blain, time to meet the mayor."

THIRTY-EIGHT

Phoenix and the other stage participants gathered with her assistant, chattering about stage instructions. Pasquali and Gabe waited by the back door of City Hall. Moments later, Manuel Foreva rushed in with a little girl's jacket in his fist. When he saw Pasquali and Gabe, he smiled.

"Manny, we'd like to have a quick word with you." Pasquali ushered him into a dusty library by the door. Gabe followed.

"Manny, we don't have much time before TR Day kicks off, so I gotta make this quick." Pasquali eyes bored into Manuel's, communicating God knows how many pieces of unstated, obscure leverage Pasquali had over a man like him. Over anyone in Twin Rivers for that matter.

"I know Senator Bryant and Enos were old friends," Pasquali said. "Close friends. And I know you loved Enos. It makes sense you have a continuing friendship with the senator. Personally, I don't care if you make some extra cash giving information to Bryant now and then. Maybe about The Trade, or Phoenix. But I need you to make a phone call for me, and say exactly what I tell you to say. If you do it, then nobody—not Michael, not Phoenix, and not the state police—ever need to hear a word about the shit I have on you."

Without awaiting a response, Gabe dialed the number while Pasquali instructed a white-faced Manuel. Gabe held the phone a few inches from Manuel's face so he and Pasquali could hear the call. It rang only once, even though it was a Sunday.

"Senator Bryant's Helena office," a female voice said.

"I need to speak to Senator Bryant. Tell him it's an emergency. It's Manuel Foreva."

After a long hesitation, Senator Bryant picked up an extension somewhere.

"I've told you how to contact my assistant, and—"

"Senator, TR Day is off."

"What?"

"I said TR Day is off."

No response, then some muffling with the phone. "It's not off, I just spoke to the mayor." Pasquali gestured to Manuel. Encouragement.

"It's on, but it's off," Manuel said, repeating Pasquali's whispers.

The senator huffed.

Gabe studied Manuel's face. An able man but not a quick one. Raised to follow orders, tend cattle, and guard a marijuana plantation. *TR Day is off. It's on, but it's off.* Manuel had no idea what those phrases meant. Of course he didn't. Even if he engaged in some questionable side work now and then, in his bones he was almost a Terwilliger—a confusing thing to be in recent years days. Manuel still gripped Ayalette's jacket.

Pasquali's hard eyes prompted Manuel to continue with the script. Manuel, God bless him, was not much of an actor. It now sounded like he was reading.

"What should I do?" Manuel asked. "About our friend?"

Bryant paused. "I have no idea what you're talking about." Annoyed. But not angry. A pro.

Gabe took the phone. "Senator, this is Gabriel Lantagne. We met yesterday."

No response, but no hang up.

"Nice op-ed piece this morning, Beau. Prescient, some might say. Written by a man with real vision. Clairvoyance, even. I wanted to let you know I thought about what you said about my father. About judgment. And while he might have been the state's highest law enforcement officer, I'm not. It's my judgment that this entire TR Day situation should remain between friends. That is, you, me, and a small group of my friends. I'm sure you understand my judgment here. Now I gotta go. We've got some dynamite to defuse and some witnesses to interview. All confidential, of course. But we'll make tapes. Real ones this time. Sorry to interrupt your meeting."

The senator was still breathing on the phone when Gabe hit end.

"You're actually gonna let Blain accept the award?" Gabe asked.

"Shit, yes," Pasquali said.

"That's crazy."

"No it ain't." Pasquali held up his iPhone, displaying a live video feed from the ravine.

THIRTY-NINE

MAY 17, 2009, 12:20 P.M. – TWIN RIVERS DAY, TWIN RIVERS, MONTANA

Gabe stood on stage next to Phoenix, but mostly kept his eyes on Pasquali near the River Street entrance at the front corner of City Hall. Pasquali watched his phone intently.

The county cheered when Gabe accepted his award, but he declined to speak. When Jeremy Blain stepped forward, a small group of enthusiastic supporters cheered from the front of the stage. Apparently Pandora's Box had closed for the afternoon. When Blain shook hands with Phoenix and reached towards her for the award, Gabe glanced at Pasquali, who held his phone up, squinting at it. Then he smiled at Gabe and mouthed one word: Kapow.

The cheers increased dramatically when Phoenix discussed the certification of the prison contract and the availability of the first installment of the Twin Rivers stimulus package. After the speech, Pasquali and Gabe followed Blain back through City Hall. Blain, ahead of them and out of earshot, walked like a gymnast who just nailed a perfect ten on the rings, not like a guy whose life as he knew it was about to end.

"What are you gonna do with him?" Gabe asked Pasquali.

Pasquali stopped in the hallway, fixing his gaze on the man as he got closer to the back door of City Hall.

"I don't know that I'm gonna do anything with him, as long as he leaves Caroline County, which I believe is precisely his plan."

Gabe got it. Pasquali was one arrest away from becoming a national hero. The talk shows, the book deals, the fame. But he did not care, because that wouldn't help Twin Rivers. Pasquali wanted the town to survive. Which required the prison contract. Gabe had to admit, the guy had standards.

Blain pushed open the heavy door and slipped into the sunny parking lot.

Gabe and Pasquali sprinted down the hallway next to each other, but to Gabe it felt like slow motion. The initial gunshot, muffled by the closed door, was followed by a series of two and then several more. Pasquali kicked the door open, gun drawn. It took what seemed like several seconds for Gabe to understand what he was seeing.

A thin brunette girl screaming. Blain on the ground, scurrying on his arms backwards towards them. And finally, a man firing a pistol wildly at Blain.

"No, Gracie!" the girl yelled. "No, Stop!"

The crazy-eyed, longhaired man fired again, this time from only yards away. He then turned his gun on the girl, who was now on her knees, screaming in a begging position. Gabe then heard a series of loud explosions and the gunman flew back off his feet. His cast-wrapped right arm banged against the cement and came to rest awkwardly under him.

People from the street, trudging towards the festival, began to scream and run, some towards them, some away. Gabe could hear nothing. He walked to Blain, who lay in a pool of blood. A creeping stain expanded quickly across the lower part of his shirt. His chest heaved, yet his hands remained at his sides, not gripping the wound. Gabe knelt down, reaching for Blain and scanning for additional wounds on the upper body. He noticed the contrast, the starkness of the red blood on the white shirt, neatly packaged under the new black suit. Then Gabe felt an arm around him.

"You're shot, Gabe, lie down," Pasquali said.

Gabe saw bright lights, then a camera. As he lost consciousness, he heard a woman gasping and weeping softly, even amid all the screams and swirling sirens. He never understood why he heard the quiet crying above everything else, or why it made such an impression on him.

FORTY

It was one of those dreams where Gabe knew it was a dream. He guzzled one chilled glass of ice water after another, sucking each of them bone dry. Yet the thirst continued. The dream was something of a comedy of errors, Gabe endeavoring to procure cold, sustaining drinks in various simple situations. A McDonald's drive–thru. A frigid water fountain in the park. The hose behind the house he grew up in. But the thirst remained.

Suddenly he was awake. He heard the noise before he opened his eyes. A television. He opened his eyes and saw Myrlene sitting next to him, watching the television in the upper corner of the room. Strangely, in the seconds before he realized where he was and why he was there, he felt an awkwardness in making a sound or any deliberate attempt to turn Myrlene's head. Finally, he said her name, which came out a whisper over his dry tongue.

"Gabe, you're up!" She hit a red button on a cord by his side and stepped off her stool. She looked to the door as if unsure what to do. "How do you feel?"

"Fucking thirsty."

A female doctor glanced at a couple of machines. "You're looking good, Mr. Lantagne. I'm Dr. Weiss. You were shot in the lower abdomen and the bullet had to be removed. It missed your stomach, but wreaked some havoc in your lower intestine. We'll talk more later. Your prognosis is good. You should watch a little television and sleep some more."

Gabe knew Dr. Weiss whether she remembered him or not. As the hospital's only full-time doctor, she had been a witness in several of his cases, testifying professionally and usually without cross-examination about one petty medical matter or another. An attractive thirty-five or so, she moved and talked with the commanding hurry of a big-city doctor. She was also Deputy Glower's wife, another odd Twin Rivers coupling. Another town secret, perhaps not.

Gabe had a thousand questions, but could muster only, "Water."

"Sorry about that. You're being hydrated as we speak, but it takes a while to catch. You're also on heavy painkillers that dehydrate you, so you may feel a little thirsty. Go to sleep."

He looked at Myrlene's face, which seemed as it always did. Expressionless balance. He turned back to the doctor to protest, but never got around to it.

The next time he woke up, the previous time itself seemed a dream, but Myrlene was still there, only now on a couch reading.

"Hey there," Gabe said.

"Hey," she replied in a tired voice.

After a few moments of small talk, Gabe asked what happened.

Myrlene shrugged, as if the mundane question demanded old news. It was. "You've been here four days. At first they were saying critical condition. Then you had surgery, and it's been uphill every day since."

"And you've been here every day?"

"Not just me. National news crews for two days. Pasquali, Phoenix, everybody from the courthouse, your aunt and uncle, and, you won't believe this, Senator Bryant."

Gabe raised his eyebrows.

"Yeah, look." She gestured toward the table under the television, covered with flower baskets and cards. "I put out the word that no more flowers were needed, to send donations to the indigent defense commission in Helena."

"Was I supposed to be dead or something?"

"What the hell do I know, the flowers kept coming."

"Bryant left a card?"

Myrlene pointed. "That big display on the left, that's him." Gabe focused on her skinny arm, its self-conscious, double-jointed movement.

"That guy Gracie, the stripper's nutty husband, shot you. He killed Jeremy Blain, and then Pasquali shot him dead. The press has been all over the place, but it's calmed down a little… oh look—"

She stood, scampered over to the couch, and quickly turned up the volume with a thin black remote, her expertise gained over the last four days shining through.

Phoenix stood in front of City Hall in front of flashing cameras. She addressed a large crowd.

"God, that doesn't even look like River Street," Gabe said.

"No shit," Myrlene said. "This is a press conference called by Phoenix, her first official comment on what happened."

"First official comment in four days?"

"She said she wouldn't comment until she knew your situation. It was actually kind of sweet, for her."

Phoenix held the podium firmly with both hands but her glowing face commanded the attention. The press was in the middle of questions.

"Absolutely not," she said. "Before the prisoners even arrive, we'll have the highest law-enforcement-to-citizen ratio anywhere in America. This is a small town, where we all know each other, and despite the other day, a peaceful, nonviolent place with little crime."

"Haven't there been two murders within miles of the prison in the last two weeks?" an unseen reporter asked.

"I'm going to let Sheriff Genovese Pasquali address questions about crime in Caroline County. Sheriff?"

Pasquali stepped from off-camera to the podium, and Gabe smiled. On television, his pasty face, thick jowls, and deep-set eyes presented such a startling contrast to Phoenix's effervescence that Gabe actually felt sorry for him. Pasquali's genius was in the small setting, the back room, the subtle gestures of the high-stakes poker game. He owned the confined environment where a tilt of an eyebrow or a minor inflection told him all he needed to know while he conveyed nothing. On television though, he was nothing but the country bumpkin sheriff. Which was perfect.

"Let me explain something to you folks. I've been Sheriff here for thirty-nine years and in that time, we have had exactly fourteen homicides in Caroline County. Five of 'em were DUI-related, two of 'em involved fights between intoxicated men at bars, four of 'em were domestic incidents, and one, insurance fraud. As for the two recent cases, one was the act of deluded and jealous wife-abuser, and the other represents the only unsolved murder in modern Caroline County history. The victim was a retired career police officer who worked cases around the state, and the investigation is still underway. But I can assure everybody, neither of the recent murders had anything whatever to do with Twin Rivers Penitentiary."

Pasquali stepped away, no doubt realizing that all the questions were for the mayor.

"Has Councilman Lantagne recovered?"

Phoenix beamed. "Yes, I saw him this morning and was informed he's in full recovery mode."

"Are you running for governor?"

This time Phoenix's smile turned to a charming and very hearty laugh."If I do, we have the perfect mayoral candidate to step into my shoes."

Then a reporter asked if he could put a question to Pasquali. "Have autopsies been completed on Jeremy Blain and his murderer?"

Pasquali stepped to the podium, the normal charm of his smile lost by the cameras, but ever so fitting for his role. "You people beat all. I personally saw the assailant gun down Mr. Blain, and I shot the assailant myself. At least twelve witnesses saw the entire event. The cause of death in both cases is obvious. But if you have to know, the death certificates were put on file today."

"Will there be funerals? Where?"

"Mr. Blain's arrangements, I'm told, are to remain private," Phoenix announced.

The news cut to a clip of TR Day. Jeremy Blain accepting his award. And then a partially censored picture of Blain lying on the street, the screen pixilated to block any view of the inching bloodstain on his stomach.

A nurse stepped up from behind Myrlene and snatched the remote. "Enough for now. This guy needs to sleep. He's got some visitors slated for tomorrow."

FORTY-ONE

MAY 22, 2009 – TWIN RIVERS, MONTANA

Hospital rules confined Gabe to a wheelchair, but he was free to move around, a freedom he elected to exercise by rolling himself to the elevator and downstairs in the hopes somebody would be outside smoking a cigarette. Caroline County Municipal Hospital was a tiny but well-equipped facility, one of the county's many amenities whose existence had previously puzzled Gabe. What thousand-person county had its own hospital? In any event, the answer to those questions had settled into his mind as if he had known them forever, as if he had been part of their creation.

No smokers, but Pasquali strolled alone from his truck to the hospital entrance. Pasquali nodded and sat on a bench. "Sack o' shit."

"Nice job on the news," Gabe said.

"I guess from now on we're in for a bit of attention."

Gabe asked a deliberately unfocused question. "How are things progressing?"

Pasquali immediately answered it as if he knew what it addressed. "The Trade is dead. One and a half tons shipped out, grow-houses destroyed—a successful thirty-year business decimated within a week."

"You sad about it?"

Pasquali appeared to think on the answer. "Not sad. But you get used to things. For thirty years I've walked around with a mild tension, knowing but not knowing what it had to do with, and that little tension becomes part of who you are. When it goes, yeah, it's a relief, but it's like a part of your personality is gone." Pasquali paused again. "We got a nice town here, and

I've always been proud of that. The Trade was part of it. Now, it's on to something else."

"The next generation, huh? Twin Rivers goes legit."

"Phhhh."

"So what's bothering you then?" Gabe asked.

Pasquali removed a crushed envelope from his back pocket. "All these years, we were breaking the law, but it never hurt nobody. That's how we saw it. Egan, Enos, even your dad. Probably Senator what's-his-name. Everybody's just a little complicit, that's all you need. Other than that, this was a great American town. Hell, a conservative town. And so we learned to cut corners and keep secrets, and eventually the number of secrets gets so high, they become part of the town's soul. But in all those years, I never lay down on a real case. Not something important."

The old sheriff looked tired, pale, maybe even unhealthy.

"Gillespie," Pasquali said, "didn't deserve to die. He was an outsider who came here because it was a nice quiet place. Now I'm not blaming you, but I know he was killed because he was diggin' into your case. And I think we both know Bryant is dirty. I'll tell you something else: Gillespie was not killed by that knucklehead Scruggs or by our unfortunately deceased Islamic tourist."

Pasquali must have had some kind of evidence to back up that claim, but Gabe did not ask. Somehow he knew both statements to be true.

"Nobody knows this, but we use prepaid cell phones, always bought outside town. Me, Egan, Terwilliger, Manuel, even Phoenix. We all have our regular numbers, but we use the prepaids to call each other. About the Trade."

Pasquali was building to a point in his own gradual way.

"I did know about the prepaids," Gabe said. "At least about Phoenix's. She gave me a number once. I figured, you know, public official, the lawsuit, she's got enemies. Didn't seem strange."

"When we were in the truck the other night," Pasquali said, "and you got the call from Phoenix, you held up the phone to show me it was her. I knew right then you didn't think that number was a secret from me. But Phoenix had been using a different prepaid with me. So I memorized that number you showed me and, well hell, I had no time to think about it until after TR Day, but then I realized I still remembered it."

Pasquali handed the sealed white envelope to Gabe. "Here's the record for that phone for the last two weeks. And don't ask me how I got it. But this will show who Phoenix called or got calls from, including the night she showed up at Gillespie's."

Gabe said, "Open it."

Pasquali looked at Gabe sternly then sighed. "What's done is done. Either there's a call on that record that suggests who told Phoenix to go to Gillespie's, or there's not. Even if there is, even if it could be proven to have come from Senator Bryant, would we really know anything? A warning call, to scare her off, or a mission-accomplished call, either way."

Gabe was about to respond, but Pasquali continued. "It hurts me to beg off a murder case, and I'll always know I sold Gillespie out, not to mention myself, but what's the alternative? To bring Phoenix Jamborsky into a murder investigation now? Consider that for a moment. The prison contract? The stimulus? Plus she knows everything about this town. Hell, part of the reason this whole thing worked was that everybody involved had their hands around everybody else's balls. Mutual assured destruction. Which would leave what? A broken town full of prosecuted criminals? An embarrassment to the entire country?

And Michael, and Egan, Ayalette, and my deputies, and all the families who think this is just a nice place to live? And then I started thinking about Phoenix."

Pasquali looked squarely at Gabe. "I can read people, Gabe. It's my skill. Phoenix is the best liar I've ever met. She'd cover up anything, but she wouldn't condone a killing…not in advance."

"So why give me the envelope? What can I do with it?"

"The next generation. I don't feel like it's my decision to make. At least not alone. You, my friend, not Phoenix and not me, will be charting the stars for Twin Rivers, Part II. The sequel. You decide what you wanna do about it. I'm closing the case unless I hear from you." He gripped Gabe on the shoulder and Gabe felt kindness in his thick hand. "I trust you to make the call on this."

Everybody just a little complicit, that's all you need. Mutual assured destruction indeed.

Gabe's true affinity for Pasquali notwithstanding, he now saw the true meaning of the Weasel Junction Way. How the town had survived. Look out for each other, sure. Trust each other, not exactly. Enos, Michael, and Pasquali had formed the iron triangle of Caroline County. Gabe, Phoenix, and Pasquali were now three sides of a similar triangle. A triangle of trust, deceit, and overlapping secrets in which all knew some and none knew all. After all, even while admitting her own misdeeds, Phoenix had maintained the absurd lie that Pasquali had not helped her cover up Enos's murder. Pasquali had not exposed her either. Not completely anyway. *I never quite believed it was a suicide.* Wow, no wonder Manuel had made that phone call to the senator so fast. He would have called Vladimir Putin if Pasquali had asked him to. To these people, the careful balance of truth and deception made perfect sense. And just as Pasquali knew nothing about Phoenix's manipulation of Beau Bryant, Gabe would never fully understand Weasel Junction's history. Only, maybe, its future.

"You know, Sheriff, Phoenix might be the best liar you've ever met, but she's not the best liar I've ever met."

Pasquali smiled broadly now, and for the first time, Gabe noticed the man had a perfect set of gleaming white teeth. A truly beautiful smile. So funny that God would grant that particular gift to an old country cop.

"I prefer to think of myself as a poker player," Pasquali said. "You, you're a chess player. Trying to guess moves way down the line. For me, it's the short game. Play cards, win or lose, and move on. Always another hand, right?"

"Does anyone, including Phoenix, know who Blain really was?"

"That little piece of information remains where it belongs. I don't try to read moves that far down the line. No chess for me, just poker."

"Then tell me, Geno. How many people know he's still alive?"

Pasquali's eyes narrowed and he shifted his belt buckle. And in that second of hesitation, he lost his chance to deny it. "Exactly the right number, my friend."

"Where is he?" Pasquali's expression rendered it clear that he planned to keep this one to himself as well. Most of it anyway.

"We owed the boy one," Pasquali said, as if to suggest that burying the Blain issue was a matter of goodwill rather than Weasel Junction politics at its very best. "He asked me for two things. I gave him the one I could. And I gave him his freedom so he could try for the other."

Gabe just watched Pasquali.

"He wanted to know if the fuse at the ravine blew during TR Day. I told him yes. Then he said needed to go home. To save his brother."

Gabe sat alone outside the hospital watching Pasquali walk away. Moments later, a nurse came out looking for him. "Mr.

Lantagne? The mayor is on the phone. Says she has some great news for you, wanted me to find you right away."

The nurse turned Gabe's wheelchair and hurried him to the elevator, to his room, and then right up to the phone next to his bed. "I'll ring in the call."

"Wait," Gabe said. "Put this in the safe for me, will you?"

The nurse took the sealed white envelope. Gabe picked up the phone to speak to the newly declared candidate for Governor of Montana.

FORTY-TWO
JULY 2009 – EDINBURGH, SCOTLAND

Ian McLanahan was tired. He had learned to live with the travel, the constant moving from place to place, the phone calls at all hours. But he would never fully manage the stress. Then again, he had always known he was special. If he were not special, he would have been dead or in prison a long time ago rather than an international freedom fighter. He chuckled. And a filthy rich one at that. He looked out the window down on the Royal Mile, the strip of bars and shops leading along the famous street to Edinburgh Castle. Perhaps he would shower and go have a drink. But first business.

He entered the sitting room without turning on the light. His fingers deftly spun the dial on the floor safe. It opened, and he deposited three stacks of tightly bound cash.

I'm a political fundraiser, he often told his mother, who looked at him questioningly when he handed her generous gifts. A devout Afghani emigrant, she did know enough to realize that political fundraisers in Britain don't carry around tens of thousands of dollars in cash.

Ian shut the safe and spun the dial. He had access to dozens of safe rooms in Britain, this one a long-term rental by a wealthy friend. A friend sympathetic to the cause. Sort of.

Ian stood, turned on the light, and then nearly jumped out of his skin."My God, my God, praise God!" He fell to his knees and then backed himself into a chair. "We thought you were dead! Praise God."

"Hello, Karim," Ahmed said, quietly. Ahmed looked not only balder than months before, but calmer, older. Or something.

"We knew the Americans captured and killed you, pretending you were an American killed by another American over a woman. There's nothing more you could have done, but, but, why are you here…?"

"Shut up, Karim." Ahmed watched Karim closely, trying to see if he knew that Ahmed had already contacted his mother and gotten her the money to leave the village with Abu. To get as far away as possible from Omar and the camp. With any luck, they were living with cousins in Islamabad, where Ahmed hoped to meet them. If Karim had already known that he was alive, it meant his mother and Abu were either under Omar's control or dead. But he could tell that Karim had truly believed him to be dead.

"Omar will be so pleased. We must tell him."

"He will soon be in possession of that information."

Ian leaned forward, and Ahmed saw his eyes flicker towards the pistol. Recognition. Almost. The pistol was not in Ahmed's hand but on the low wooden coffee table, right between them.

"Ahmed… do you have a gun on the table?"

"You aren't asking yourself the right question, Karim. The right question is, do I feel lucky?"

Ian just stared, eyes wide in abject horror.

"Well, do you?"

FORTY-THREE

MAY 2010 – EUGENE, OREGON

Shannon woke to the annoying radio alarm. Her roommate's alarm. Still, it was time for class anyway. She swung her legs onto the ground and rubbed her eyes. Jackie was already at her desk, cramming for another few moments for the physics final. Shannon herself was not worried. She was ready.

The last final of the last semester of her last year at college. A real college. In a few weeks she would graduate from the University of Oregon, and the best part was that she planned to take the summer off to travel. South America. A hike through Peru and then quick visits to Brazil and Argentina. How her life had changed.

She still dreamed of Jeremy, a guy she'd hardly known but somehow still had feelings for. He had shared with her the lowest week of her life before his own ended. She would never get over the guilt—that somehow she was at fault because Gracie killed him for protecting her. And that was not even all of it, because Jeremy had not only lost his life to help her, but continued giving in a way she never could have predicted.

That terrible day in the back of City Hall, the shooting, the questioning by police, the swarming reporters. The melee had ended with Shannon drunk on her bed, crying and crying on the shabby motel sheets. She sat up, begging God to put her to sleep. And then she had glanced at the desk and seen the black bag poking out from under it. Not her bag. Not a bag she had ever seen before. She shakily walked towards it, pulled it out, and unzipped it. Even drunk she had never been a bad counter. One hundred thousand dollars.

Jackie slammed her laptop shut. "I'll never pass this thing."

Shannon walked to the sink to brush her teeth, looked at herself in the mirror, and spoke quietly to herself as she did every morning.

Thank you for this life, and thank you, Jeremy Blain.

FORTY-FOUR
AUGUST 2012 – TWIN RIVERS, MONTANA

"There's our girl," Pasquali said. Gabe, Myrlene, Sheriff Glower, and Pasquali sat equidistant from each other on the leather couch in front of the television at the Weasel Junction Hunt Club.

Phoenix's beaming face filled the screen under the caption *Montana Governor, Keynote Address, 2012 Republican National Convention.*

"Oh, I'm gonna puke," Myrlene said.

Phoenix had just finished her speech, during which she persuasively declared that Beau Bryant was the man to defeat the President. The man with the judgment to realize that America had real enemies in the world.

"Hey, deputy, we need another round of beers in here," Pasquali yelled.

"I'm on it, sir," Scruggs called out from the kitchen.

"I don't give a shit about your career, Gabe," Myrlene said. "I know she made you mayor, but I'm voting for the President. That bitch endorsing Bryant is enough of a reason for me. Plus his new fundraising scandal. Not even Phoenix can talk Bryant's way out of that one."

"Darlin', you sure don't understand politics," Pasquali said.

"Oh yeah? What don't I understand?"

"Phoenix probably leaked that fundraising shit." And everybody laughed, the sad-but-true kind of laughter that nevertheless warmed their hearts.

Governor Jamborsky worked her way through the cheering delegates.

EPILOGUE

MAY 2022 – SIXTY MILES NORTHWEST OF CHITRAL, PAKISTAN

His drivers, his guides, and even his identification falsely referred to him as a freelance reporter named Campbell. Though years older, he kept pace with his Pakistani guides, following them step for step through the rocky passes ever deeper into a place that was hardly a country but more like a law-free zone. His guides were themselves led by a man about his age, a close aide to the man Campbell had traveled across the world to meet. Alone. Campbell had decided he should meet the mysterious leader by himself, and the President agreed.

Campbell had been known by various titles over the years, including Deputy Chief of Staff and State Department Liaison. Now most referred to him as Ambassador, though he worked at no embassy and never had. A fixer, perhaps? An emissary? Or, as one writer put it, the conscience of the President.

The sole picture the administration had of Rafique depicted him standing next to a horse, looking past the camera. His hand rested on the horse's neck, as if to comfort it before an attempt to mount. Rafique was younger than Campbell but looked far older, his painfully thin frame and troubled eyes telling the story of a man who internalized too much. The type of person who believed he was responsible for everything. It was Rafique's face that first drew him to Campbell's attention. It was the face that made Campbell hopeful. After months of research into the man's contacts and family, Campbell was still not sure.

Some believed that Rafique—the first leader to assert a measure of order over perhaps the world's most uncontrollable region—was a man bent on preventing an impending war that until then seemed inevitable. The President's dilemma was whether these rumors about Rafique and his level of influence could possibly be true, and if so, what to do about them.

"Mr. Campbell." The guide in front of him called turned and pointed down the ridge into a valley. A camp filled tents, and with men. Hundreds, and armed.

Campbell took a deep breath, hoping that his educated guess was correct.

Campbell walked with his lead guide straight through the camp. He saw no reason to hesitate and had declined his guides' suggestion for a meal or a rest before meeting Rafique. His local garb did nothing to deter the curious stares of several hundred men as he walked boldly through a camp no American had ever before seen.

"He waits for you." His guide placed his hand on Campbell's back, a touch which must have alerted him to Campbell's inner apprehension. "No reason whatever to be nervous. Rafique is the gentlest man you will ever meet. I promise it."

Campbell was not afraid. His history of similar jaunts had taken him to other dangerous meetings. No, his perceptible agitation was not about fear, but excitement. As if he had been waiting for this circle to close for years.

Campbell's lead guide stopped suddenly about ten feet from the tent, as if he had reached an invisible demarcation beyond which the onlookers knew he should not pass. He motioned with one sweeping arm for Campbell to continue. Campbell strode forward, parted the tent flap and entered. Choosing not to focus on the man's face until seated, he sat on the ground in front of Rafique, and then met his eyes, surprised to see a beaming smile under the deep crow's-feet he'd examined in the photograph so many times. Then, he finally knew for sure. This was his man.

"Abu."

"Gabriel," Rafique said.

"The President sends her respects and commends you for responding to our request," Gabe said.

"And I thank her for making such a request," Abu said.

They needed no further words to acknowledge the story that bound them together. Instead, they spoke of the war both hoped to prevent.

OTHER NOVELS & SHORT STORIES
BY CHRISTOPHER LEIBIG

The Black Rabbit

Almost Mortal

Intervention

Paradise City

Made in the USA
Middletown, DE
24 May 2023

31312692R00166